The Little Mermaid

AND OTHER TALES

The Little Mermaid
AND OTHER TALES

HANS CHRISTIAN

ANDERSEN

Compiled and edited by Julia Simon-Kerr

HarperFestival®
A Division of HarperCollins*Publishers*

Hans Christian Andersen published his first three acknowledged fairy tales in 1835.
HarperCollins®, ☕®, and HarperFestival® are trademarks of HarperCollins Publishers Inc.
The Little Mermaid and Other Tales
Printed in the United States of America. All rights reserved.
www.harperchildrens.com
For information address HarperCollins Children's Books, a division of HarperCollins Publishers,
1350 Avenue of the Americas, New York, NY 10019.
Library of Congress catalog card number: 2004111659
Typography by Scott Richards
1   2   3   4   5   6   7   8   9   10
❖
First HarperFestival edition, 2005

Contents

The Little Mermaid

AND OTHER TALES

The Little Mermaid

Far out in the ocean, where the water is as blue as the prettiest cornflower, and as clear as crystal, it is very, very deep; so deep, indeed, that no cable could fathom it; many church steeples, piled one upon another, would not reach from the ground beneath to the surface of the water above. There dwell the Sea King and his subjects.

We must not imagine that there is nothing at the bottom of the sea but bare yellow sand. No, indeed; the most singular flowers and plants grow there; the leaves and stems of which are so pliant that the slightest agitation of the water causes them to stir as if they had life. Fishes, both large and small, glide between the branches, as birds fly among the trees here upon land. In the deepest spot of all stands the castle of the Sea King. Its walls are built of coral, and the long, gothic windows are of the clearest amber. The roof is formed of shells that open and close as the water flows over them. Their appearance is very beautiful, for in each lies a glittering pearl, which would be fit for the crown of a queen.

The Sea King had been a widower for many years, and his aged mother kept house for him. She was a very wise woman, and exceedingly proud of her high birth. On that account she wore twelve oysters on her tail, while others, also of high rank, were only allowed to wear six. She was, however, deserving of very great praise, especially for her care of the little sea princesses, her granddaughters. They were six beautiful children, but the youngest was the prettiest of them all. Her skin was as clear and delicate as a rose leaf, and her eyes as blue as the deepest sea; but, like all the others, she had no feet, and her body ended in a fish's tail. All day long they played in the great halls of the castle, or among the living flowers that grew out of the walls. The large amber windows were open, and the fish swam in, just as the swallows fly into our houses when we open the windows, except that the fish swam up to the princesses, ate out of their hands, and allowed themselves to be stroked.

Outside the castle there was a beautiful garden, in which grew bright red and dark blue flowers, and blossoms like flames of fire. The fruit glittered like gold, and the leaves and stems waved to and fro continually. The earth itself was the finest sand, but blue as the flame of burning sulphur. Over everything lay a peculiar blue radiance, as if it were surrounded by the air from above, through which the blue sky shone, instead of the dark depths of the sea. In calm weather the sun could be seen, looking like a purple flower, with the light streaming from the calyx.

Each of the young princesses had a little plot of ground in the garden, where she might dig and plant as she pleased. One arranged her flowerbed into the form of a whale; another thought it better to make hers like the figure of a little mermaid; but that of the youngest was round like the sun, and contained flowers as red as his rays at sunset. She was a strange child, quiet and thoughtful; and while her sisters would be delighted with the wonderful things that they obtained from the wrecks of vessels, she cared for nothing but her pretty red flowers, like the sun, except for a beautiful marble statue. It was the representation of a handsome boy, carved out of pure white stone, which had fallen to the bottom of the sea from a wreck. She planted by the statue a rose-colored weeping willow. It grew splendidly, and very soon hung its fresh branches over the statue, almost down to the blue sands. The shadow had a violet tint, and waved to and fro like the branches. It seemed as if the crown of the tree and the root were at play, and trying to kiss each other.

Nothing gave her so much pleasure as to hear about the world above the sea. She made her old grandmother tell her all she knew of the ships and of the towns, the people and the animals. To her it seemed most wonderful and beautiful to hear that the flowers of the land should have fragrance, and not those below the sea; that the trees of the forest should be green; and that the fishes among the trees could sing so sweetly that it was quite a pleasure to hear them. Her grandmother called the little birds fishes, otherwise the princess would not have understood her, for she had never seen birds.

"When you have reached your fifteenth year," said the grandmother, "you will have permission to rise up out of the sea, to sit on the rocks in the moonlight, while the great ships are sailing by; and then you will see both forests and towns."

In the following year, one of the sisters would be fifteen; but as each was a year younger than the other, the youngest would have to wait five years before her turn came to rise up from the bottom of the ocean, and see the earth as we do. However, each promised to tell the others what she saw on her first visit, and what she thought the most beautiful; for their grandmother could not tell them enough; there were so many things on which they wanted information.

None of them longed so much for her turn to come as the youngest, she who had the longest time to wait, and who was so quiet and thoughtful. Many nights she stood by the open window, looking up through the dark blue water and watching the fish as they splashed about with their fins and tails. She could see the moon and stars shining faintly; but through the water they looked larger than they do to our eyes. When something like a black cloud passed between her and them, she knew that it was either a whale swimming over her head or a ship full of human beings, who never imagined that a pretty little mermaid was standing beneath them, holding out her white hands toward the keel of their ship.

As soon as the eldest was fifteen, she was allowed to rise to the surface of the ocean. When she came back, she had hundreds of things to talk about; but the most beautiful, she said, was to lie in the moonlight on a sandbank, in the quiet sea near the coast, and to gaze on a large town nearby, where the lights were twinkling like hundreds of stars; to listen to the sounds of the music, the noise of carriages, and the voices of human beings; and then to hear the merry bells peal out from the church steeples; and because she could not go near to all those wonderful things, she longed for them more than ever.

Oh, did not the youngest sister listen eagerly to all these descriptions? Afterward, when she stood at the open window looking up through the dark blue water, she thought of the great city, with all its bustle and noise, and even fancied she could hear the sound of the church bells, down in the depths of the sea.

In another year the second sister received permission to rise to the surface of the water and to swim about where she pleased. She rose just as the sun was setting, and this, she said, was the most beautiful sight of all. The whole sky looked like gold, while violet and rose-colored clouds, which she could not describe, floated over her; and, still more rapidly than the clouds, flew a large flock of wild swans toward the setting sun, looking like a long white veil across the sea. She also swam toward the sun; but it sunk into the waves, and the rosy tints faded from the clouds and from the sea.

The third sister's turn followed; she was the boldest of them all, and she swam up a broad river that emptied itself into the sea. On the banks she saw green hills covered with beautiful vines; palaces and castles peeped out from amid the proud trees of the forest; she heard the birds singing, and the rays of the sun were so powerful that she was obliged often to dive down under the water to cool her burning face. In a narrow creek she found a whole troop of little human children, quite naked, and sporting about in the water. She wanted to play with them, but they fled in a great fright; and then a little black animal came to the water. It was a dog, but she did not know that, for she had never before seen one. This animal barked at her so terribly that she became frightened and rushed back to the open sea. But she said she should never forget the beautiful forest, the green hills, and the pretty little children who could swim in the water, although they had not fish's tails.

The fourth sister was more timid; she remained in the midst of the sea, but she said it was quite as beautiful there as nearer the land. She could see for so many miles around her, and the sky above looked like a bell of glass. She had seen the ships, but at such a great distance that they looked like seagulls. The dolphins sported in the waves, and the great whales spouted water from their nostrils till it seemed as if a hundred fountains were playing in every direction.

The fifth sister's birthday occurred in the winter, so when her turn came, she saw what the others had not seen the first time they went up. The sea looked quite green, and large icebergs were floating about, each like a pearl, she said, but larger and loftier than the churches built by men. They were of the most singular shapes and glittered like diamonds. She had seated herself upon one of the largest and let the wind play with her long hair, and she remarked that all the ships sailed by rapidly and steered as far away as they could from the iceberg, as if they were afraid of it. Toward evening, as the sun went down, dark clouds covered the sky, the thunder rolled and the lightning flashed, and the red light glowed on the icebergs as they rocked and tossed on the heaving sea. On all the ships the sails were reefed with fear and trembling, while she sat calmly on the floating iceberg, watching the blue lightning, as it darted its forked flashes into the sea.

When first the sisters had permission to rise to the surface, they were each delighted with the new and beautiful sights they saw; but now, as grown-up girls, they could go when they pleased, and they had become indifferent about it. They wished themselves back again in the water, and after a month had passed they said it was much more beautiful down below and pleasanter to be at home. Yet often, in the evening hours, the five sisters would twine their arms around each other, and rise to the surface in a row. They had more beautiful voices than any human being could have; and before the approach of a storm, and when they expected a ship would be lost, they swam before the vessel, and sang sweetly of the delights to be found in the depths of the sea, and begged the sailors not to fear if they sank to the bottom. But the sailors could not understand the song; they took it for the howling of the storm. And these things were never to be beautiful for them, for if the ship sank, the men were drowned, and their dead bodies alone reached the palace of the Sea King.

When the sisters rose, arm in arm, through the water in this way, their youngest sister would stand quite alone, looking after them, ready to cry, only that the mermaids have no tears, and therefore they suffer more. "Oh, were I but fifteen years old," said she. "I know that I shall love the world up there, and all the people who live in it."

At last she reached her fifteenth year. "Well, now, you are grown up," said the old dowager, her grandmother, "so you must let me adorn you like your other sisters." She placed a wreath of white lilies in the youngest's hair, and every flower petal was half a pearl. Then, the old lady ordered eight great oysters to attach themselves to the tail of the princess to show her high rank.

"But they hurt me so," said the little mermaid.

"Pride must suffer pain," replied the old lady. Oh, how gladly the princess would have shaken off all this grandeur and laid aside the heavy wreath! The red flowers in her own garden would have suited her much better, but she could not help herself. So she said, "Farewell," and rose as lightly as a bubble to the surface of the water.

The sun had just set as she raised her head above the waves; but the clouds were tinted with crimson and gold, and through the glimmering twilight beamed the evening star in all its beauty. The sea was calm, and the air mild and fresh. A large ship, with three masts, lay becalmed on the water with only one sail set, for not a breeze stiffed, and the sailors sat idle on deck or among the rigging. There was music and song on board; and, as darkness came on, a hundred colored lanterns were lighted, as if the flags of all nations waved in the air.

The little mermaid swam close to the cabin windows. Now and then, as the waves lifted her up, she could look in through clear glass windowpanes and see a number of well-dressed people within. Among them was a young prince, the most beautiful of all, with large black eyes. He was sixteen years of age, and his birthday was being kept with much rejoicing. The sailors were dancing on deck, but when the prince came out of the cabin, more than a hundred rockets rose in the air, making it as bright as day. The little mermaid was so startled that she dived underwater; and when she again stretched out her head, it appeared as if all the stars of heaven were falling around her, she had never seen such fireworks before. Great suns spurted fire about, splendid fireflies flew into the blue air, and everything was reflected in the clear, calm sea beneath. The ship itself was so brightly illuminated that all the people, and even the smallest rope, could be distinctly and plainly seen. And how handsome the young prince looked, as he pressed the hands of all present and smiled at them, while the music resounded through the clear night air.

It was very late, yet the little mermaid could not take her eyes from the ship or from the beautiful prince. The colored lanterns had been extinguished, no more rockets rose in the air, and the cannon had ceased firing; but the sea became restless, and a moaning, grumbling sound could be heard beneath the waves. Still the little mermaid remained by the cabin window, rocking up and down on the water, which enabled her to look in. After a while, the sails were quickly unfurled, and the noble ship continued her passage; but soon the waves rose higher, heavy clouds darkened the sky, and lightning appeared in the distance. A dreadful storm was approaching. Once more the sails were reefed, and the great ship pursued her flying course over the raging sea. The waves rose as high as a mountain, as if they would have overtopped the mast; but the ship dived like a swan between them, and then rose again on their lofty, foaming crests. To the little mermaid this appeared pleasant sport; not so to the sailors. At length the ship groaned and creaked; the thick planks gave way under the lashing of the sea as it broke over the deck; the mainmast snapped asunder like a reed; the ship lay over on her side; and the water rushed in.

The little mermaid now perceived that the crew was in danger; even she herself was obliged to be careful to avoid the beams and planks of the wreck which lay scattered on the water. At one moment it was so pitch-dark that she could not see a single object, but a flash of lightning revealed the whole scene. She could see everyone who had been on board except the prince. When the ship parted, she had seen him sink into the deep waves, and she was glad, for she thought he would now be with her. Then she remembered that human beings could not live in the water, so that when he got down to her father's palace he would be quite dead. But he must not die. So she swam about among the beams and planks which strewed the surface of the sea, forgetting that they could crush her to pieces. Then she dived deeply under the dark waters, rising and falling with the waves, till at length she managed to reach the young prince, who was fast losing the power of swimming in that stormy sea. His limbs were failing him, his beautiful eyes were closed, and he would have died had not the little mermaid come to his assistance. She held his head above the water and let the waves drift them where they would.

In the morning the storm had ceased, but of the ship not a single fragment could be seen. The sun rose up red and glowing from the water, and its beams brought back the hue of health to the prince's cheeks, but his eyes remained closed. The mermaid kissed his high, smooth forehead and stroked back his wet hair. He seemed to her like the marble statue in her little garden, and she kissed him again and wished that he might live.

Presently they came in sight of land. She saw lofty blue mountains, upon which the white snow rested as if a flock of swans were lying upon them. Near the coast were beautiful green forests, and close by stood a large building, whether a church or a convent she could not tell. Orange and citron trees grew in the garden, and before the door stood lofty palms. The sea here formed a little bay, in which the water was quite still but very deep; so she swam with the handsome prince to the beach, which was covered with fine, white sand, and there she laid him in the warm sunshine, taking care to raise his head higher than his body. Then bells sounded in the large white building, and a number of young girls came into the garden.

The little mermaid swam out farther from the shore and placed herself between some high rocks that rose out of the water. Then she covered her head and neck with the foam of the sea so that her little face might not be seen and watched to see what would become of the poor prince.

She did not wait long before she saw a young girl approach the spot where he lay. She seemed frightened at first, but only for a moment. Then, she fetched a number of people, and the mermaid saw that the prince came to life again and smiled upon those who stood around him. But to her he sent no smile; he knew not that she had saved him. This made her very unhappy, and when he was led away into the great building, she dived down sorrowfully into the water and returned to her father's castle.

She had always been silent and thoughtful, and now she was more so than ever. Her sisters asked her what she had seen during her first visit to the surface of the water, but she would tell them nothing.

Many an evening and morning did she rise to the place where she had left the prince. She saw the fruits in the garden ripen till they were gathered, the snow on the tops of the mountains melt away; but she never saw the prince, and therefore she returned home, always more sorrowful than before. It was her only comfort to sit in her own little garden and fling her arm around the beautiful marble statue that was like the prince; but she gave up tending her flowers, and they grew in wild confusion over the paths, twining their long leaves and stems around the branches of the trees, so that the whole place became dark and gloomy.

At length she could bear it no longer and told one of her sisters all about it. Then the others heard the secret, and very soon it became known to two mermaids whose intimate friend happened to know who the prince was. She had also seen the festival on board ship, and she told them where the prince came from and where his palace stood.

"Come, little sister," said the other princesses. Then they entwined their arms and rose up in a long row to the surface of the water, close by the spot where they knew the prince's palace stood. It was built of bright yellow shining stone, with long flights of marble steps, one of which reached quite down to the sea. Splendid gilded cupolas rose over the roof, and between the pillars that surrounded the whole building stood lifelike statues of marble. Through the clear crystal of the lofty windows could be seen noble rooms, with costly silk curtains and hangings of tapestry, while the walls were covered with beautiful paintings that were a pleasure to look at. In the center of the largest saloon a fountain threw its sparkling jets high up into the glass cupola of the ceiling, through which the sun shone down upon the water and upon the beautiful plants growing around the basin of the fountain.

Now that she knew where he lived, she spent many an evening and many a night on the water near the palace. She would swim much nearer the shore than any of the others ventured to do. Indeed once she went quite up the narrow channel under the marble balcony, which threw a broad shadow on the water. Here she would sit and watch the young prince, who thought himself quite alone in the bright moonlight. She saw him many times of an evening sailing in a pleasant boat, with music playing and flags waving. She peeped out from among the green rushes, and if the wind caught her long silvery-white veil, those who saw it believed it to be a swan, spreading out its wings.

On many a night, too, when the fishermen with their torches were out at sea, she heard them relate so many good things about the doings of the young prince that she was glad she had saved his life when he had been tossed about half-dead on the waves. And she remembered that his head had rested on her bosom and how heartily she had kissed him; but he knew nothing of all this, and could not even dream of her.

The little mermaid grew more and more fond of human beings and wished more and more to be able to wander about with those whose world seemed to be so much larger than her own. They could fly over the sea in ships and mount the high hills that were far above the clouds; and the lands they possessed, their woods and their fields, stretched far away beyond the reach of her sight. There was so much that she wished to know, and her sisters were unable to answer all her questions. Then she applied to her old grandmother, who knew all about the upper world, which she very rightly called the lands above the sea.

"If human beings don't drown," asked the little mermaid, "can they live forever? Don't they ever die as we do here in the sea?"

"Yes," replied the old lady, "they must also die, and their term of life is even shorter than ours. We sometimes live to three hundred years, but when we cease to exist here we only become the foam on the surface of the water, and we have not even a grave down here of those we love. We have not immortal souls, we shall never live again; but, like the green seaweed, when once it has been cut off, we can never flourish more. Human beings, on the contrary, have a soul that lives forever, lives after the body has been turned to dust. It rises up through the clear, pure air beyond the glittering stars. As we rise out of the water, and behold all the land of the earth, so do they rise to unknown and glorious regions that we shall never see."

"Why have not we an immortal soul?" asked the little mermaid mournfully. "I would give gladly all the hundreds of years that I have to live, to be a human being only for one day and to have the hope of knowing the happiness of that glorious world above the stars."

"You must not think of that," said the old woman. "We feel ourselves to be much happier and much better off than human beings."

"So I shall die," said the little mermaid, "and as the foam of the sea I shall be driven about never again to hear the music of the waves, or to see the pretty flowers nor the red sun. Is there anything I can do to win an immortal soul?"

"No," said the old woman, "unless a man were to love you so much that you were more to him than his father or mother; and if all his thoughts and all his love were fixed upon you, and the priest placed his right hand in yours, and he promised to be true to you here and hereafter, then his soul would glide into your body and you would obtain a share in the future happiness of humankind. He would give a soul to you and retain his own as well, but this can never happen. Your fish's tail, which among us is considered so beautiful, is thought on earth to be quite ugly. They do not know any better, and they think it necessary to have two stout props, which they call legs, in order to be handsome."

Then the little mermaid sighed and looked sorrowfully at her fish's tail. "Let us be happy," said the old lady, "and dart and spring about during the three hundred years that we have to live, which is really quite long enough. After that we can rest ourselves all the better. This evening we are going to have a court ball."

It is one of those splendid sights that we can never see on earth. The walls and the ceiling of the large ballroom were of thick but transparent crystal. Many hundreds of colossal shells, some of a deep red, others of a grass green, stood on each side in rows, with blue fire in them, which lighted up the whole saloon and shone through the walls, so that the sea was also illuminated. Innumerable fishes, great and small, swam past the crystal walls. On some of them the scales glowed with a purple brilliancy, and on others they shone like silver and gold. Through the halls flowed a broad stream, and in it danced the mermen and the mermaids to the music of their own sweet singing.

No one on earth has such a lovely voice as theirs. The little mermaid sang more sweetly than them all. The whole court applauded her with hands and tails; and for a moment her heart felt quite gay, for she knew she had the loveliest voice of any on earth or in the sea. But she soon thought again of the world above her, for she could not forget the charming prince, nor her sorrow that she had not an immortal soul like his. Therefore, she crept away silently out of her father's palace, and while everything within was gladness and song, she sat in her own little garden sorrowful and alone. Then she heard the bugle sounding through the water, and thought, *He is certainly sailing above, he on whom my wishes depend, and in whose hands I should like to place the happiness of my life. I will venture all for him, and to win an immortal soul. While my sisters are dancing in my father's palace, I will go to the sea witch. I have always been so much afraid of her, but she can give me counsel and help.*

And then the little mermaid went out from her garden and took the road to the foaming whirlpools, behind which the sorceress lived. She had never been that way before. Neither flowers nor grass grew there; nothing but bare, gray, sandy ground stretched out to the whirlpool, where the water, like foaming millwheels, whirled around everything that it seized and cast it into the fathomless deep. Through the midst of these crushing whirlpools the little mermaid was obliged to pass to reach the dominions of the sea witch. Also for a long distance the only road lay right across a quantity of warm, bubbling mire, called by the witch her turfmoor. Beyond this stood her house, in the center of a strange forest, in which all the trees and flowers were polyps, half animals and half plants. They looked like serpents with a hundred heads growing out of the ground. The branches were long slimy arms, with fingers like flexible worms, moving limb after limb from the root to the top. All that could be reached in the sea they seized upon and held fast, so that it never escaped from their clutches.

The little mermaid was so alarmed at what she saw that she stood still, and her heart beat with fear, and she very nearly turned back. But she thought of the prince and of the human soul for which she longed, and her courage returned. She fastened her long flowing hair around her head, so that the polyps might not seize hold of it. She laid her hands together across her bosom, and then she darted forward as a fish shoots through the water, between the supple arms and fingers of the ugly polyps, which were stretched out on each side of her. She saw that each held in its grasp something it had seized with its numerous little arms, as if they were iron bands. The white skeletons of human beings who had perished at sea and had sunk down into the deep waters, skeletons of land animals, oars, rudders, and chests of ships were lying tightly grasped by their clinging arms; even a little mermaid, whom they had caught and strangled. This seemed the most shocking of all to the little princess.

She now came to a space of marshy ground in the wood, where large, fat water snakes were rolling in the mire and showing their ugly, drab-colored bodies. In the midst of this spot stood a house, built with the bones of shipwrecked human beings. There sat the sea witch, allowing a toad to eat from her mouth, just as people sometimes feed a canary with a piece of sugar. She called the ugly water snakes her little chickens and allowed them to crawl all over her chest.

"I know what you want," said the sea witch. "It is very unwise of you, but you shall have your way, and it will bring you sorrow, my pretty princess. You want to get rid of your fish's tail and to have two supports instead of it, like human beings on earth, so that the young prince may fall in love with you and that you may have an immortal soul." And then the witch laughed so loud and disgustingly that the toad and the snakes fell to the ground and lay there wriggling about. "You are but just in time," said the witch, "for after sunrise tomorrow I should

not be able to help you till the end of another year. I will prepare a draught for you, with which you must swim to land
tomorrow before sunrise and sit down on the shore and drink
it. Your tail will then disappear and shrink up into what
humans calls legs, and you will feel great pain, as if a sword
were passing through you. But all who see you will say that
you are the prettiest little human being they ever saw. You will
still have the same floating gracefulness of movement, and no
dancer will ever tread so lightly; but at every step you take it
will feel as if you were treading upon sharp knives and that
the blood must flow. If you will bear all this, I will help you."

"Yes, I will," said the little princess in a trembling voice,
as she thought of the prince and the immortal soul.

"But think again," said the witch, "for when once your
shape has become like a human being, you can no more be a
mermaid. You will never return through the water to your
sisters or to your father's palace again. And if you do not win the
love of the prince, so that he is willing to forget his father and
mother for your sake and to love you with his whole soul and
allow the priest to join your hands that you may be
husband and wife, then you will never have an immortal soul.
The first morning after he marries another your heart will break,
and you will become foam on the crest of the waves."

"I will do it," said the little mermaid, and she became
pale as death.

"But I must be paid also," said the witch, "and it is not a
trifle that I ask. You have the sweetest voice of any who dwell
here in the depths of the sea, and you believe that you will be
able to charm the prince with it also, but this voice you must
give to me. The best thing you possess will I have for the price
of my draught. My own blood must be mixed with it, that it may

be as sharp as a two-edged sword."

"But if you take away my voice," said the little mermaid, "what is left for me?"

"Your beautiful form, your graceful walk, and your expressive eyes; surely with these you can enchain a man's heart. Well, have you lost your courage? Put out your little tongue that I may cut it off as my payment, then you shall have the powerful draught."

"It shall be," said the little mermaid.

Then the witch placed her cauldron on the fire, to prepare the magic draught.

"Cleanliness is a good thing," said she, scouring the vessel with snakes, which she had tied together in a large knot. Then she pricked herself in the breast and let the black blood drop into it. The steam that rose formed itself into such horrible shapes that no one could look at them without fear. Every moment the witch threw something else into the vessel, and when it began to boil, the sound was like the weeping of a crocodile. When at last the magic draught was ready, it looked like the clearest water.

"There it is for you," said the witch. Then she cut off the mermaid's tongue, so that she became mute and would never again speak or sing.

"If the polyps should seize hold of you as you return through the wood," said the witch, "throw over them a few drops of the potion, and their fingers will be torn into a thousand pieces." But the little mermaid had no occasion to do this, for the polyps sprang back in terror when they caught sight of the glittering draught, which shone in her hand like a twinkling star. So she passed quickly through the wood and the marsh, and between the rushing whirlpools.

She saw that in her father's palace the torches in the ballroom were extinguished, and all within asleep. But she did not venture to go in to them, for now she was mute and going to leave them forever; she felt as if her heart would break. She stole into the garden, took a flower from the flowerbeds of each of her sisters, kissed her hand a thousand times toward the palace, and then rose up through the dark blue waters.

The sun had not risen when she came in sight of the prince's palace and approached the beautiful marble steps, but the moon shone clear and bright. Then the little mermaid drank the magic draught, and it seemed as if a two-edged sword went through her delicate body. She fell into a swoon and lay like one dead. When the sun arose and shone over the sea, she recovered and felt a sharp pain. But just before her stood the handsome young prince. He fixed his coal-black eyes upon her so earnestly that she cast down her own, and then became aware that her fish's tail was gone and that she had as pretty a pair of white legs and tiny feet as any little maiden could have. But she had no clothes, so she wrapped herself in her long, thick hair.

The prince asked her who she was and where she came from, and she looked at him mildly and sorrowfully with her deep blue eyes; but she could not speak. Every step she took was as the witch had said it would be; she felt as if treading upon the points of needles or sharp knives. But she bore it willingly and stepped as lightly by the prince's side as a soap bubble, so that he and all who saw her wondered at her graceful swaying movements.

She was very soon arrayed in costly robes of silk and muslin and was the most beautiful creature in the palace. But she was mute, and could neither speak nor sing. Beautiful female slaves, dressed in silk and gold, stepped forward and sang before the prince and his royal parents. One sang better than all the others, and the prince clapped his hands and smiled at her. This was great sorrow to the little mermaid; she knew how much more sweetly she herself could sing once, and she thought, *Oh, if he could only know that! I have given away my voice forever to be with him.*

The slaves next performed some pretty fairylike dances to the sound of beautiful music. Then the little mermaid raised her lovely white arms, stood on the tips of her toes, and glided over the floor, and danced as no one yet had been able to dance. At each moment her beauty became more revealed, and her expressive eyes appealed more directly to the heart than the songs of the slaves.

Everyone was enchanted, especially the prince, who called her his little foundling; and she danced again quite readily to please him, although each time her foot touched the floor it seemed as if she trod on sharp knives. The prince said she should remain with him always, and she received permission to sleep at his door on a velvet cushion.

He had a page's dress made for her, that she might accompany him on horseback. They rode together through the sweet-scented woods, where the green boughs touched their shoulders, and the little birds sang among the fresh leaves. She climbed with the prince to the tops of high mountains; and although her tender feet bled so that even her steps were marked, she only laughed and followed him till they could see the clouds beneath them looking like a flock of birds traveling to distant lands.

While at the prince's palace, and when all the household were asleep, she would go and sit on the broad marble steps, for it eased her burning feet to bathe them in the cold seawater; and then she thought of all those below in the deep.

Once during the night her sisters came up arm in arm, singing sorrowfully, as they floated on the water. She beckoned to them, and then they recognized her and told her how she had grieved them. After that, they came to the same place every night. Once she saw in the distance her old grandmother, who had not been to the surface of the sea for many years, and the old Sea King, her father, with his crown on his head. They stretched out their hands toward her, but they did not venture so near the land as her sisters did.

As the days passed, she loved the prince more fondly, and he loved her as he would love a little child, but it never came into his head to make her his wife; yet, unless he married her, she could not receive an immortal soul; and, on the morning after his marriage with another, she would dissolve into the foam of the sea.

Do you not love me the best of them all? the eyes of the little mermaid seemed to say, when he took her in his arms and kissed her fair forehead.

"Yes, you are dear to me," said the prince, "for you have the best heart, and you are the most devoted to me. You are like a young maiden whom I once saw, but whom I shall never meet again. I was in a ship that was wrecked, and the waves cast me ashore near a holy temple, where several young maidens performed the service. The youngest of them found me on the shore and saved my life. I saw her but twice, and she is the only one in the world whom I could love. But you are like her, and you have almost driven her image out of my mind. She belongs to the holy temple, and my good fortune has sent you to me instead of her, and we will never part."

He doesn't know that it was I who saved his life, thought the little mermaid. *I carried him over the sea to the woods where the temple stands. I sat beneath the foam, and watched till the human beings came to help him. I saw the pretty maiden that he loves better than he loves me.* The mermaid sighed deeply, but she could not shed tears. *He says the maiden belongs to the holy temple; therefore, she will never return to the world. They will meet no more. While I am by his side, and see him every day. I will take care of him, and love him, and give up my life for his sake.*

Very soon it was said that the prince must marry and that the beautiful daughter of a neighboring king would be his wife, for a fine ship was being fitted out. Although the prince gave out that he merely intended to pay a visit to the king, it was generally supposed that he really went to see his daughter. A great company was to go with him. The little mermaid smiled and shook her head. She knew the prince's thoughts better than any of the others.

"I must travel," he had said to her. "I must see this beautiful princess. My parents desire it, but they will not make me bring her home as my bride. I cannot love her. She is not like the beautiful maiden in the temple, whom you resemble. If I were forced to choose a bride, I would rather choose you, my mute foundling, with those expressive eyes." And then he kissed her rosy mouth, played with her long wavy hair, and laid his head on her heart, while she dreamed of human happiness and an immortal soul.

"You are not afraid of the sea, my mute child," said he, as they stood on the deck of the noble ship that was to carry them to the country of the neighboring king. And then he told her of storm and of calm, of strange fishes in the deep beneath them, and of what the divers had seen there. She smiled at his descriptions, for she knew better than anyone what wonders were at the bottom of the sea.

In the moonlight, when all onboard were asleep, except the man at the helm who was steering, she sat on the deck, gazing down through the clear water. She thought she could distinguish her father's castle, and upon it her aged grandmother, with the silver crown on her head, looking through the rushing tide at the keel of the vessel. Then her sisters came up on the waves and gazed at her mournfully, wringing their white hands. She beckoned to them and smiled, and wanted to tell them how happy and well off she was; but the cabin boy approached, and when her sisters dived down he thought it was only the foam of the sea that he saw.

The next morning the ship sailed into the harbor of a beautiful town belonging to the king whom the prince was going to visit. The church bells were ringing, and from the high towers sounded a flourish of trumpets. Soldiers, with flying colors and glittering bayonets, lined the rocks through which they passed. Every day was a festival; balls and entertainments followed one another.

But the princess had not yet appeared. People said that she was being brought up and educated in a religious house, where she was learning every royal virtue. At last she came. Then the little mermaid, who was very anxious to see whether she was really beautiful, was obliged to acknowledge that she had never seen a more perfect vision of beauty. Her skin was delicately fair, and beneath her long dark eyelashes her laughing blue eyes shone with truth and purity.

"It was you," said the prince, "who saved my life when I lay dead on the beach," and he folded his blushing bride in his arms. "Oh, I am too happy," said he to the little mermaid. "My fondest hopes are all fulfilled. You will rejoice at my happiness, for your devotion to me is great and sincere."

The little mermaid kissed his hand and felt as if her heart were already broken. His wedding morning would bring death to her, and she would change into the foam of the sea.

All the church bells rung, and the heralds rode about the town proclaiming the betrothal. Perfumed oil was burning in costly silver lamps on every altar. The priests waved the censers, while the bride and bridegroom joined their hands and received the blessing of the bishop. The little mermaid, dressed in silk and gold, held up the bride's train. But her ears heard nothing of the festive music, and her eyes saw not the holy ceremony. She thought of the night of death that was coming to her, and of all she had lost in the world.

On the same evening the bride and bridegroom went onboard ship. Cannons were roaring, flags waving, and in the center of the ship a costly tent of purple and gold had been erected. It contained elegant couches for the reception of the bridal pair during the night.

The ship, with swelling sails and a favorable wind, glided away smoothly and lightly over the calm sea. When it grew dark a number of colored lamps were lighted, and the sailors danced merrily on the deck. The little mermaid could not help thinking of her first rising out of the sea, when she had seen similar festivities and joys. She joined in the dance, poised herself in the air as a swallow when it pursues its prey, and all present cheered her with wonder. She had never danced so elegantly before. Her tender feet felt as if cut with sharp knives, but she cared not for it; a sharper pang had pierced through her heart. She knew this was the last evening she should ever see the prince, for whom she had forsaken her kindred and her home. She had given up her beautiful voice and suffered unheard-of pain daily for him, while he knew nothing of it. This was the last evening that she would breathe the same air with him or gaze on the starry sky and the deep sea. An eternal night, without a thought or a dream, awaited her. She had no soul and now she could never win one.

All was joy and gaiety onboard the ship till long after midnight. She laughed and danced with the rest, while the thoughts of death were in her heart. The prince kissed his beautiful bride, while she played with his raven hair, till they went arm in arm to rest in the splendid tent.

Then all became still onboard the ship. The helmsman, alone awake, stood at the helm. The little mermaid leaned her white arms on the edge of the vessel and looked toward the east for the first blush of morning, for that first ray of dawn that would bring her death. She saw her sisters rising out of the flood. They were as pale as herself, but their long beautiful hair waved no more in the wind and had been cut off.

"We have given our hair to the witch," said they, "to obtain help for you, that you may not die tonight. She has given us a knife: Here it is, see it is very sharp. Before the sun rises you must plunge it into the heart of the prince. When the warm blood falls upon your feet they will grow together again and form into a fish's tail; and you will be once more a mermaid and return to us to live out your three hundred years before you die and change into the salt sea foam. Haste, then; he or you must die before sunrise. Our old grandmother moans so for you that her white hair is falling out from sorrow, as ours fell under the witch's scissors. Kill the prince and come back. Hasten: Do you not see the first red streaks in the sky? In a few minutes the sun will rise, and you must die." And then they sighed deeply and mournfully, and sank down beneath the waves.

The little mermaid drew back the crimson curtain of the tent and beheld the fair bride with her head resting on the prince's breast. She bent down and kissed his fair brow, then looked at the sky on which the rosy dawn grew brighter and brighter. Then she glanced at the sharp knife and again fixed her eyes on the prince, who whispered the name of his bride in his dreams. She was in his thoughts, and the knife trembled in the hand of the little mermaid. Then she flung it far away from her into the waves. The water turned red where it fell, and the drops that spurted up looked like blood. She cast one more lingering, half-fainting glance at the prince, and then threw herself from the ship into the sea and felt her body dissolving into foam.

The sun rose above the waves, and its warm rays fell on the cold foam of the little mermaid, who did not feel as if she were dying. She saw the bright sun, and all around her floated hundreds of transparent beautiful beings. She could see through them the white sails of the ship, and the red clouds in the sky. Their speech was melodious, but too ethereal to be heard by mortal ears, as they were also unseen by mortal eyes. The little mermaid perceived that she had a body like theirs, and that she continued to rise higher and higher out of the foam.

"Where am I?" asked she, and her voice sounded ethereal, as the voice of those who were with her. No earthly music could imitate it.

"Among the daughters of the air," answered one of them. "A mermaid has not an immortal soul, nor can she obtain one unless she wins the love of a human being. On the power of another hangs her eternal destiny. But the daughters of the air, although they do not possess an immortal soul, can, by their good deeds, procure one for themselves. We fly to warm countries and cool the sultry air that destroys people with its pestilence. We carry the perfume of the flowers to spread health and restoration. After we have striven for three hundred years to do all the good in our power, we receive an immortal soul and take part in human happiness. You, poor little mermaid, have tried with your whole heart to do as we are doing. You have suffered and endured and raised yourself to the spirit world by your good deeds. And now, by striving for three hundred years in the same way, you may obtain an immortal soul."

The little mermaid lifted her clear eyes toward the sun and felt them, for the first time, filling with tears. On the ship, in which she had left the prince, there was life and noise. She saw him and his beautiful bride searching for her. Sorrowfully they gazed at the pearly foam, as if they knew she had thrown herself into the waves. Unseen she kissed the forehead of the bride and fanned the prince, and then mounted with the other daughters of the air to a rosy cloud that floated through the ether.

"After three hundred years, we shall float into God's kingdom," said she. "And we may even get there sooner," whispered one of her companions. "Unseen we can enter people's houses, where there are children, and for every day on which we find a good child, who is the joy of his parents and deserves their love, our time of probation is shortened. The child does not know when we fly through the room that we smile with joy at his good conduct, for we can count one year less of our three hundred years. But when we see a naughty or a wicked child, we shed tears of sorrow, and for every tear a day is added to our time of trial!"

The Emperor's New Clothes

Many years ago, there was an emperor who was so excessively fond of new clothes that he spent all his money on dress. He did not trouble himself in the least about his soldiers; nor did he care to go either to the theater or the chase, unless he could show off his new clothes. He had a different suit for each hour of the day. For another king or emperor, people said, "He is sitting in council," but it was always said of him, "The emperor is sitting in his closet."

Time passed merrily in the large town where the emperor lived. Strangers arrived every day at the court. One day two rogues, calling themselves weavers, made their appearance. They gave out that they knew how to weave fabric of the most beautiful colors and elaborate patterns. Not only that, but also the clothes manufactured from this material had the wonderful property of remaining invisible to anyone who was unfit for the office he held, or who was extraordinarily simple in character.

These must, indeed, be splendid clothes! thought the emperor. *If I had such a suit, I might at once find out what people in my realms are unfit for their office, and also distinguish the wise from the foolish! This cloth must be woven for me immediately.* And he caused large sums of money to be given to both the weavers in order that they might begin their work at once.

So the two pretend weavers set up two looms and affected to work very busily, although in reality they did nothing at all. They asked for the most delicate silk and the purest gold thread, put both into their own knapsacks, and then continued to pretend to work at the empty looms until late at night.

I should like to know how the weavers are getting on with my cloth, thought the emperor to himself after some little time had elapsed. He was, however, rather embarrassed when he remembered that a simpleton, or one unfit for his office, would be unable to see the fabric. To be sure, he thought he had nothing to risk in his own person; but yet, he would prefer sending somebody else to bring him intelligence about the weavers and their work before he troubled himself in the affair. All the people throughout the city had heard of the wonderful property the cloth was to possess, and all were anxious to learn how wise, or how ignorant, their neighbors might prove to be.

"I will send my faithful old minister to the weavers," said the emperor at last, after some deliberation. "He will be best able to see how the cloth looks, for he is a man of sense, and no one can be more suitable for his office than he is."

So the faithful old minister went into the hall, where the knaves were working with all their might at their empty looms. *What can be the meaning of this?* thought the old man, opening his eyes very wide. *I cannot discover the least bit of thread on the looms.* However, he did not express his thoughts aloud.

The impostors requested him very courteously to be so good as to come nearer their looms, and then asked him whether the design pleased him and whether the colors were not very beautiful, at the same time pointing to the empty frames. The poor old minister looked and looked, but he could not see anything on the looms, for a very good reason. There was nothing there to see. *What!* thought he again. *Is it possible that I am a simpleton? I have never thought so myself, and no one must know it now if I am so. Can it be that I am unfit for my office? No, that must not be said either. I will never confess that I could not see the cloth.*

"Well, Sir Minister!" said one of the knaves, still pretending to work. "You do not say whether the fabric pleases you."

"Oh, it is excellent!" replied the old minister, looking at the loom through his spectacles. "This pattern, and the colors, yes, I will tell the emperor without delay how very beautiful I think them."

"We shall be much obliged to you," said the impostors, and then they named the different colors and described the pattern of the pretended stuff. The old minister listened attentively to their words, in order that he might repeat them to the emperor. Then, the knaves asked for more silk and gold, saying that it was necessary to complete what they had begun. However, they put all that was given them into their knapsacks and continued to work with as much apparent diligence as before at their empty looms.

Soon the emperor sent another officer of his court to see how the men were getting on and to ascertain whether the cloth would soon be ready. It was just the same with this gentleman as with the minister. He surveyed the looms on all sides, but could see nothing at all but the empty frames.

"Does not the stuff appear as beautiful to you, as it did to my lord the minister?" asked the impostors of the emperor's second ambassador, at the same time making the same gestures as before and talking of the design and colors that were not there.

I certainly am not stupid! thought the messenger. *It must be that I am not fit for my good, profitable office! That is very odd. However, no one shall know anything about it.* And accordingly he praised the stuff he could not see and declared that he was delighted with both colors and patterns. "Indeed, please your Imperial Majesty," said he to his sovereign when he returned. "The cloth that the weavers are preparing is extraordinarily magnificent."

The whole city was talking of the splendid cloth that the emperor had ordered to be woven at his own expense.

Finally the emperor himself wished to see the costly fabric, while it was still on the loom. Accompanied by a select number of officers of the court, among whom were the two men who had already admired the cloth, he went to the crafty impostors, who, as soon as they were aware of the emperor's approach, went on working more diligently than ever, although they still did not pass a single thread through the looms.

"Is not the work absolutely magnificent?" said the two trusted officials. "If Your Majesty will only be pleased to look at it! What a splendid design! What glorious colors!" and at the same time they pointed to the empty frames, for they imagined that everyone else could see this exquisite piece of workmanship.

How is this? said the emperor to himself. *I can see nothing! This is indeed a terrible affair! Am I a simpleton, or am I unfit to be an emperor? This is the worst thing that could happen to me.* At the same time he said aloud, "The cloth is charming. It has my complete approbation." And he smiled most graciously and looked closely at the empty looms, for on no account would he say that he could not see what two of the officers of his court had praised so much. All his retinue now strained their eyes, hoping to discover something on the looms, but they could see no more than the others. Nevertheless, they all exclaimed, "Oh, how beautiful!" and advised His Majesty to have some new clothes made from this splendid material for the approaching procession. "Magnificent! Charming! Excellent!" resounded on all sides, and everyone was uncommonly pleased. The emperor shared in the general satisfaction and presented the impostors with the ribbon of an order of knighthood, to be worn in their buttonholes, and the title of Knights of the Loom.

The night before the day on which the procession was to take place the rogues stayed up and had sixteen lights burning so that everyone might see how anxious they were to finish the emperor's new suit. They pretended to roll the cloth off the looms, cut the air with their scissors, and sewed with needles without any thread in them. "See!" cried they, at last. "The emperor's new clothes are ready!"

And then the emperor arrived, with all the grandees of his court. The rogues raised their arms, as if they were holding something up, saying, "Here are Your Majesty's trousers! Here is the scarf! Here is the mantle! The whole suit is as light as a cobweb. One might fancy one has nothing at all on when dressed in it. That, however, is the great virtue of this delicate cloth."

"Yes, indeed!" said all the courtiers, although not one of them could see anything of this exquisite cloth.

"If Your Imperial Majesty will be graciously pleased to take off your clothes, we will fit on the new suit in front of the looking glass."

The emperor was accordingly undressed, and the rogues pretended to array him in his new suit as the emperor turned around, from side to side, before the looking glass.

"How splendid His Majesty looks in his new clothes, and how well they fit!" everyone cried out. "What a design! What colors! These are indeed royal robes!"

"The canopy that is to be borne over Your Majesty, in the procession, is waiting," announced the chief master of the ceremonies.

"I am quite ready," answered the emperor. "Do my new clothes fit well?" he asked, turning himself around again before the looking glass, in order that he might appear to be examining his handsome suit.

The lords-in-waiting, who were to carry His Majesty's train, felt about on the ground, as if they were lifting up the ends of the cloth, and pretended to be carrying something, for they would by no means betray anything like simplicity or unfitness for their office.

So the emperor walked under his high canopy in the midst of the procession, through the streets of his capital. All the people standing by and those at the windows cried out, "Oh! How beautiful are our Emperor's new clothes! What a magnificent train there is to the mantle, and how gracefully the scarf hangs!" In short, no one would admit that he could not see these much-admired clothes, because, in doing so, he would have declared himself either a simpleton or unfit for his office. Certainly, none of the emperor's various suits had ever made so great an impression as this invisible one.

"But the emperor has nothing at all on!" said a little child.

"Listen to the voice of innocence!" exclaimed his father, and what the child had said was whispered from one to another.

"But he has nothing at all on!" at last cried out all the people. The emperor was vexed, for he knew that the people were right, but he thought the procession must go on now! And the lords-in-waiting took greater pains than ever to appear holding up a train, although, in reality, there was no train to hold.

The Princess and the Pea

There was once a prince who wished to marry a princess, but then she must be a real princess. He traveled all over the world in hopes of finding such a lady, but there was always something wrong. Princesses he found in plenty, but whether they were real princesses it was impossible for him to decide, for now one thing, now another, seemed to him not quite right about the ladies. At last he returned to his palace quite downcast, because he wished so much to have a real princess for his wife.

One evening a fearful tempest arose; it thundered and lightninged, and the rain poured down from the sky in torrents. It was as dark as pitch. All at once there was heard a violent knocking at the door, and the old king, the prince's father, went out himself to open it.

It was a princess who was standing outside the door. What with the rain and the wind, she was in a sad condition. The water trickled down from her hair, and her clothes clung to her body. She said she was a real princess.

Ah! we shall soon see that! thought the old queen mother. However, she said not a word of what she was going to do, but went quietly into the bedroom, took all the bedclothes off the bed, and put three little peas on the bedstead. She then laid twenty mattresses one upon another over the three peas and put twenty featherbeds over the mattresses.

Upon this bed the princess was to pass the night.

The next morning she was asked how she had slept. "Oh, very badly indeed!" she replied. "I have scarcely closed my eyes the whole night through. I do not know what was in my bed, but I had something hard under me and am all over black and blue. It has hurt me so much!"

Now it was plain that the lady must be a real princess, since she had been able to feel the three little peas through the twenty mattresses and twenty featherbeds. None but a real princess could have had such a delicate sense of feeling.

The prince accordingly made her his wife, being now convinced that he had found a real princess. The three peas were, however, put into the cabinet of curiosities, where they are still to be seen, provided they are not lost.

Wasn't this a lady of real delicacy!

The Shoes of Fortune

I. A Beginning

Every author has some peculiarity in his descriptions or in his style of writing. Those who do not like him magnify it, shrug up their shoulders, and exclaim—there he is again! I, for my part, know very well how I can bring about this movement and this exclamation. It would happen immediately if I were to begin here, as I intended to do, with: "Rome has its Corso, Naples its Toledo"—"Ah, that Andersen. There he is again!" they would cry. Yet I must, to please my fancy, continue quite quietly, and add: "But Copenhagen has its East Street."

Here, then, we will stay for the present. In one of the houses not far from the new market a party was invited—a very large party, in order, as is often the case, to get a return invitation from the others. One half of the company was already seated at the card table; the other half awaited the result of the hostess's question: "Now let us see what we can do to amuse ourselves."

Gradually, the conversation grew more interesting. Among other things, they spoke of the Middle Ages. Some praised that period as far more interesting, far more poetic than our own too sober present. Indeed Councillor Knap defended this opinion so warmly that the hostess declared immediately on his side, and both exerted themselves with unwearied eloquence. The councillor boldly declared the time of King Hans to be the noblest and the most happy period.*

While the conversation continued on this subject and was only for a moment interrupted by the arrival of a journal that contained nothing worth reading, we will just step out into the antechamber, where cloaks, raincoats, sticks, umbrellas, and shoes were deposited. Here sat two female figures, a young and an old one. One might have thought at first they were servants come to accompany their mistresses home; but on looking nearer, one soon saw they could scarcely be ordinary servants. Their forms were too noble for that, their skin too fine, the cut of their dress too striking. Two fairies were they. The younger, it is true, was not Dame Fortune herself, but the waiting maid of one of Dame Fortune's attendants who carry about the lesser good things that she distributes. The other looked extremely gloomy—it was Care. She always attends to her own serious business herself, as then she is sure of having it done properly. The two fairies were telling each other where they had been during the day. The messenger of Fortune had only executed a few unimportant commissions, such as saving a new bonnet from a shower of rain, but what she had yet to perform was something quite unusual.

"I must tell you," said she, "that today is my birthday. And in honor of it, a pair of walking shoes, or galoshes, has

* A.D. 1482–1513

been entrusted to me, which I am to introduce to mankind. These shoes possess the property of instantly transporting anyone who has them on to the place or the period in which that person most wishes to be. Every wish, as regards time or place or state of being, will be immediately fulfilled, and so at last people will be happy."

"Do you seriously believe that?" replied Care, in a severe tone of reproach. "No, whoever wears the shoes will be very unhappy and will assuredly bless the moment when he feels that he has freed himself from them."

"Stupid nonsense!" said the other angrily. "I will put them here by the door. Someone will make a mistake for certain and take the wrong ones—he will be a happy man."

Such was their conversation.

II. What Happened to the Councillor

It was late. Councillor Knap, lost in thought about the times of King Hans, intended to go home, and malicious Fate managed matters so that his feet, instead of finding their way to his own galoshes, slipped into the magic shoes of Fortune. Thus adorned the good man walked out of the well-lighted rooms onto East Street. But by the magic power of the shoes he had been carried back to the times of King Hans, on which account his foot very naturally sank in the mud and puddles of the street, there having been in those days no pavement in Copenhagen.

"Well! This is terrible! How dirty it is here!" exclaimed the councillor. "As to a pavement, I can find no traces of one, and all the lamps, it seems, have gone to sleep."

The moon was not yet very high. It was besides rather foggy, so that in the darkness all objects seemed mingled in chaotic confusion. At the next corner hung a votive lamp before a picture of the Madonna, but the light it gave was little better than none at all. Indeed, he did not observe it before he was exactly under it, and his eyes fell upon the bright colors of the pictures that represented the well-known group of the Virgin and the infant Jesus.

That is probably a waxwork show, thought he; *and the people have delayed taking down their sign in hopes of a late visitor or two.*

Then two figures in the costume of the time of King Hans passed quickly by him.

How strange they look! thought the councilor. *The good folks must be coming from a masquerade!*

Suddenly the sound of drums and fifes was heard. The bright blaze of a fire shot up from time to time, and its ruddy gleams seemed to contend with the bluish light of the torches. The councillor stood still and watched a most strange procession pass by. First came a dozen skillful drummers, then came guards, some armed with crossbows. The principal person in the procession was a priest. Astonished at what he saw, the councillor asked what was the meaning of the procession and who the man was.

"That's the Bishop of Zealand," was the answer.

"Good Heavens! What has taken possession of the bishop?" sighed the councillor, shaking his head. It certainly could not be the bishop, even though he was considered the most absentminded man in the whole kingdom, and people told the drollest anecdotes about him.

While reflecting on the matter, and without looking right or left, the councillor went through East Street and across the Habro-Platz. But the bridge leading to Palace Square had disappeared; scarcely trusting his senses, the nocturnal wanderer discovered a shallow piece of water, and here fell in with two men who were rocking very comfortably in a boat.

"Does your honor want to cross the ferry to the Holme?" asked they.

"Across to the Holme!" said the councillor, who knew nothing of the age in which he at that moment was. "No, I am going to Christian's Haven, to Little Market Street." Both men stared at him in astonishment.

"Only just tell me where the bridge is," said he. "It is really unpardonable that there are no lamps here; and it is as dirty as if one had to wade through a morass." The longer he spoke with the boatmen, the less they could understand each other.

"I don't understand your Bornholmish dialect," said he at last, angrily, turning his back upon them. He still couldn't find the bridge; however, and there was no railway either.

"It is really disgraceful what a state this place is in," muttered he to himself. Never had his own times, with which he was always grumbling, seemed so miserable as on this evening. *I'll take a hackney coach!* thought he. But where were the hackney coaches? Not one was to be seen.

"I must go back to the New Market. There, it is to be hoped, I shall find some coaches, for if I don't, I shall never get safe to Christian's Haven." So off he went in the direction of East Street and had nearly got to the end of it when the moon came out from behind a cloud.

"God bless me! What wooden scaffolding is that which they have set up there?" cried he involuntarily, as he caught sight of the East Gate, which, in those days, was at the end of East Street.

He found, however, a little side door open, and through this he went and stepped through to the other side where he expected to find the New Market. Instead he saw a huge desolate plain. Some wild bushes stood up here and there, while across the field flowed a broad canal or river. Some wretched hovels for the Dutch sailors, resembling great boxes and after which the place was named, lay about in confused disorder on the opposite bank.

"I either behold a *fata morgana*, or I am regularly tipsy," groaned the councillor. "But what's this?"

He turned around anew, firmly convinced that he was seriously ill. He gazed at the street formerly so well known to him and now so strange in appearance, and looked at the houses more attentively. Most of them were of wood, slightly put together. Many had a thatched roof.

"No—I must be far from well," sighed he, "and yet I drank only one glass of punch. But even that was too much for me—it was, too, really very wrong to give us punch and hot salmon for supper. I shall speak about it at the first opportunity. I have half a mind to go back again and say what I suffer. But no, that would be too silly, and Heaven only knows if they are up still." Then he looked for the house, but it had vanished.

"It is really dreadful," groaned he with increasing anxiety; "I cannot recognize East Street again. There is not a single decent shop from one end to the other! Nothing but wretched huts can I see anywhere, just as if I were at

Ringstead. Oh! I am ill! I can scarcely bear myself any longer. Where the deuce can the house be? It must be here on this very spot, yet there is not the slightest resemblance between this house and the one I left, to such a degree has everything changed this night! At all events here are some people up and stirring. Oh! Oh! I am certainly very ill."

He came to a half-open door, through a chink of which a faint light shone. It was a sort of hostelry of those times, a kind of public house. The room had some resemblance to the clay-floored halls in Holstein. A pretty numerous company, consisting of seamen, Copenhagen merchants, and a few scholars, sat here in deep conversation over their pewter mugs and gave little heed to the person who entered.

"By your leave!" said the councillor to the hostess, who came bustling toward him. "I've felt so queer all of a sudden. Would you have the goodness to send for a hackney coach to take me to Christian's Haven?"

The woman examined him with eyes of astonishment and shook her head. She then addressed him in German. The councillor thought she did not understand Danish and therefore repeated his wish in German. This, in connection with his costume, strengthened the good woman in the belief that he was a foreigner. That he was ill, she comprehended directly, so she brought him a pitcher of water, which tasted certainly pretty strong of the sea, although it had been fetched from the well.

The councillor supported his head on his hand, drew a long breath, and thought over all the wondrous things he saw around him. "Is this the Daily News of this evening?" he asked mechanically, as he saw the hostess push aside a large sheet of paper.

She did not understand what he meant, but she handed him the paper without replying. It was a coarse woodcut, representing a splendid meteor "as seen in the town of Cologne."

"That is very old!" said the councillor, whom this piece of antiquity began to make considerably more cheerful. "Pray how did you come into possession of this rare print? It is extremely interesting, although the whole is a mere fable. Such meteors are easily explained today—they are the reflections of the aurora borealis, and it is highly probable they are caused principally by electricity."

Those persons who were sitting nearest him and heard his speech, stared at him in wonderment. One of them rose, took off his hat respectfully, and said with a serious countenance, "You are no doubt a very learned man, Monsieur."

"Oh, no," answered the councillor, "I can only join in conversation on this topic and on that, as indeed one must do according to the demands of the world at present."

"*Modestia* is a fine virtue," continued the gentleman. "However, as to your speech, I must say *mihi secus videtur*. Yet I am willing to suspend my *judicium*."

"May I ask with whom I have the pleasure of speaking?" asked the councillor.

"I am a Bachelor of Divinity," answered the gentleman with a stiff reverence.

This reply fully satisfied the councillor; the title suited the dress. *He is certainly*, thought he, *some village schoolmaster—some queer old fellow, such as one still meets with in Jutland.*

"This is no *locus docendi*, it is true," began the clerical gentleman, "yet I beg you earnestly to let us profit by your learning. Your reading in the ancients is, *sine dubio*, of vast extent?"

"Oh yes, I've read some to be sure," replied the councillor. "I like reading all useful old works, but I do not on that account despise the modern ones. 'Tis only the stories of everyday life that I cannot bear—we have more than enough of those."

"Everyday stories?" said our bachelor inquiringly.

"I mean those newfangled novels, twisting and writhing themselves in the dust of commonplace, that are so common today."

"Oh!" exclaimed the clerical gentleman, smiling. "There is much wit in them; besides they are read at court. The king likes the history of Sir Iffven and Sir Gaudian particularly, which treats of King Arthur and his Knights of the Round Table. He has more than once joked about it with his high vassals."

"I have not read that novel," said the councillor. "It must be quite a new one that Heiberg has published lately."

"No," answered the theologian of the time of King Hans. "That book is not written by a Heiberg, but was imprinted by Godfrey von Gehmen."

"Oh, is that the author's name?" said the councillor. "It is a very old name, and, as well as I recollect, he was the first printer that appeared in Denmark."

"Yes, he is our first printer," replied the clerical gentleman hastily.

So far all went on well. One of the worthy merchants now spoke of the dreadful pestilence that had raged in the country a few years back, meaning that of 1484. The councillor imagined it was the cholera that was meant, which people made so much fuss about; and the discourse passed off satisfactorily enough. The war of the buccaneers of 1490 was so recent that it could not fail being alluded to. The English pirates had, they said, most shamefully taken their ships while in the roadstead. The councillor, before whose eyes the Herostratic* event of 1801 still floated vividly, agreed entirely with the others in abusing the rascally English. With other topics he was not so fortunate. Every moment brought about some new confusion and threatened to create a perfect Babel, for the worthy bachelor was really too ignorant, and the simplest observations of the councillor sounded to him too daring and phantastical. They looked at one another from the crown of the head to the soles of the feet. And when matters grew to too high a pitch, then the bachelor spoke in Latin in the hope of being better understood—but it was of no use.

"What's the matter?" asked the hostess, plucking the councillor by the sleeve. And now his recollection returned, for in the course of the conversation he had entirely forgotten all that had preceded it.

"Merciful God, where am I!" exclaimed he in agony. All his ideas and feelings of overpowering dizziness, against which he struggled with the utmost power of desperation, encompassed him with renewed force. "Let us drink claret and mead, and Bremen beer," shouted one of the guests— "and you shall drink with us!"

Two maidens approached. One wore a cap of two colors, denoting the class of persons to which she belonged. They poured out the liquor and bowed their heads, while a cold perspiration trickled down the poor councillor's back.

---

* Herostratus, or Eratostratus—an Ephesian, who wantonly set fire to the famous temple of Diana, in order to commemorate his name by so uncommon an action.

"What's to be the end of this! What's to become of me!" he groaned. But his hosts were so polite that he felt obligated, in spite of his opposition, to drink with the rest. Eventually they took hold of the worthy man, who, hearing on every side that he was intoxicated, did not in the least doubt the truth of this assertion. On the contrary, he implored the ladies and gentlemen present to procure him a hackney coach. They, however, thought he was speaking Russian.

Never before, he thought, had he been in such a coarse and ignorant company. One might almost fancy the people had turned heathens again. "It is the most dreadful moment of my life. The whole world is leagued against me!" But suddenly it occurred to him that he might stoop down under the table and then creep unobserved out of the door. He did so, but just as he was going, the others remarked what he was about. They laid hold of him by the legs, and now, happily for him, off fell his fatal shoes—and with them the charm was at an end.

The councillor saw quite distinctly before him a lantern burning, and behind this a large handsome house. All seemed to him in proper order as usual. It was East Street, splendid and elegant as we now see it. He lay with his feet toward a doorway, and exactly opposite sat the watchman asleep.

"Gracious Heaven!" said he. "Have I lain here in the street and dreamed? Yes, 'tis East Street! How splendid and light it is! But really it is terrible what an effect that one glass of punch must have had on me!"

Two minutes later, he was sitting in a hackney coach and driving to Christian's Haven. He thought of the distress and agony he had endured, and praised from the very bottom of his heart the happy modern reality—our own time—which, with all its deficiencies, is yet much better than that in which, so much against his inclination, he had lately been.

III. The Watchman's Adventure

"Why, there is a pair of galoshes, as sure as I'm alive!" said the watchman, awaking from a gentle slumber. "They belong no doubt to the lieutenant who lives over the way. They lie close to his door."

The worthy man was inclined to ring and deliver them at the house, for there was still a light in the window. But he did not like disturbing the other people in their beds, and so very considerately he left the matter alone.

"Such a pair of shoes must be very warm and comfortable," said he. "The leather is so soft and supple." They fitted his feet as though they had been made for him. "'Tis a curious world we live in," continued he, soliloquizing. "There is the lieutenant, now, who might go quietly to bed if he chose, where no doubt he could stretch himself at his ease, but does he do it? No, he saunters up and down his room because, probably, he has enjoyed too many of the good things of this world at his dinner. That's a happy fellow! He has neither an infirm mother, nor a whole troop of everlastingly hungry children to torment him. Every evening he goes to a party, where his nice supper costs him nothing. Would to Heaven I could but change with him! How happy should I be!"

While expressing his wish, the charm of the shoes, which he had put on, began to work. The watchman entered into the being and nature of the lieutenant. He stood in the handsomely furnished apartment and held between his fingers a small sheet of rose-colored paper, on which some verses were written—written indeed by the officer himself, for who has not, at least once in his life, had a lyrical moment? And if one then marks down one's thoughts, poetry is produced. But here was written:

Oh, Were I Rich!

"Oh, were I rich! Such was my wish, yea such
When hardly three feet high, I longed for much.
Oh, were I rich! An officer was I,
With sword, and uniform, and plume so high.
And the time came, and officer was I!
But yet I grew not rich. Alas, poor me!
Have pity, Thou, who all man's wants dost see.

"I sat one evening sunk in dreams of bliss,
A maid of seven years old gave me a kiss,
I at that time was rich in poesy
And tales of old, though poor as poor could be;
But all she asked for was this poesy.
Then was I rich, but not in gold, poor me!
As Thou dost know, who all men's hearts canst see.

"Oh, were I rich! Oft asked I for this boon.
The child grew up to womanhood full soon.
She is so pretty, clever, and so kind;
Oh, did she know what's hidden in my mind—
A tale of old. Would she to me were kind!
But I'm condemned to silence! Oh, poor me!

As Thou dost know, who all men's hearts canst see.

"Oh, were I rich in calm and peace of mind,
My grief you then would not here written find!
O thou, to whom I do my heart devote,
Oh, read this page of glad days now remote,
A dark, dark tale, which I tonight devote!
Dark is the future now. Alas, poor me!
Have pity Thou, who all men's pains dost see."

Such verses as these people write when they are in love!
But a wise man will not print them. Here one of the sorrows of
life, in which there is real poetry, gave itself vent; not that
barren grief that the poet may only hint at, but never depict in
its detail—misery and want: that animal necessity, in short, to
snatch at least at a fallen leaf of the breadfruit tree, if not at
the fruit itself. The higher the position in which one finds one-
self transplanted, the greater is the suffering. Everyday necessity is the stagnant pool of life—no lovely picture reflects
itself therein. Lieutenant, love, and lack of money—that is a
symbolic triangle, or much the same as the half of the shat-
tered die of Fortune. This the lieutenant felt most poignantly,
and this was the reason he leaned his head against the window
and sighed so deeply.

"The poor watchman out there in the street is far happier
than I. He knows not what I term privation. He has a home, a
wife, and children, who weep with him over his sorrows, who
rejoice with him when he is glad. Oh, far happier were I, could
I exchange with him my being—with his desires and with his
hopes perform the weary pilgrimage of life! Oh, he is a
hundred times happier than I!"

At this moment the watchman was again watchman. It was the shoes that caused the metamorphosis by means of which he took upon him the thoughts and feelings of the officer. But, as we have just seen, he felt himself in his new situation much less contented, and now preferred the very thing which but some minutes before he had rejected. So then the watchman wished himself again a watchman.

"That was an unpleasant dream," said he, "but 'twas droll enough altogether. I fancied that I was the lieutenant over there, and yet the thing was not very much to my taste after all. I missed my good old mother and the dear little ones, who almost tear me to pieces for sheer love."

He seated himself once more and nodded: The dream continued to haunt him, for he still had the shoes on his feet. A falling star shone in the dark firmament. "There falls another star," said he, "but what does it matter. There are always enough left. I should not much mind examining the little glimmering things somewhat nearer, especially the moon, for that would not slip so easily through a man's fingers. When we die—so at least says the student, for whom my wife does the washing—we shall fly about as light as a feather from one such a star to the other. That's, of course, not true, but 'twould be pretty enough if it were so. If I could but once take a leap up there, my body might stay here on the steps for all I care."

There are certain things in the world to which one ought never to give utterance except with the greatest caution; but doubly so when we have the Shoes of Fortune on our feet. Now just listen to what happened to the watchman.

As to ourselves, we all know the speed produced by the employment of steam. We have experienced it either on railroads or in boats when crossing the sea. But such a flight is like the traveling of a sloth in comparison with the velocity with which light moves. It flies nineteen million times faster than the best racehorse, and yet electricity is quicker still. Death is an electric shock that our heart receives; the freed soul soars upward on the wings of electricity. The sun's light wants eight minutes and some seconds to perform a journey of more than twenty million of our Danish* miles. Borne by electricity, the soul wants even some minutes less to accomplish the same flight. To it the space between the heavenly bodies is not greater than the distance between the homes of our friends in town is for us, even if they live a short way from each other. Such an electric shock in the heart, however, costs us the use of the body here below—unless, like the watchman of East Street, we happen to have on the Shoes of Fortune.

In a few seconds the watchman had done the fifty-two thousand Danish miles up to the moon, which was formed out of matter much lighter than our earth, and is, so we should say, as soft as newly fallen snow. He found himself on one of the many circular mountain ridges with which we are acquainted by means of Dr. Madler's "Map of the Moon." Within, down it sunk perpendicularly into a caldron, about a Danish mile in depth; while below lay a town whose appearance we can, in some measure, realize to ourselves by beating the white of an egg in a glass of water. The matter of which it was built was just as soft, and formed similar towers and domes and pillars, transparent and rocking in the thin air; while above his head our earth was rolling like a large fiery ball.

He perceived immediately a quantity of beings who were

* A Danish mile is nearly 4¾ English

certainly similar to what we call "men," yet they looked different from us. A far more active imagination than that of the pseudo-Herschel* must have had created them. And if they had been placed in groups, and copied by some skillful painter's hand, one would, without doubt, have exclaimed involuntarily, "What a beautiful arabesque!"

They had a language, too. No one could have expected that the soul of the watchman would understand it. Be that as it may, his soul did comprehend it, for in our souls there germinate far greater powers than we poor mortals, despite all our cleverness, have any notion of. Do we not show an astounding dramatic talent in all our dreams? There every acquaintance appears and speaks upon the stage, so entirely in character and with the same tone of voice that none of us, when awake, are able to imitate it. How well can we recall persons to our mind, of whom we have not thought for years, when suddenly they step forth "every inch a man," resembling the real personages, even to the finest features, and become the heroes or heroines of our world of dreams. In reality, such remembrances are rather unpleasant: Every sin, every evil thought, may, like a clock with alarm or chimes, be repeated at random. Then the question is if we can trust ourselves to give an account of every unbecoming word in our heart and on our lips.

The watchman's spirit understood the language of the inhabitants of the moon pretty well. The Selenites* disputed variously about our earth and expressed their doubts if it could be inhabited. The air, they said, must certainly be too

* This relates to a book published some years ago in Germany, said to be written by Herschel, which contained a description of the moon and its inhabitants, written with such a semblance of truth that many were deceived by the imposture. Probably a translation of the celebrated moon hoax, written by Richard A. Locke, and originally published in New York.
* Dwellers in the moon.

dense to allow any rational dweller in the moon the necessary free respiration. They considered the moon alone to be inhabited. They imagined it was the real heart of the universe or planetary system, on which the genuine Cosmopolites, or citizens of the world, dwelled. What strange things people—no, what strange things Selenites sometimes take into their heads!

About politics they had a good deal to say. But little Denmark must take care what it is about and not run counter to the moon. That great realm might in an ill-humor bestir itself and dash down a hailstorm in our faces, or force the Baltic to overflow the sides of its gigantic basin.

We will, therefore, not listen to what was spoken. But we will rather proceed, like good quiet citizens, to East Street, and observe what happened meanwhile to the body of the watchman.

He sat lifeless on the steps. The morning star,* that is to say, the heavy wooden staff headed with iron spikes, and which had nothing else in common with its sparkling brother in the sky, had glided from his hand, while his eyes were fixed with glassy stare on the moon where his honest soul still wandered it.

"What's the hour, watchman?" asked a passerby. But when the watchman gave no reply, the merry roisterer, who was now returning home from a noisy drinking bout, took it into his head to try what a tweak of the nose would do, on which the supposed sleeper lost his balance. The body lay motionless, stretched out on the pavement: The man was

---

* The watchmen in Germany had formerly carried, and in some places they still carry, on their rounds at night a sort of mace or club, known in ancient times by the above denomination.

dead. When the patrol came up, all his comrades, who comprehended nothing of the whole affair, were seized with a dreadful fright, for dead he was, and he remained so. The proper authorities were informed of the circumstance, people talked a good deal about it, and in the morning the body was carried to the hospital.

Now that would be a very pretty joke, if the spirit when it came back and looked for the body in East Street, were not to find one. No doubt the soul would, in its anxiety, run off to the police, and then to the lost and found office to announce that "the finder will be handsomely rewarded," and at last find it in the hospital. Yet we may boldly assert that the soul is shrewdest when it shakes off every fetter and every sort of leading string—the body only makes it stupid.

The seemingly dead body of the watchman wandered, as we have said, to the hospital, where it was brought into the general viewing room. The first thing that was done here was naturally to pull off the galoshes forcing the spirit, that was merely gone out on adventures, to return with the quickness of lightning to its earthly tenement. It took its direction toward the body in a straight line, and a few seconds after, life began to show itself in the man. He asserted that the preceding night had been the worst that ever the malice of fate had allotted him. He would not for two silver marks again go through what he had endured while moon-stricken. But now, however, it was over. The same day he was discharged from the hospital perfectly cured, but the shoes remained behind.

IV. An Important Moment
—An Evening's "Dramatic Readings"
—A Most Strange Journey

Every inhabitant of Copenhagen knows what the entrance to Frederick's Hospital looks like. But as it is possible that others, who are not Copenhagen people, may also read this little work, we will beforehand give a short description of it.

The extensive building is separated from the street by a pretty high railing, the thick iron bars of which are so far apart that, in all seriousness, it is said some very thin fellow had of a night occasionally squeezed himself through to go and pay his little visits in the town. The part of the body most difficult to manage on such occasions was, no doubt, the head. Here, as is so often the case in the world, long-headed people get through best. So much, then, for the introduction.

One of the young men, whose head, in a physical sense only, might be said to be of the thickest, had the watch that evening. The rain poured down in torrents, yet despite these two obstacles, the young man had his reasons for wanting to go out, if only for a quarter of an hour. He thought it unnecessary to tell the door-keeper he was leaving since he could easily slip through the iron railings. On the floor in front of him lay the galoshes, which the watchman had forgotten. He never dreamed for a moment that they belonged to Fortune, and they promised to do him good service in the wet, so he put them on. The question now was, if he could squeeze himself through the grating, for he had never tried before. Well, there he stood.

"Would to Heaven I had got my head through!" said he, involuntarily. And instantly through it slipped, easily and without pain, notwithstanding it was pretty large and thick. But now the rest of the body was to be got through!

"Ah! I am much too stout," groaned he aloud, while fixed as in a vice. "I had thought the head was the most difficult part of the matter—oh! Oh! I really cannot squeeze myself through!"

He now wanted to pull his overhasty head back again, but he could not. For his neck there was room enough, but for nothing more. His first feeling was of anger; then his spirits sank. The Shoes of Fortune had placed him in the most dreadful situation, and, unfortunately, it never occurred to him to wish himself free. The pitch-black clouds poured down their contents in still heavier torrents. Not a creature was to be seen in the streets. He couldn't reach up to the bell and to cry aloud for help would have availed him little. Besides, how ashamed would he have been to be found caught in a trap, like an out-witted fox! How was he to twist himself through! He saw clearly that it was his irrevocable destiny to remain a prisoner till dawn, or, perhaps, even late in the morning. Then the smith must be fetched to file away the bars, but all that would not be done so quickly as he could think about it. The whole Charity School, just opposite, would be in motion; all the new booths, with their not very courtierlike swarm of seamen, would join them out of curiosity and would greet him with a wild "hurrah!" while he was standing in his pillory. There would be a mob, hissing and rejoicing and jeering—"Oh, my blood is mounting to my brain; 'tis enough to drive one mad! I shall go wild! I know not what to do. Oh! Were I but free, my dizziness would stop. Oh, if only my head were free!"

You see he ought to have said that sooner, for the moment he expressed the wish his head was free. And cured of all his paroxysms of love, he hastened off to his room, where the pains consequent on the fright the shoes had prepared for him did not so soon take their leave.

But you must not think that the affair is over now. It grows much worse.

The night passed, the next day also, but nobody came to fetch the shoes.

In the evening "Dramatic Readings" were to be given at the little theater in King Street. The house was filled to suffocation. Among other pieces to be recited was a new poem by H. C. Andersen, called "My Aunt's Spectacles," the contents of which were pretty nearly as follows:

"A certain person had an aunt, who boasted of particular skill in fortune-telling with cards and who was constantly being stormed by persons that wanted to have a peep into the future. But she was full of mystery about her art, in which a certain pair of magic spectacles did her essential service. Her nephew, a merry boy, who was his aunt's darling, begged so long for these spectacles that, at last, she lent him the treasure after having informed him, with many exhortations, that in order to execute the interesting trick, he need only repair to some place where a great many persons were assembled. Then, from a higher position, whence he could overlook the crowd, he should look at the people through his spectacles. Immediately, 'the inner man' of each individual would be displayed before him, like a game of cards, in which he unerringly might read what the future of every person presented was to be. Well pleased, the little magician hastened away to prove the powers of the spectacles in the theater, no place seeming to him more fitted for such a trial. He begged permission of the worthy audience and set his spectacles on his nose. A motley phantasmagoria presented itself before him, which he described in a few satirical touches, yet without expressing his opinion openly. He told the people enough to set them all thinking and guessing. But in order to hurt nobody, he wrapped his witty oracular judgments in a transparent veil, or rather in a lurid thundercloud, shooting forth bright sparks of wit that they might fall in the powder magazine of the expectant audience."

The humorous poem was admirably recited, and the speaker much applauded. Among the audience was the young man of the hospital, who seemed to have forgotten his adventure of the preceding night. He had on the shoes, for as yet no lawful owner had appeared to claim them. And besides it was so very dirty out-of-doors, they were just the thing for him, he thought.

The beginning of the poem he praised with great generosity. He even found the idea original and effective. But that the end of it, like the Rhine, was very insignificant and proved, in his opinion, the author's want of invention.

Meanwhile, he was haunted by the idea—he should like to possess such a pair of spectacles himself. Then, perhaps, by using them circumspectly, one would be able to look into people's hearts, which, he thought, would be far more interesting than merely to see what was to happen next year, for that we should all know in proper time, but the other never.

"I can now," said he to himself, "fancy the whole row of ladies and gentlemen sitting there in the front row. If one

could but see into their hearts—yes, that would be a
revelation—a sort of bazaar. In that lady yonder, so strangely
dressed, I should find for certain a large milliner's shop; in
that one the shop is empty, but a thorough cleaning would be
good for it. And, of course there would also be some well
stocked shops. Alas!" sighed he, "I know one in which the
merchandise is fine. But that shop already has a shopkeeper
and he's the only bad thing in the whole shop. All would be
splendidly decked out, and we should hear, 'Walk in,
gentlemen, pray walk in. Here you will find all you please to
want.' Ah! I wish I could walk like a nice thought through
their hearts!"

And behold! to the Shoes of Fortune this was the cue. The
whole man shrunk together, and a most uncommon journey
through the hearts of the front row of spectators began. The
first heart through which he came was that of a middle-aged
lady, but he instantly fancied himself in the room of the "institution for the cure of the crooked and deformed," where casts
of misshapen limbs are displayed in naked reality on the wall.
Yet there was this difference. In the institution the casts were
taken at the entry of the patient, but here they were retained
and guarded in the heart while the sound persons went away.
For every bodily or mental deformity of the friends she had
lost had been carefully stored and catalogued.

He soon passed into another female heart, but this one
seemed to him like a great cathedral. The white dove of innocence fluttered over the altar. How gladly would he have sunk
upon his knees, but he must hurry away to the next heart. Yet
he still heard the pealing tones of the organ, and he himself
seemed to have become a newer and a better man. He felt
almost worthy to enter the neighboring sanctuary. This was a

poor garret, inhabited by a sick bedridden mother. But God's warm sun streamed through the open window and lovely roses nodded from the wooden flower boxes on the roof. In the tree outside, two sky-blue birds sang rejoicingly, while the sick mother implored God's richest blessings on her daughter.

Next, the man crept on hands and knees through a butcher's shop. On every side, and above and below, there was nothing but flesh. It was the heart of a most respectable rich man, whose name is certain to be found in the directory.

He then came to the heart of the wife of this worthy gentleman. It was an old, dilapidated, moldering dovecote. The husband's portrait was used as a weathervane, which was connected in some way or other with the doors, and so they opened and shut of their own accord, whenever the stern old husband turned around.

Hereupon he wandered into a boudoir formed entirely of mirrors, like the one in Castle Rosenburg. But here the glasses magnified to an astonishing degree. On the floor, in the middle of the room, sat, like a Dalai Lama, the insignificant "Self" of the person, quite pleased with his own greatness.

He then seemed to be stuffed into a needle case full of pointed needles of every size.

This is certainly the heart of an old maid, thought he. But he was mistaken. It was the heart of a young military man, a man, as people said, of talent and feeling.

In the greatest perplexity, he now came out of the last heart in the row. He was unable to put his thoughts in order and fancied that his too lively imagination had run away with him.

"Good heavens!" sighed he. "I have surely a disposition to

madness—'tis dreadfully hot here. My blood boils in my veins and my head is burning like a coal." And then he remembered the important event of the evening before, how his head had got jammed in between the iron railings of the hospital. "That's what it is, no doubt," said he. "I must do something in time. Under such circumstances a Russian bath might do me good. I only wish I were already on the upper bank."*

And so there he lay on the uppermost bank in the vapor bath, but with all his clothes on, in his boots and galoshes, while the hot drops fell scalding from the ceiling on his face.

"Holloa!" cried he, leaping down. The bathing attendant, on his side, uttered a loud cry of astonishment when he beheld in the bath a man completely dressed. The other, however, retained sufficient presence of mind to whisper to him, " 'Tis a bet, and I have won it!"

But the first thing he did as soon as he got home was to have a large blister put on his chest and back to draw out his madness.

The next morning he had a sore chest and a bleeding back, and, except the fright, that was all that he had gained by the Shoes of Fortune.

V. Metamorphosis of the Copying Clerk

The watchman, whom we have certainly not forgotten, remembered meanwhile the galoshes he had found and taken with him to the hospital. He went to claim them, and as neither the lieutenant nor anybody else in the street claimed

---

* In these Russian (vapor) baths the person extends himself on a bank or form, and as he gets accustomed to the heat, moves to another higher up toward the ceiling, where, of course, the vapor is warmest. In this manner he ascends gradually to the highest.

them as his property, delivered them over to the police office.*

"Why, I declare the shoes look just like my own," said one of the clerks, eyeing the newly found treasure whose hidden powers even he, sharp as he was, was not able to discover. "Not even a shoemaker would know one pair from the other," said he, soliloquizing, and putting the homeless galoshes beside his own in the corner.

"Here, sir!" said an out of breath policeman, who brought him a pile of papers.

The copying clerk turned around and spoke a while with the officer about the reports and legal documents in question, but when he had finished and his eye fell again on the shoes, he was unable to say whether those to the left or those to the right belonged to him. *At all events it must be those that are wet*, thought he. But this time, in spite of his cleverness, he guessed quite wrong, for they were the galoshes of Fortune

So he put them on, stuck his papers in his pocket, and took a few more under his arm, intending to look them through at home to make the necessary notes. It was noon, and the weather that had threatened rain began to clear up, while gaily dressed holiday folks filled the streets. *A little walk to Fredericksburg would do me no great harm*, thought he, *for I, poor beast of burden that I am, have so much to annoy me that I don't know what a good appetite is. 'Tis a bitter crust, alas, at which I am condemned to gnaw!*

Nobody could be more steady or quiet than this young man. We therefore wish him joy of the excursion with all our heart, and it will certainly be beneficial for a person who leads

---

* As on the continent, in all law and police practices, nothing is verbal, but any circumstance, however trifling, is reduced to writing. The labor, as well as the number of papers that thus accumulate, is enormous. In a police office, consequently, we find copying clerks among many other scribes of various denominations, of which, it seems, our hero was one.

so sedentary a life. In the park he met a friend, one of our young poets, who told him that the following day he would leave for a long-intended vacation.

"So you are going away again!" said the clerk. "You are a very free and happy being. We others are chained by the leg and held fast to our desk."

"Yes, but it is a chain, friend, which ensures you the blessed bread of existence," answered the poet. "You need feel no care for the coming morrow. When you are old, you receive a pension."

"True," said the clerk, shrugging his shoulders, "and yet you are the better off. To sit at one's ease and write poetry— that is a pleasure. Everybody has something agreeable to say to you, and you are always your own master. No, friend, you should see what it's like to sit from one year's end to the other occupied with and judging the most trivial matters."

The poet shook his head; the copying clerk did the same. Each one kept to his own opinion, and so they separated.

"It's a strange race, those poets!" said the clerk, who was very fond of soliloquizing. "I should like some day, just for a trial, to take such a trade upon me and be a poet myself. I am very sure I should write no such melancholy verses as the others. Today is a perfect day for a poet. Nature seems anew to celebrate its awakening into life. The air is so unusually clear, the clouds sail on so buoyantly, and from the green grass a fragrance is exhaled that fills me with delight. For many a year I have not felt as I do at this moment."

You could tell already, by the previous effusion, that he had become a poet. To give further proof of it, however, would in most cases be insipid, for it is a foolish notion to fancy a poet different from other people. Among the latter there may be far more poetical natures than many an acknowledged poet, when examined more closely, could boast of. The difference only is that the poet possesses a better mental memory and so is able to retain the feeling and the thought till they can be embodied in words, a faculty that the others do not possess. But the transition from a commonplace nature to one that is richly endowed demands always a more or less breakneck leap over a certain abyss that yawns threateningly below. And thus must the sudden change with the clerk strike the reader.

"The sweet air!" continued he of the police office in his dreamy imaginings. "How it reminds me of the violets in the garden of my aunt Magdalena! Yes, then I was a little wild boy, who did not go to school very regularly. O heavens! 'Tis a long time since I have thought on those times. The good old soul! She lived behind the Exchange. She always had a few twigs or green shoots in water—let the winter rage without as it might. The violets exhaled their sweet breath, while I pressed against the windowpanes covered with fantastic frostwork the copper coin I had heated on the stove, and so made peepholes. What splendid vistas were then opened to my view! What change— what magnificence! Yonder in the canal lay the ships frozen up and deserted by their whole crews, with a screaming crow for the sole occupant. But when the spring, with a gentle stirring motion, announced its arrival, a new and busy life arose. With songs and hurrahs the ice was sawed away. The ships were fresh tarred and rigged, that they might sail away to distant lands. But I have remained here—must always remain here, sitting at my desk in the office, and patiently see other people fetch their passports to go abroad. Such is my fate!

Alas!" sighed he, and was again silent. "Great heaven! What is
come to me! Never have I thought or felt like this before! It must
be the summer air that affects me with feelings almost as dis-
quieting as they are refreshing."

He felt in his pocket for the papers. "These police reports
will soon stem the torrent of my ideas and hinder any rebellious
overflowing of the timeworn banks of official duties," he said to
himself consolingly, while his eye ran over the first page: DAME
SIGBRITH, tragedy in five acts. "What is that? And yet it is unde-
niably my own handwriting. Have I written the tragedy?
Wonderful, very wonderful! And this—what have I here?
INTRIGUE ON THE RAMPARTS; or THE DAY OF REPENTENCE—a vaude-
ville. The deuce! Where did I get all this rubbish? Someone
must have slipped it slyly into my pocket for a joke. And here's
a letter to me; a crumpled letter and the seal broken." It was not
a very polite epistle from the manager of a theater, in which both
pieces were flatly refused.

"Hem! hem!" said the clerk breathlessly, and quite
exhausted he seated himself on a bank. His thoughts were so
elastic, his heart so tender; and involuntarily he picked one of
the nearest flowers. It is a simple daisy, just bursting out of the
bud. What the botanist tells us after a number of imperfect lec-
tures, the flower proclaimed in a minute. It related the mythos
of its birth, told of the power of the sunlight that spread out its
delicate leaves, and forced them to infuse the air with their
incense. Then his mind wandered to the manifold struggles of
life, which in like manner awaken the budding flowers of feeling in our bosom. Light and air contend with chivalric emula-
tion for the love of the fair flower that bestowed her chief favors
on the latter. Full of longing she turned toward the light, and
as soon as it vanished, rolled her tender leaves together and

slept in the embraces of the air. "It is the light that makes me beautiful," said the flower.

"But 'tis the air that enables thee to breathe," said the poet's voice.

Close by stood a boy who was digging with a stick in a wet ditch. The drops of water splashed up to the green leafy branches, and the clerk thought of the million of tiny creatures that in a single drop were thrown up to a height that was as great for them, as it would be for us if we were to be hurled above the clouds.

While he thought of this and of the whole metamorphosis he had undergone, he smiled and said, "I must be asleep and dreaming, but it is wonderful how one can dream so naturally and know besides so exactly that it is but a dream. If only tomorrow on awaking, I could remember it all so vividly! I seem in unusually good spirits. My perception of things is clear. I feel as light and cheerful as though I were in heaven. But I know for a certainty that if tomorrow a dim remembrance of it should swim before my mind, it will then seem nothing but stupid non-sense, as I have often experienced in the past—especially before I enlisted under the banner of the police, for that dispels all the visions of an unfettered imagination. All we hear or say in a dream that is fair and beautiful is like the gold of the sub-terranean spirits. It is rich and splendid when it is given us, but viewed by daylight we find only withered leaves. Alas!" he sighed quite sorrowful, and gazed at the chirping birds that hopped contentedly from branch to branch, "They are much better off than I! To fly must be a heavenly art, and happy do I prize that creature in which it is innate. Yes! Could I exchange my nature with any other creature, I would like to be a happy little lark!"

He had hardly uttered these hasty words when the coat-tails and sleeves of his coat folded themselves together into wings, the clothes became feathers, and the galoshes talons. He observed it perfectly and laughed in his heart.

"Now then, there is no doubt that I am dreaming, but I never before was aware of such silly dreams as these."

And up he flew into the green branches and sang, but in the song there was no poetry, for the spirit of the poet was gone. The shoes, as is the case with anybody who does what he has to do properly, could only attend to one thing at a time. The clerk wanted to be a poet, and he was one. He now wished to be a merry chirping bird, but when he was turned into one, the former peculiarities ceased immediately. "It really is quite amusing," said he. "The whole day long I sit in the office amid the driest law papers, and at night I fly in my dream as a lark in the gardens of Fredericksburg. One might really write a very pretty comedy upon it."

He fluttered down into the grass, turned his head gracefully on every side, and with his bill pecked the pliant blades of grass, which, in comparison to his present size, seemed as majestic as the palm branches of northern Africa. Unfortunately the pleasure lasted but a moment. All of a sudden, everything turned black as night, as if some vast object had been thrown over him. It was a large oilskin cap, which a sailor boy from the quay had thrown over the struggling bird. A coarse hand sought its way carefully in under the broad rim and seized the clerk over the back and wings. In the first moment of fear, he called, indeed, as loud as he could, "You impudent little blackguard! I am a copying clerk at the police office, and you know you cannot insult anyone belonging to the constabulary force without punishment. Besides, you good-for-nothing rascal, it is strictly forbidden to catch birds in the royal gardens of Fredericksburg, but your blue uniform betrays where you come from." This fine tirade sounded, however, to the ungodly sailor boy like a mere *peep peep*. He gave the noisy bird a knock on his beak and walked on.

He was soon met by two schoolboys of the upper class—that is to say in terms of wealth, for with regard to learning they were in the lowest class in the school, and they bought the bird. So the copying clerk came back to Copenhagen as guest, or rather as prisoner, of a family living on Gother Street.

"'Tis well that I'm dreaming," said the clerk, "or I really should get angry. First I was a poet, now sold for a few pence as a lark. No doubt it was that accursed poetic nature that has metamorphosed me into such a poor harmless little creature. It is really pitiable, particularly when one gets into the hands of a little blackguard versed in all sorts of cruelty to animals. All I should like to know is how the story will end."

The two schoolboys, the proprietors now of the transformed clerk, carried him into an elegant room. A stout stately dame received them with a smile, but she expressed much dissatisfaction that a common field bird, as she called the lark, should appear in such high society. For today, however, she would allow it; but they must shut him in the empty cage that was standing in the window.

"Perhaps he will amuse my good Polly," added the lady, looking with a loving smile at a large green parrot that swung himself backward and forward most comfortably in his ring inside a magnificent brass-wired cage. "Today is Polly's birthday," said she with a vapid grin, "and the little brown field bird must wish him joy."

Mr. Polly uttered not a syllable in reply, but swung to and fro with dignified condescension, while a pretty canary, as yellow as gold, that had lately been brought from his sunny fragrant home, began to sing aloud.

"Noisy creature! Will you be quiet!" screamed the lady of the house, covering the cage with an embroidered white pocket handkerchief.

"Chirp, chirp!" sighed the canary. "What a dreadful snowstorm." He sighed again and was silent.

The copying clerk, or, as the lady said, the brown field bird, was put into a small cage close to the canary and not far from "my good Polly." The only human sounds that the parrot could bawl out were, "Come, let us be men!" Everything else that he said was as unintelligible to everybody as the chirping of the canary, except to the clerk, who was now a bird, too. He understood his companion perfectly.

"I flew about beneath the green palms and the blossoming almond trees," sang the canary. "I flew around, with my brothers and sisters, over the beautiful flowers and over the glassy lakes where the bright water plants nodded to me from below. There, too, I saw many brilliant parrots that told the funniest stories and the wildest fairy tales without end."

"Oh! Those were uncouth birds," answered the parrot. "They had no education and talked of whatever came into their head.

"If my mistress and all her friends can laugh at what I say, so should you, too, I think. It is a great fault to have no sense of humor—come, let us be men."

"Do you remember the charming maidens that danced beneath the outspread tents beside the bright fragrant flowers? Or the sweet fruits, and the cooling juice in the wild plants of our never-to-be-forgotten home?" said the former inhabitant of the Canary Isles, continuing his song.

"Oh, yes," said the parrot, "but I am far better off here. I am well fed and get friendly treatment. I know I am a clever fellow, and that is all I care about. Come, let us be men. You are of a poetic nature, as it is called—I, on the contrary, possess profound knowledge and inexhaustible wit. You have genius, but clear-sighted, calm discretion does not take such lofty flights and utter such high natural tones. For this they have covered you over—they never do the like to me, for I cost more. Besides, they are afraid of my beak, and I have always a witty answer at hand. Come, let us be men!"

"O warm spicy land of my birth," sang the canary bird. "I will sing of thy dark-green bowers, of the calm bays where the pendent boughs kiss the surface of the water. I will sing of the rejoicing of all my brothers and sisters where the cactus grows in wanton luxuriance."

"Spare us your sorrowful tones," said the parrot giggling. "Rather speak of something at which one may laugh heartily. Laughing is an infallible sign of the highest degree of mental development. Can a dog or a horse laugh? No, but they can cry. The gift of laughing was given to humans alone. Ha! ha! ha!" screamed Polly, and added his stereotype witticism. "Come, let us be men!"

"Poor little Danish gray bird," said the canary. "You have been caught, too. It is, no doubt, cold enough in your woods, but there at least is the breath of liberty. Therefore, fly away. In the hurry they have forgotten to shut your cage, and the upper window is open. Fly, my friend. Fly away. Farewell!"

Instinctively the clerk obeyed. With a few strokes of his wings he was out of the cage. But at the same moment the door, which was only ajar and which led to the next room, began to creak, and supple and creeping came the large tomcat into the room and began to pursue him. The frightened canary fluttered about in his cage. The parrot flapped his wings and cried, "Come, let us be men!" The clerk felt a mortal fright and flew through the window, far away over the houses and streets. At last he was forced to rest a little.

The house across the street from where he landed had something familiar about it. A window stood open, and he flew in. It was his own room. He perched upon the table.

"Come, let us be men!" said he, involuntarily imitating the chatter of the parrot, and at the same moment he was again a copying clerk, but he was sitting in the middle of the table. "Heaven help me!" cried he. "How did I get up here—and so buried in sleep, too? After all, that was a very unpleasant, disagreeable dream that haunted me! The whole story is nothing but silly, stupid nonsense!"

VI. The Best That the Galoshes Gave

The following day, early in the morning, while the clerk was still in bed, someone knocked at his door. It was his neighbor, a young theological student, who lived on the same floor.

"Lend me your galoshes," he asked. "It is very wet in the garden, but the sun is shining so invitingly that I should like to go out a little."

He put on the galoshes, and he was soon below in a teeny garden, where between two immense walls a plum tree and an apple tree were standing. Even such a little garden as this was considered luxurious in the metropolis of Copenhagen.

The young man wandered up and down the narrow paths. The clock struck six; he heard the horn of a post boy outside the wall.

"Oh, to travel! To travel!" he exclaimed, overcome by painful and passionate remembrances. "That is my great goal! That is the happiest thing in the world! Then at last would my agonizing restlessness be calmed! But it must be far, far away! I would love to see magnificent Switzerland, to tour Italy, and—"

It was a good thing that the power of the galoshes worked as instantaneously as lightning in a powder magazine would do; otherwise the poor man with his overactive wishes would have traveled about the world too much to suit himself or to please us. In short, he was traveling. He was in the middle of Switzerland, but packed up with eight other passengers in the inside of an eternally creaking stagecoach. His head ached till it almost split, his weary neck could hardly bear the heavy load, and his feet, pinched by his tight boots, were terribly swollen. He was in an intermediate state between sleeping and waking, at odds with himself, with his company, with the country, and with the government. In his right pocket he had his letter of credit; in the left, his passport and in a small leather purse some gold pieces, carefully sewn up in the bosom of his waistcoat. Every time he dozed off he dreamed that one or the other of these valuables was lost, wherefore he started up in a panic. His first movement would then trace a magic triangle from the right pocket to the left and then up toward the bosom to feel if he had his treasures safe or not. Umbrellas, walking sticks, hats, and sundry other articles were hanging from the roof inside the carriage, and hindered the imposing view. He now endeavored as well as he was able to dispel his gloom, which was caused by outward chance circumstances merely, and on the bosom of nature imbibe the milk of purest human enjoyment.

The surrounding landscape was grand, solemn, and dark. The gigantic pine forests on the pointed crags seemed almost like little tufts of heather colored by the surrounding clouds. It began to snow, and a cold wind blew.

"Augh!" sighed he. "If only we were on the other side of the Alps, then we should have summer, and I could get my letters of credit cashed. This anxiety over them prevents me from enjoying Switzerland. If only I were on the other side!"

And so saying he *was* on the other side in Italy, between Florence and Rome. Lake Thrasymene, lit up by the evening sun, lay like flaming gold between the dark blue mountain ridges. Here, where Hannibal defeated Flaminius, the grape vines now held each other in their green embraces. Lovely, half-naked children tended a herd of black swine, beneath a group of fragrant laurel trees by the roadside. Could we paint this picture properly, then would everybody exclaim, "Beautiful, unparalleled Italy!" But neither the young student said so, nor anyone of his grumbling companions in the coach of the *vetturino*.

Poisonous flies and gnats swarmed into the coach by the thousands. In vain the travelers waved myrtle branches about like mad. The audacious flies did not cease to sting, nor was there a single person in the well-crammed carriage whose face was not swollen and sore from their ravenous bites. The poor horses, tortured almost to death, suffered most from this plague. The flies alighted upon them in large disgusting swarms, and if the coachman got down and scraped them off, hardly a minute elapsed before they were there again.

Once the sun set, a freezing chill enveloped the travelers. It was like a horrid gust coming from a burial vault on a warm summer's day. But yet all around the mountains took on a wonderful green hue. It was a glorious prospect, but the travelers' stomachs were empty, their bodies tired. All that they cared and longed for was good night quarters; yet where would they stay? They looked much more intently for lodging than at the charms of nature, which everywhere were so profusely displayed.

The road led through an olive grove, and here the solitary inn was situated. Ten or twelve crippled beggars had encamped outside. The healthiest of them resembled, to use an expression of Marryat's, "Hunger's eldest son when he had come of age." The others were either blind and had withered legs and crept about on their hands or had withered arms and fingerless hands. It was the most wretched misery, among the filthiest rags.

"Excellenza, miserabili!" they sighed, thrusting forth their deformed limbs to view. Even the hostess, with bare feet, uncombed hair, and dressed in a garment of doubtful color, received the guests grumblingly. The doors were fastened with a loop of string. Half the stones of the floors had been torn up. Bats fluttered wildly about the ceiling. And as to the smell—it was beyond description.

"It would be better to have dinner in the stable," said one of the travelers. "There, at all events, one knows what one is breathing."

The windows were quickly opened, to let in a little fresh air. Quicker, however, than the breeze, the withered, sallow arms of the beggars were thrust in, accompanied by the eternal whine of *"Miserabili, miserabili, excellenza!"* On the walls were displayed innumerable inscriptions, written in nearly every language of Europe, some in verse, some in prose, most of them not very laudatory of *"bella Italia."*

The meal was served. It consisted of a soup of salted water, seasoned with pepper and rancid oil. The last ingredient played a very prominent part in the salad. Stale eggs and roasted cocks' combs furnished the grand dish of the meal. The wine even was not without a disgusting taste—it was like a medicinal draught.

At night the passengers' boxes and trunks were placed against the rickety doors. One of the travelers kept watch while the others slept. The sentry was our young student. How close it was in the chamber! The heat oppressive to the point of suffocation—the gnats hummed and stung unceasingly— the *"miserabili"* outside whined and moaned in their sleep.

"Traveling would be agreeable enough," said he groaning, "if one only had no body, or could send it to rest while the spirit went on its pilgrimage unhindered, whither the voice within might call it. Wherever I go, I am pursued by a longing that is insatiable—that I cannot explain to myself and that tears my very heart. I always want something better than what I have. But what is it, and where is it to be found? Yet, I know in reality what it is I wish for. Oh! Most happy were I, could I but reach that one aim—could but reach the happiest goal of all!" And as he spoke the word he was again in his home. The long white curtains hung down from the windows, and in the middle of the floor stood a black coffin. In it he lay in the sleep of death. His wish was fulfilled—the body rested, while the spirit went unhindered on its pilgrimage. "Let no one deem himself happy before his end" were the words of

Solon, and here was a new and brilliant proof of the wisdom of the old apothegm.

Every corpse is a sphynx of immortality. Here, too, on the black coffin the sphynx gave us no more answer than what he who lay inside had written two days before:

> "O mighty Death! Thy silence teaches nought;
>   Thou leadest only to the near grave's brink;
> Is it broken now the ladder of my thoughts?
>   Do I instead of mounting only sink?
>
> Our heaviest grief the world oft seeth not,
>   Our sorest pain we hide from stranger eyes:
> And for the sufferer there is nothing left
>   But the green mound that o'er the coffin lies."

Two figures were moving in the chamber. We knew them both. It was the fairy of Care and the emissary of Fortune. They both bent over the corpse. "Do you now see," said Care, "what happiness your galoshes have brought to mankind?"

"To him, at least, who slumbers here they have brought an imperishable blessing," answered the other.

"Ah, no!" replied Care. "He went of his own accord; he was not called away. His spiritual power was not strong enough for the glorious tasks for which he is destined. I will do him a favor."

And she took the galoshes from his feet; his sleep of death was ended, and he who had been thus called back again to life arose from his dread couch in all the vigor of youth. Care vanished, and with her the galoshes. She has no doubt taken them for herself, to keep for all eternity.

The Snow Queen: A Tale in Seven Stories

FIRST STORY.

Which Treats of a Mirror and of the Splinters

Now then, let us begin. When we are at the end of the story, we shall know more than we know now; but to begin:

Once upon a time there was an evil troll. Indeed he was the most mischievous of all trolls—he was the devil. One day he was in a very good humor, for he had made a mirror with the power of causing all that was good and beautiful when it was reflected therein to look small and insignificant, and that which was good-for-nothing and looked ugly was shown magnified and increased in ugliness. In this mirror the most beautiful landscapes looked like boiled spinach, and the sweetest people were turned into frights or appeared to stand on their heads, their faces so distorted as to be unrecognizable. And if anyone had a mole, you might be sure that it would be magnified and spread over both nose and mouth.

"That's glorious fun!" said the troll. If a good thought passed through a man's mind, then a grin was seen in the mirror. The devil-troll laughed heartily at his clever discovery. All the little trolls who went to his school—for he kept a troll school—told each other that a miracle had happened. They thought it would now be possible to see how the world really looked. They ran all over with the mirror until there was not a land or a person who hadn't been distorted by the mirror. So then they thought they would fly up to the sky and use the mirror there. The higher they flew with the mirror, the more terribly it grinned. They could hardly hold onto it. Higher and higher still they flew, nearer and nearer to the stars, when suddenly the mirror shook so terribly with grinning that it flew out of their hands and fell to the earth, where it was dashed in a hundred million and more pieces.

From that moment, the mirror worked much more evil than before. Some of the pieces were barely the size of a grain of sand, and they flew about in the wide world. If they got into people's eyes, there they stayed, making everything look bad. Then people could see only that which was evil because the very smallest bit had the same power that the whole mirror had possessed. Some people even got a splinter in their heart, and then it made one shudder, for their heart became like a lump of ice. Some of the broken pieces were so large that they were used for windowpanes, through which one could not see one's friends. Other pieces were put in spectacles, and that was a sad affair when people put on their glasses to see well and rightly. Then the wicked troll-devil laughed till he almost choked, for all this tickled his fancy. The fine splinters still flew about in the air. And now we shall hear what happened next.

SECOND STORY.

A Little Boy and a Little Girl

In a large town, where there are so many houses and so many people that there is no room left for everybody to have a little garden, and where, on this account, most people are obliged to content themselves with flowers in pots, there lived two little children, who had a garden somewhat larger than a flowerpot. They were not brother and sister, but they cared for each other as much as if they were. Their parents lived next door to each other. They inhabited two garrets, where the roof of the one house joined that of the other. A gutter ran between the houses and there was to each house a small window. One needed only to step over the gutter to get from one window to the other.

Outside the windows, the children's parents had large wooden boxes in which vegetables for the kitchen were planted, and little rose trees besides. There was a rose in each box, and they grew splendidly. The parents had put the boxes across the gutter, so that they nearly reached from one window to the other and looked just like two walls of flowers. The tendrils of the peas hung down over the boxes, and the rose trees shot up long branches, twined around the windows, and then bent toward each other. It was almost like a triumphant arch of foliage and flowers. The boxes were very high up, and the children knew that they must not climb out of them, but they often obtained permission to sit on their little stools among the roses, where they could play delightfully.

In winter there was an end of this fun. The windows were often frozen over, but the children heated copper farthings on the stove and when they pressed the hot coins on the window-pane, they made perfect peepholes, quite nicely rounded. Out of each peeped a gentle friendly eye—it was the little boy and the little girl who were looking out. His name was Kay, hers was Gerda. In summer, with one jump, they could get to each other; but in winter they were obliged first to go down the long stairs, and then up the long stairs again while the snow drifted outside.

"The white bees are swarming," said Kay's old grandmother, watching the snowflakes.

"Do the white bees have a queen?" asked the little boy, for he knew that the honeybees always have one.

"Yes," said the grandmother, "she flies where the swarm hangs in the thickest clusters. She is the largest of all. She can never remain quietly on the ground, but goes up again into the black clouds. Many a winter's night she flies through the streets of the town and peeps in at the windows, and then they freeze in such a strange manner that they look like flowers."

"Yes, I have seen that," said both the children, and so they knew that it was true.

"Can the Snow Queen come in?" said the little girl.

"Do let her come in!" said the little boy. "Then I'd put her on the stove, and she'd melt."

His grandmother just patted his head and told him more stories.

In the evening, when little Kay was at home and half undressed, he climbed up on the chair by the window and peeped out of the little hole. A few snowflakes were falling, and one, the largest of all, remained lying on the edge of a flowerpot.

The flake of snow grew larger and larger, and at last it was like a young lady, dressed in the finest white gauze made of a million little flakes like stars. She was so beautiful and delicate. She was of ice, of dazzling, sparkling ice, yet she lived. Her eyes gazed fixedly, like two stars, but there was neither quiet nor repose in them. She nodded toward the window and beckoned with her hand. The little boy was frightened and jumped down from the chair. It seemed to him as if, at the same moment, a large bird flew past the window.

The next day there was a sharp frost, and then the spring came. The sun shone, the green leaves appeared, the swallows built their nests, the windows were opened, and the little children again sat in their pretty garden, high up on the gutters at the top of the house.

That summer the roses flowered in unusual beauty. The little girl had learned a hymn that mentioned roses, and made her think of her own flowers. She sang the verse to the little boy, who then sang it with her:

"The rose in the valley is blooming so sweet,
And angels descend there the children to greet."

And the children held each other by the hand, kissed the roses, looked up at the clear sunshine, and spoke as though they really saw angels there. What lovely summer days those were! How delightful to be out in the air, near the fresh rosebushes that seem as if they would never finish blossoming!

Kay and Gerda looked at the picture book full of beasts and of birds, and it was then—the clock in the church tower was just striking five—that Kay said, "Oh! I feel such a sharp pain in my heart, and now something has got into my eye!"

The little girl put her arms around his neck. He blinked his eyes, but there was nothing to see.

"I think it is out now," said he, but it was not. It was, in fact, one of those pieces of glass from the troll's mirror that had got into his eye, and poor Kay had got another piece right in his heart. Soon it would become a block of ice. It did not hurt any longer, but there it was.

"What are you crying for?" Kay asked. "You look so ugly! There's nothing the matter with me. Ah," said he at once, "that rose is cankered! And look, this one is quite crooked! After all, these roses are very ugly! They are just like the box they are planted in!" And then he gave the box a good kick with his foot and pulled both the roses up.

"What are you doing?" cried the little girl. As he perceived her fright, he pulled up another rose, got in at the window, and hastened off from dear little Gerda.

Afterward, when she brought her picture book, he asked, "What horrid beasts have you there?" And if his grandmother told them stories, he always interrupted her. Besides, if he could manage it, he would get behind her, put on her spectacles, and imitate her way of speaking. He copied all her ways, and then everybody laughed at him. He was soon able to imitate the gait and manner of everyone in the street. Everything that was peculiar and displeasing in them, Kay knew how to imitate. At such times all the people said, "The boy is certainly very clever!" But it was the glass he had got in his eye. The glass that was sticking in his heart made him tease even little Gerda, whose whole soul was devoted to him.

His games now were quite different to what they had formerly been; they were so very knowing. One winter's day, when the flakes of snow were flying about, he spread the tails of his blue coat and caught the snow as it fell.

"Look through this magnifying glass, Gerda," said he. Every flake seemed larger and appeared like a magnificent flower or beautiful star. It was splendid to look at!

"Look, how clever!" said Kay. "That's much more interesting than real flowers! They are as exact as possible. There is not a fault in them, if they did not melt!"

It was not long after this that Kay came one day with large gloves on and his little sled at his back, and yelled right into Gerda's ear, "I have permission to go out into the square where the others are playing." And off he was in a moment.

In the marketplace, some of the boldest of the boys often tied their sleds to carts as they passed by, and so they were pulled along and got a good ride. It was great fun! Just as they were in the very height of their game, a large sleigh passed by. It was painted quite white, and there was someone in it wrapped up in a rough white mantle of fur and a fleecy white fur cap. The sleigh drove around the square twice, and Kay tied on his sled as quickly as he could, and off he drove with it. On they went quicker and quicker into the next street, and the person who drove turned around to Kay and nodded to him in a friendly manner, just as if they knew each other. Every time he was going to untie his sled, the person would nod again, and then Kay stayed put. They went on like this till they came outside the gates of the town.

Then the snow began to fall so thickly that the little boy could not see an arm's length before him, but the sleigh sped on. He let go the string he held in his hand in order to get loose from the sleigh, but it was of no use. The little sled was stuck and it rushed on with the quickness of the wind. He then cried as loud as he could, but no one heard him. The snow drifted and the sleigh flew on, and sometimes it gave a jerk as though they were driving over hedges and ditches. He was quite frightened. He tried to recite a prayer, but he could only remember his multiplication tables.

The snowflakes grew larger and larger till at last they looked just like great white fowls. Suddenly the large sleigh stopped, and the person who drove stood up. It was a lady. Her cloak and cap were made of snow. She was tall and slender, and of a dazzling whiteness. It was the Snow Queen.

"We have traveled fast," said she, "but it is freezing cold. Come under my bearskin." And she put Kay in the sleigh beside her and wrapped the fur around him. He felt as though he were sinking in a snow drift.

"Are you still cold?" she asked, and then she kissed his forehead. Ah! Her kiss was colder than ice. It penetrated right to his heart, which was already almost a frozen lump. It seemed to him as if he were about to die—but after a moment more it was quite pleasant to him, and he no longer noticed the cold that was around him.

"My sled! Do not forget my sled!" That was the first thing he remembered. It was there tied to one of the white chickens, who flew along with it on his back behind the large sleigh. The Snow Queen kissed Kay once more, and at that moment he forgot little Gerda, Grandmother, and all whom he had left at his home.

"Now you will have no more kisses," said the Snow Queen, "or they might kill you!"

Kay looked at her. She was very beautiful. He could not imagine a more clever or a more lovely countenance. She no longer appeared made of ice as she had when she sat outside the window and beckoned to him. In his eyes she was perfect. He did not fear her at all, and he told her that he could do math in his head—even fractions, and that he knew the number of square miles there were in the different countries, and how many inhabitants they had. She smiled while he spoke. It then seemed to him as if what he knew was not enough, and he looked upward into the large huge empty sky above him. And on she flew with him, flew high over the black clouds, while the storm groaned and whistled as though it were singing some old tune. On they flew over woods and lakes, over seas, and many lands. Beneath them the chilling storm rushed fast, the wolves howled, the snow crackled. Above them flew large screaming crows, but higher up appeared the moon, quite large and bright. Kay gazed at the moon during the long, long winter's night, while by day he slept at the feet of the Snow Queen.

THIRD STORY.

Of the Flower Garden and the Woman Who Understood Witchcraft

But what became of little Gerda when Kay did not return? Where could he be? Nobody knew. No one could tell her. All the boys knew was that they had seen him tie his sled to another large and splendid one, which drove down the street and out of the town. Nobody knew where he was. Many sad tears were shed, and little Gerda wept long and bitterly. At last she said he must be dead, that he had been drowned in the river that flowed close to the town. Oh! Those were very long and dismal winter evenings!

At last spring came with its warm sunshine.

"Kay is dead and gone!" said little Gerda.

"That I don't believe," said the sunshine.

"Kay is dead and gone!" she said to the swallows.

"That I don't believe," said they, and at last little Gerda did not think so any longer either.

"I'll put on my red shoes," said she one morning. "Kay has never seen them, and then I'll go down to the river and ask what it knows."

It was quite early. She kissed her old grandmother, who was still asleep, put on her red shoes, and went alone to the river.

"Is it true that you have taken my friend? I will make you a present of my red shoes, if you will give him back to me."

And, as it seemed to her, the blue waves nodded in a strange manner. Then, she took off her red shoes, the most precious things she possessed, and threw them both into the river. But they fell close to the bank, and the little waves bore them immediately to land. It was as if the stream would not take what was dearest to her, for in reality it had not got little Kay. But Gerda thought that she had not thrown the shoes out far enough, so she clambered into a boat that lay among the rushes, went to the farthest end, and threw out the shoes. But the boat was not tied down, and her movement made it drift from the shore. As soon as Gerda noticed this she hastened to get back. But before she could do so, the boat was more than a yard from the land and was gliding quickly onward.

Little Gerda was very frightened and began to cry, but no one heard her except the sparrows. They could not carry her to land, but they flew along the bank and sang as if to comfort her, "Here we are! Here we are!" The boat drifted with the stream, little Gerda sat quite still without shoes, for they were swimming behind the boat. She could not reach them, because the boat went much faster than they did.

The banks on both sides of the river were beautiful with lovely flowers, venerable trees, and slopes with sheep and cows—but not a human being was to be seen.

"Perhaps the river will carry me to little Kay," said she, and then she grew less sad. She rose and looked for many hours at the beautiful green banks. Presently she sailed by a large cherry orchard, where there was a little cottage with curious red and blue windows. It was thatched, and before it two wooden soldiers stood sentry and presented arms when anyone went past.

Gerda called to them, for she thought they were alive, but they, of course, did not answer. She got very close to them, for the stream drifted the boat quite near the land.

Gerda called still louder, and an old woman then came out of the cottage, leaning upon a crooked stick. She had a large broad-brimmed hat on, painted with the most splendid flowers.

"Poor little child!" said the old woman. "How did you get out there on the large rapid river, to be driven about so in the wide world!" And then the old woman went into the water, caught hold of the boat with her crooked stick, drew it to the bank, and lifted little Gerda out.

Gerda was glad to be on dry land again; but she was a little afraid of the strange old woman.

"But come and tell me who you are, and how you came here," said the woman.

Gerda told her all, and the old woman shook her head and said, "Ahem! ahem!" When Gerda had told her everything and asked her if she had seen little Kay, the woman answered that he had not passed there, but he no doubt would come. She told her not to be cast down, but taste her cherries and look at her flowers, which were finer than any in a picture book, each of which had a story to tell. She then took Gerda by the hand, led her into the little cottage, and locked the door.

The windows were very high up. The glass was red, blue, and green, and the sunlight shone through quite wondrously in all sorts of colors. On the table stood the most exquisite cherries, and Gerda ate as many as she chose, for she had permission to do so. While she was eating, the old woman combed her hair with a golden comb, and her hair curled and shone with a lovely golden color around that sweet little face, which was so round and so like a rose.

"I have often longed for such a dear little girl," said the old woman. "Now you shall see how well we get along." While she combed little Gerda's hair, the child forgot her foster brother Kay more and more, for the old woman understood magic. She was no evil being; she only practiced witchcraft a little for her own private amusement, and now she wanted very much to keep little Gerda. She therefore went out in the garden, stretched out her crooked stick toward the rosebushes, which, beautifully as they were blooming, all sank into the earth until no one could tell where they had stood. The old woman feared that if Gerda saw the roses, she would then think of her own roses, remember little Kay, and run away from her.

Then she led Gerda into the flower garden. Oh, what fragrance and what loveliness was there! Every flower that one could think of, and of every season, stood there in fullest bloom. No picture book could be more colorful or beautiful. Gerda jumped for joy and played till the sun set behind the tall cherry tree. She then had a pretty bed with a red silk coverlet filled with blue violets. She fell asleep and had as pleasant dreams as ever a queen on her wedding day.

The next morning Gerda went to play with the flowers in the warm sunshine. Many days passed. Gerda recognized every flower, and, numerous as they were, it still seemed to her that one was missing, although she did not know which. One day while she was looking at the old woman's sunhat painted with flowers, the most beautiful of them all seemed to her to be a rose. The old woman had forgotten to take it from her hat when she made the others vanish in the earth. But so it is when one's thoughts are not collected.

"What!" said Gerda. "Are there no roses here?" She ran about among the flowerbeds and looked and looked, but there was not one to be found. She then sat down and wept. Her hot tears fell just where a rosebush had sunk, and when her warm tears watered the ground, the bush shot up suddenly as fresh and blooming as when it had been swallowed up. Gerda kissed the roses, thought of her own dear roses at home, and with them of little Kay.

"Oh, how long I have stayed!" said the little girl. "I intended to look for Kay! Don't you know where he is?" she asked of the roses. "Do you think he is dead and gone?"

"Dead he certainly is not," said the roses. "We have been in the earth where all the dead are, but Kay was not there."

"Many thanks!" said little Gerda. And she went to the other flowers, looked into their cups, and asked, "Don't you know where little Kay is?"

But every flower stood in the sunshine and dreamed its own fairy tale or its own story. They all told her very many things, but not one knew anything of Kay.

What did the tiger lily say?

"Do you not hear the drum? *Bum! Bum!* Those are the only two tones. Always *bum! Bum!* Hark to the plaintive song of the old woman, to the call of the priests! The Hindu woman in her long robe stands upon the funeral pile. The flames rise around her and her dead husband, but the Hindu woman thinks who is living inside the circle, on him whose eyes burn hotter than the flames—on him, the fire of whose eyes pierces her heart more than the flames that soon will burn her body to ashes. Can the heart's flame die in the flame of the funeral pile?"

"I don't understand that at all," said little Gerda.

"That is my story," said the lily.

What did the morning glory say?

"Projecting over a narrow mountain path there hangs an old feudal castle. Thick evergreens grow on the dilapidated walls and around the altar where a lovely maiden is standing. She bends over the railing and looks out upon the rose. No fresher rose hangs on the branches than she. No appleblossom carried away by the wind is lighter! How her silken robe is rustling!

"'Is he not yet come?' she cries."

"Is it Kay that you mean?" asked little Gerda.

"I am speaking about my own story—about my dream," answered the morning glory.

What did the daisy say?

"Between the trees a long board is hanging—it is a swing. Two little girls are sitting in it and swinging themselves backward and forward. Their frocks are as white as snow, and long green silk ribbons flutter from their bonnets. Their brother, who is older than they are, stands up in the swing. He twines his arms around the cords to hold himself fast, for in one hand he has a little cup and in the other a clay pipe. He is blowing soap bubbles. The swing moves, and the bubbles float in charming changing colors. The last is still hanging to the end of the pipe and rocks in the breeze. The swing moves. The little black dog, as light as a soap bubble, jumps up on his hind legs to try to get into the swing. It moves; the dog falls down, barks, and is angry. They tease him; the bubble bursts! A swing, a reflection in a bursting bubble—such is my song!"

"What you say may be very pretty, but you tell it in so melancholy a manner and do not mention Kay."

What do the hyacinths say?

"There were once upon a time three sisters, quite transparent and very beautiful. The robe of the one was red, that of the second blue, and that of the third white. They danced hand in hand beside the calm lake in the clear moon-shine. They were not elfin maidens, but mortal children. A sweet fragrance filled the air, and the maidens vanished in the wood. The fragrance grew stronger. Three coffins (and in them three lovely maidens), glided out of the forest and across the lake. Shining glowworms flew around like little floating lights. Do the dancing maidens sleep, or are they dead? The fragrance of the flowers says they are corpses. The evening bell tolls for the dead!"

"You make me quite sad," said little Gerda. "I cannot help thinking of the dead maidens. Oh! Is little Kay really dead? The roses have been in the earth, and they say no."

"Ding, dong!" sounded the hyacinth bells. "We do not toll

for little Kay. We do not know him. That is our way of singing, the only one we have."

And Gerda went to the buttercups that looked forth from among the shining green leaves.

"You are a little bright sun!" said Gerda. "Tell me if you know where I can find my playfellow."

And the buttercups shone brightly and looked again at Gerda. What song could the buttercups sing? It was one that said nothing about Kay either.

"In a small courtyard the bright sun was shining in the first days of spring. The beams glided down the white walls of a neighbor's house, and close by the fresh yellow flowers were growing, shining like gold in the warm sunrays. An old grandmother was sitting outside. Her granddaughter, a poor and lovely servant, had just come for a short visit. She kissed her grandmother. There was gold, pure virgin gold in that blessed kiss. There, that is my little story," said the buttercups.

"My poor old grandmother!" sighed Gerda. "Yes, she is longing for me, no doubt. She is sorrowing for me, as she did for little Kay. But I will soon come home, and then I will bring Kay with me. It is of no use asking the flowers. They only know their own old rhymes and can tell me nothing." And she tucked up her frock to enable her to run quicker, but the narcissus gave her a knock on the leg just as she was going to jump over it. So she stood still, looked at the long yellow flower, and asked, "You perhaps know something?" and she bent down to the narcissus. And what did it say?

"I can see myself—I can see myself! Oh, how fragrant I am! Up in the little garret there stands, half-dressed, a little dancer. She stands now on one leg, now on both. She despises the whole world, yet she lives only in imagination. She pours water out of the teapot over a piece of cloth that she holds in her hand. It is the bodice of her dress. Cleanliness is a fine thing. The white dress is hanging on the hook. It was washed in the teapot and dried on the roof. She puts it on, ties a saffron-colored kerchief around her neck, and then the gown looks whiter. I can see myself—I can see myself!"

"That's nothing to me," said little Gerda. "That does not concern me." And then off she ran to the far end of the garden.

The gate was locked, but she shook the rusty handle till it loosened, and the gate opened. Then little Gerda ran off barefoot into the wide world. She looked back three times, but no one followed her. At last she could run no longer. She sat down on a large stone, and when she looked about her, she saw that the summer had passed. It was late in the autumn, but one could not know that in the beautiful garden where there was always sunshine and where there were flowers the whole year round.

"Dear me, how long I have stayed!" said Gerda. "Autumn is come. I must not rest any longer." And she got up to go farther.

Oh, how tender and wearied her little feet were! All around it looked so cold and raw. The long willow leaves were quite yellow, and the fog dripped from them like water. One leaf fell after the other. Only the blackthorn bush stood full of berries, which were so sour they set one's teeth on edge. Oh, how dark and comfortless it was in the dreary world!

FOURTH STORY.

The Prince and the Princess

Gerda was obliged to rest herself again, when, exactly opposite from where she sat, a large raven came hopping over the white snow. He had long been looking at Gerda and shaking his head. Now he said, *"Caw! Caw!"* He meant, *Good day! Good day!* He could not articulate it very well, but he felt a sympathy for the little girl and asked her where she was going all alone. The word "alone" Gerda understood quite well and felt how much was expressed by it, so she told the raven her whole history and asked if he had not seen Kay.

The raven nodded very gravely, and said, "It may be—it may be!"

"What, do you really think so?" cried the little girl, and she nearly squeezed the raven to death, so much did she kiss him.

"Gently, gently," said the raven. "I think I know. I think that it may be little Kay. But now he has forgotten you for the princess."

"Does he live with a princess?" asked Gerda.

"Yes—listen," said the raven. "But it will be difficult for me to speak your language. If you understand the raven language I can tell you better."

"No, I have not learned it," said Gerda, "but my grandmother understands it, and she can speak gibberish, too. I wish I had learned it."

"No matter," said the raven. "I will tell you as well as I

can; however, it will be bad enough." And then he told all he knew.

"In the kingdom where we now are there lives a princess, who is extraordinarily clever, for she has read all the newspapers in the whole world and has forgotten them again—so clever is she. She was recently, it is said, sitting on her throne—which is not very amusing after all—when she began humming an old tune. It went like this: 'Oh, why should I not be married?' 'That song is not without its meaning,' said she, and then she was determined to marry. But she wanted a husband who knew how to give an answer when he was spoken to, not one who only looked as if he were a great personage, for that is so tiresome. She then called all the ladies of the court together. When they heard her intention, all were very pleased, and said, 'We are very glad to hear it. It is the very thing we were thinking of.' You may believe every word I say," said the raven, "for I have a tame sweetheart that hops about in the palace quite free, and it was she who told me all this.

"The next day the newspapers appeared with a border of hearts and the initials of the princess. They announced that every good-looking young man was at liberty to come to the palace and speak to the princess. He who spoke the best and showed he felt most at home there, would be chosen for the princess's husband.

"Yes, yes," said the raven, "you must believe it. It is as true as I am sitting here. People came in crowds. There was a crush and a hurry, but no one was successful either on the first or second day. They could all talk well enough when they were out in the street, but as soon as they came inside the palace gates and saw the guards richly dressed in silver and the footmen in gold on the staircase and the large illuminated rooms, they were struck with wonder. When they stood before the throne on which the princess was sitting, all they could do was to repeat the last word they had uttered, and to hear it again did not interest her very much. It was just as if the people within were under a charm and had fallen into a trance till they came out again into the street, for then—oh, then—they could chatter enough. There was a whole row of them standing from the town gates to the palace. I was there myself to look," said the raven. "They grew hungry and thirsty, but from the palace they got nothing whatever, not even a glass of water. Some of the cleverest, it is true, had taken bread and butter with them, but none shared it with his neighbor, for each thought, *Let him look hungry, and then the princess won't have him.*"

"But Kay—little Kay," said Gerda, "when did he come? Was he among the number?"

"Patience, patience. We are just come to him. It was on the third day when a little personage without horse or carriage came marching right boldly up to the palace; his eyes shone like yours, he had beautiful long hair, but his clothes were very shabby."

"That was Kay!" cried Gerda, with a voice of delight. "Oh, now I've found him!" and she clapped her hands for joy.

"He had a little knapsack at his back," said the raven.

"No, that was certainly his sled," said Gerda, "for when he went away he took his sled with him."

"That may be," said the raven. "I did not examine him so minutely. But I know from my tame sweetheart that when he came into the courtyard of the palace and saw the bodyguard in silver and the footmen on the staircase, he was not the least abashed. He nodded and said to them, 'It must be very tiresome to stand on the stairs. For my part, I shall go in.' The rooms were all lit up—privy councillors and various excellencies were walking about barefoot and wore gold keys. It was enough to make anyone feel uncomfortable. His boots creaked, too, so loudly, but still he was not at all afraid."

"That's Kay for certain," said Gerda. "I know he had on new boots. I have heard them creaking in grandmother's room."

"Yes, they creaked," said the raven. "And on he went boldly up to the princess, who was sitting on a pearl as large as a spinning wheel. All the ladies of the court, with their attendants and attendants' attendants, and all the lords, with their gentlemen and gentlemen's gentlemen, stood around. The nearer they stood to the door, the prouder they looked. It was hardly possible to look at the gentleman's gentleman, so very haughtily did he stand in the doorway."

"It must have been terrible," said little Gerda. "And did Kay get the princess?"

"Were I not a raven, I should have taken the princess myself, although I am promised. It is said he spoke as well as I speak when I speak my raven language; this I learned from my tame sweetheart. He was bold and nicely behaved. He had not come to woo the princess, but only to hear her wisdom. She pleased him, and he pleased her."

"Yes, yes, for certain that was Kay," said Gerda. "He was so clever, he could reckon fractions in his head. Oh, won't you take me to the palace?"

"That is very easily said," answered the raven. "But how are we to manage it? I'll speak to my tame sweetheart about it. She must advise us. But I must tell you, such a little girl as you are will never get permission to enter."

"Oh, yes I shall," said Gerda. "When Kay hears that I am here, he will come out immediately to fetch me."

"Wait for me here on these steps," said the raven. He moved his head backward and forward and flew away.

The evening was closing in when the raven returned. *"Caw, caw!"* said he. "My sweetheart sends you her compliments, and here is a roll for you. She took it out of the kitchen, where there is bread enough. You are hungry, no doubt. It is not possible for you to enter the palace after all, for you are barefoot. The guards in silver and the footmen in gold would not allow it. But do not cry, you shall come in still. My sweetheart knows a little back staircase that leads to the bedchamber, and she knows where she can get the key to it."

And they went into the garden in the large avenue, where one leaf was falling after the other. When the lights in the palace had all gradually disappeared, the raven led little Gerda to the back door, which stood half open.

Oh, how Gerda's heart beat with anxiety and longing! It was just as if she had been about to do something wrong; and yet she only wanted to know if little Kay was there. Yes, he must be there. She called to mind his intelligent eyes and his long hair so vividly, she could quite see him as he used to laugh when they were sitting under the roses at home. The raven said, "He will, no doubt, be glad to see you—to hear what a long way you have come for his sake, to know how unhappy all at home were when he did not come back."

Oh, what a fright and a joy it was!

Then they were on the staircase. A single lamp was burning there. On the floor stood the tame raven, turning her head on every side and looking at Gerda, who bowed as her grandmother had taught her to do.

"My fiancé has told me so much good of you, my dear young lady," said the tame raven. "Your tale is very moving. If you will take the lamp, I will go first. We will go straight there so that we shall meet no one."

"I think there is somebody just behind us," said Gerda, and something rushed past. It was like the shadowy figures on the wall, horses with flowing manes and thin legs, huntsmen, ladies and gentlemen on horseback.

"They are only dreams," said the raven. "They come to fetch the thoughts of the high personages to the chase. But let me find, when you enjoy honor and distinction, that you possess a grateful heart."

"Tut! That's not worth talking about," said the raven of the woods.

They now entered the first saloon, which was of rose-colored satin with artificial flowers on the wall. Here the dreams were rushing past, but they hastened by so quickly that Gerda could not see the high personages. One hall was more magnificent than the other; one might indeed well be overwhelmed. At last they came into the bedchamber. The ceiling of the room resembled a large palm tree with leaves of costly glass, and in the middle, from a thick golden stem, hung two beds, each of which resembled a lily. One was white, and in this lay the princess; the other was red, and it was here that Gerda was to look for little Kay. She bent back one of the red petals and saw a brown neck. "Oh! that's Kay!" She shouted his name, held the lamp toward him and the dreams rushed back again into the chamber. The boy awoke, turned his head, and—it was not little Kay!

The prince was only like Kay about the neck, but he was still young and handsome. The princess peeked out from her white lily bed, and asked what was the matter. Then little Gerda cried and told her whole story and all that the ravens had done for her.

"Poor little thing!" said the prince and the princess. They praised the ravens very much and told them they were not at all angry with them, but they were not to do it again. However, they should have a reward.

"Do you want to fly about here at liberty," asked the princess, "or would you like to have a fixed appointment as court ravens, with all the leftovers from the kitchen?"

Both the ravens nodded and asked for a fixed appointment, for they thought of their old age, and said, "It is a good thing to have a provision for our old days."

The prince got up and let Gerda sleep in his bed, but more than this he could not do. She folded her little hands and thought, *How good people and animals are!* and she then fell asleep and slept soundly. All the dreams flew in again, and they now looked like angels. They drew a little sled, in which little Kay sat and nodded his head, but the whole was only a dream, and therefore it all vanished as soon as she awoke.

The next day Gerda was dressed from head to foot in silk and velvet. They offered to let her stay at the palace and lead a happy life, but she begged to have a little carriage with a horse in front and for a small pair of shoes. Then, she said, she would again go forth in the wide world and look for Kay.

Gerda got shoes and a muff. She was dressed very nicely, and when she was about to set off, a new carriage stopped before the door. It was of pure gold, and the coat of arms of the prince and princess shone like a star upon it. The coachman, the footmen, and the outriders, for outriders were there, too, all wore golden crowns. The prince and the princess assisted Gerda into the carriage themselves and wished her all success. The raven of the woods, who was now married, accompanied her for the first three miles. He sat beside Gerda, for it made him sick to ride backward. The other raven stood in the doorway and flapped her wings. She could not accompany Gerda because she'd had a headache ever since she'd gotten a fixed appointment and too much to eat. The carriage was lined inside with sugarplums, and in the seats were fruits and gingerbread.

"Farewell! Farewell!" cried the prince and princess, and Gerda and the raven wept. Thus passed the first miles, and then the raven bade her farewell, and this was the most painful separation of all. He flew into a tree and beat his black wings as long as he could see the carriage that shone from afar like a sunbeam.

FIFTH STORY.

The Little Robber Maiden

They drove through a dark wood, but the carriage shone like a torch, and it dazzled the eyes of the robbers so that they could not bear to look at it.

"'Tis gold! 'Tis gold!" they cried. They rushed forward, seized the horses, knocked down the guards, the coachman, and the servants and pulled little Gerda out of the carriage.

"How plump, how beautiful she is! She must have been

fed on nuts," said the old female robber, who had a long, scrubby beard and bushy eyebrows that hung down over her eyes. "She is as good as a fatted lamb! How nice she will be!" And then she drew out a knife, the blade of which shone so that it was quite dreadful to behold.

"Oh!" cried the woman at the same moment. She had been bitten in the ear by her own daughter who clung to her back and who was so wild and unmanageable that it was quite amusing to see her. "You naughty child!" said the mother, and didn't have time to kill Gerda.

"She shall play with me," said the little robber child. "She shall give me her muff and her pretty frock. She shall sleep in my bed!" And then she bit her mother again, so that she jumped and ran around in pain. The robbers laughed and said, "Look, how she is dancing with the little one!"

"I will go into the carriage," said the little robber maiden, and she would have her way, for she was very spoiled and very headstrong. She and Gerda got in, and then away they drove over the stumps of felled trees, deeper and deeper into the woods. The little robber maiden was as tall as Gerda, but stronger, broader-shouldered, and of dark complexion. Her eyes were quite black; they looked almost melancholy. She embraced little Gerda and said, "They shall not kill you as long as I am not mad at you. You are, doubtless, a princess?"

"No," said little Gerda, who then related all that had happened to her and how much she cared about little Kay.

The little robber maiden looked at her with a serious air, nodded her head slightly, and said, "They shall not kill you, even if I am angry with you: then I will do it myself." She dried Gerda's eyes and put both her hands in the handsome muff, which was so soft and warm.

At length the carriage stopped. They were in the midst of the courtyard of a robber's castle. It was full of cracks from top to bottom, and out of the openings magpies and rooks were flying. Great bulldogs, each of which looked as if it could swallow a man, jumped up, but they did not bark, for that was forbidden.

In the midst of the large, old, smoking hall burned a great fire on the stone floor. The smoke floated up to the ceiling and had to seek its own way out. In an immense cauldron, soup was boiling, and rabbits and hares were being roasted on a spit.

"You shall sleep with me and all my animals tonight," said the little robber maiden. They had something to eat and drink, and then went into a corner where straw and carpets were lying. Beside them, on laths and perches, sat nearly a hundred tame pigeons, all asleep seemingly, but yet they moved a little when the robber maiden came. "They are all mine," said she, at the same time seizing one that was next to her by the legs and shaking it so that its wings fluttered. "Kiss it!" cried the little girl, and flung the pigeon in Gerda's face. "Up there are the wild wood pigeons," continued she, pointing to several bars that were fastened over a hole high up in the wall. "They would all fly away immediately if they were not well locked up. And here is my dear old Baa." She laid hold of the horns of a reindeer that had a bright copper ring around its neck and was tethered to the spot. "We are obliged to lock this fellow in, too, or he would make his escape. Every evening I tickle his neck with my sharp knife. He is so frightened at it!" The little girl drew forth a long knife from a crack in the wall and let it glide over the reindeer's neck. The poor animal kicked. The girl laughed and dragged Gerda to bed.

"Do you intend to keep your knife while you sleep?" asked Gerda, looking at it rather fearfully.

"I' always sleep with the knife," said the little robber maiden. "There is no knowing what may happen. But tell me now, once more, all about little Kay and why you have started off in the wide world alone." And Gerda related all from the very beginning. The wood pigeons cooed above in their cage, and the others slept. The little robber maiden wound her arm around Gerda's neck, held the knife in the other hand, and snored so loud that everybody could hear her. But Gerda could not close her eyes, for she did not know whether she was to live or die. The robbers sat around the fire and sang, and drank. The old female robber jumped about so that it was quite dreadful for Gerda to see her.

Then the wood pigeons said, *"Coo! Coo!* We have seen little Kay! A white hen carries his sled. He himself sat in the carriage of the Snow Queen, who passed here, down just over the wood, as we lay in our nest. She blew upon us young ones, and all died except we two. *Coo! Coo!"*

"What is that you say up there?" cried little Gerda. "Where did the Snow Queen go to? Do you know anything about it?"

"She is no doubt gone to Lapland, for there is always snow and ice there. Only ask the reindeer, who is tethered there."

"Yes, there is ice and snow! There it is glorious and beautiful!" said the reindeer. "One can spring about in the large shining valleys! The Snow Queen has her summer tent there, but her castle is high up toward the North Pole, on the island called Spitzbergen."

"Oh, Kay! Poor little Kay!" sighed Gerda.

"Will you be quiet?" said the robber maiden. "If you won't, I shall make you."

In the morning Gerda told her all that the wood pigeons had said, and the little maiden looked very serious. But she nodded her head and said, "That's no matter—that's no matter. Do you know where Lapland lies?" she asked of the reindeer.

"Who should know better than I?" said the animal, and his eyes sparkled. "I was born and bred there—there I leaped about on the fields of snow."

"Listen," said the robber maiden to Gerda. "You see that the men are gone, but my mother is still here and will remain. However, late in the morning she takes a draught out of the large flask, and then she sleeps a little. Then I will do something for you." She jumped out of bed and rushed to her mother. With her arms around her neck and pulling her by the beard, she said, "Good morrow, my own sweet nanny goat of a mother." And her mother took hold of her nose and pinched it till it was red and blue, but this was all done out of pure love.

When the mother had taken a sip from her flask and was having a nap, the little robber maiden went to the reindeer and said, "I should very much like to give you still many a tickling with the sharp knife, for then you are so amusing. However, I will untether you and help you out, so that you may go back to Lapland. But you must make good use of your legs, and take this little girl for me to the palace of the Snow Queen, where her playfellow is. You have heard, I suppose, all she said, for she spoke loud enough, and you were listening."

The reindeer gave a bound for joy. The robber maiden lifted up little Gerda and took the precaution to bind her fast on the reindeer's back. She even gave her a small cushion to sit on. "Here are your fur leggings, for it will be cold. But the muff I shall keep for myself, for it is so very pretty. But I do not wish you to be cold. Here is a pair of lined gloves of my mother's—they'll reach up to your elbow. On with them! Now your hands look like my ugly old mother's!"

Gerda wept for joy.

"I can't bear to see you fretting," said the little robber maiden. "This is just the time when you ought to look pleased. Here are two loaves and a ham for you, so that you won't starve." The bread and the meat were fastened to the reindeer's back. The little maiden opened the door, called in all the dogs, and then with her knife cut the rope that fastened the animal and said to him, "Now, off with you, but take good care of the little girl!"

And Gerda stretched out her hands in the big mittens toward the robber maiden and said, "Farewell!" The reindeer flew over bush and bramble through the great wood, over moor and heath, as fast as he could go.

"Achoo, achoo!" was heard in the sky. It was just as if somebody was sneezing.

"Those are my old northern lights," said the reindeer. "Look how they gleam!" And on he now sped still quicker— day and night on he went. The loaves were consumed, and the ham, too. And then they were in Lapland.

SIXTH STORY.

The Lapland Woman and the Finland Woman

Suddenly they stopped before a little house, which looked very miserable. The roof reached to the ground, and the door was so low that the family were obliged to creep upon their stomachs when they went in or out. Nobody was at home except an old Lapland woman, who was frying fish by the light of an oil lamp. And the reindeer told her Gerda's story, but first he told his own, for that seemed to him of much greater importance. Gerda was so cold that she could not speak.

"Poor thing," said the Lapland woman, "you have far to run still. You have more than a hundred miles to go before you get to Finland. There the Snow Queen has her country house and burns blue lights every evening. I will give you a few words from me, which I will write on a dried codfish, for paper I have none. This you can take with you to the Finland woman, and she will be able to give you more information than I can."

When Gerda had warmed herself and had eaten and drunk, the Lapland woman wrote a few words on a dried codfish, begged Gerda to take care of them, put her on the reindeer, bound her fast, and away sprang the animal. "Achoo, achoo!" was again heard in the air; the most charming blue lights burned the whole night in the sky, and at last they came to Finland. They knocked at the chimney of the Finland woman, for as to a door, she had none.

There was such a heat inside that the Finland woman herself went about almost naked. She was tiny and dirty. She immediately loosened little Gerda's clothes and pulled off her thick gloves and boots—for otherwise the heat would have been too great—and after laying a piece of ice on the Reindeer's head, read what was written on the fish skin. She read it three times. She then knew it by heart, so she put the fish into the cupboard, for it might very well be eaten, and she never threw anything away.

Then the reindeer related his own story first, and afterward that of little Gerda. The Finland woman winked her eyes, but said nothing.

"You are so clever," said the reindeer. "I know you can twist all the winds of the world together in a knot. If a sailor loosens one knot, then he has a good wind. If a second, then it blows pretty stiffly. If he undoes the third and fourth, then it rages so that the forests are upturned. Won't you give the little maiden a potion that she may possess the strength of twelve men and vanquish the Snow Queen?"

"The strength of twelve men!" said the Finland woman. "Much good that would be!" Then she went to a cupboard and drew out a large skin rolled up. When she had unrolled it, strange characters were to be seen written on it. The Finland woman read at such a rate that the perspiration trickled down her forehead.

But the reindeer begged so hard for little Gerda, and Gerda looked so imploringly with tearful eyes at the Finland woman that she winked and drew the reindeer aside into a corner, where they whispered together, while the animal got some fresh ice put on his head.

"'Tis true little Kay is at the Snow Queen's and finds everything there quite to his taste. He thinks it the very best place in the world, but the reason of that is, he has a splinter of glass in his eye and in his heart. These must be got out first, otherwise he will never go back to mankind, and the Snow Queen will retain her power over him."

"But can you give little Gerda nothing to take that will give her power over everything?"

"I can give her no more power than what she has already. Don't you see how much that is? Don't you see how men and animals are forced to serve her; how well she gets through the world barefoot? She must not hear of her power from us. That power lies in her heart, because she is a sweet and innocent child! If she cannot get to the Snow Queen by herself and rid little Kay of the glass, we cannot help her. Two miles hence the garden of the Snow Queen begins. There you may carry the little girl. Set her down by the large bush with red berries standing in the snow. Don't stay talking, but hasten back as fast as possible." And now the Finland woman placed little Gerda on the reindeer's back, and off he ran with all imaginable speed.

"Oh! I have not got my boots! I have not brought my gloves!" cried little Gerda. She knew she was without them because of the biting frost, but the reindeer dared not stand still. On he ran till he came to the great bush with the red berries. There he set Gerda down and kissed her while large bright tears flowed from the animal's eyes, and then back he went as fast as possible. There stood poor Gerda, without shoes or gloves, in the very middle of dreadful, icy Finland.

She ran on as fast as she could. Suddenly, a whole regiment of snowflakes came toward her, but they did not fall from above. The sky was quite bright and shining from the aurora borealis. The flakes rushed along the ground, and the nearer they came the larger they grew. Gerda well remembered how large and strange the snowflakes appeared when she once saw them through a magnifying glass. But now they were large and terrifying in another way—they were all alive. They were the outposts of the Snow Queen. They had the most wondrous shapes. Some looked like large ugly porcupines. Others like snakes knotted together with their heads sticking out. And others, again, like small fat bears, with the hair standing on end. All were of dazzling whiteness—all were living snowflakes.

Little Gerda prayed. The cold was so intense that she could see her own breath, which came like smoke out of her mouth. Her breath grew thicker and thicker until it took the form of little angels that grew more and more when they touched the earth. All had helmets on their heads and lances and shields in their hands. They increased in numbers, and when Gerda had finished her prayer, she was surrounded by a whole legion. They thrust at the horrid snowflakes with their spears, so that they flew into a thousand pieces, and little Gerda walked on bravely and in security. The angels patted her hands and feet, and then she felt the cold less and went on quickly toward the palace of the Snow Queen.

But now we shall see how Kay fared. He never thought of Gerda, and least of all that she was standing outside the palace.

SEVENTH STORY.

What Took Place in the Palace of the Snow Queen and What Happened Afterward

The walls of the palace were made of driving snow, and the windows and doors of cutting winds. There were more than a hundred rooms depending on how the snow was driven by the winds. The largest was many miles in extent. All were lighted up by the powerful aurora borealis, and all were so large, so empty, so icy cold, and so resplendent! Mirth never reigned there. There was never even a dance for the polar bears where the storm made music, and the polar bears went on their hind legs and showed off their steps. There was never a little tea party for the young white foxes. Vast, cold, and empty were the halls of the Snow Queen. The northern lights shone with such precision that one could tell exactly when they were at their highest or lowest degree of brightness. In the middle of the empty, endless hall of snow was a frozen lake. It was cracked in a thousand pieces, but each piece was so like the other that it seemed the work of a cunning artist. In the middle of this lake sat the Snow Queen when she was at home. She called it the Mirror of Understanding, and believed that it was the most unique and best thing in the world.

Little Kay had become quite blue, yes nearly black with cold, but he did not notice it, for the Snow Queen had kissed away all feeling of cold from his body, and his heart was a lump of ice. He was dragging along some pointed flat pieces of ice,

which he laid together in every possible way. He
wanted to make something with them, just as we use little flat
pieces of wood to make geometrical figures. Kay made all sorts
of figures. The most complicated was an ice puzzle of the mind.
To Kay, the figures seemed extraordinarily beautiful and of the
utmost importance because of the bit of glass that was in his
eye. He found figures to represent written words, but he never
could manage to represent just the word he wanted—that word
was "eternity." The Snow Queen had said, "If you can create
that figure, you shall be your own master, and I will make you
a present of the whole world and a pair of new skates." But he
could not do it.

"I am going now to the warm lands," said the Snow Queen.
"I must have a look down into the black cauldrons." It was the
volcanoes Vesuvius and Etna that she meant. "I will just give
them a coating of white, for that is as it ought to be. Besides, it
is good for the oranges and the grapes." And then away she
flew, and Kay sat quite alone in the empty halls of ice
that were miles long, and looked at the blocks of ice
and thought and thought till his head ached. He sat so numb
and motionless that one would have thought he was frozen
to death.

That was when little Gerda stepped through the great
portal into the palace. The gate was formed of cutting winds,
but Gerda repeated her evening prayer, and the winds were
calm as though they slept. Then the little maiden entered the
vast, empty, cold halls and saw Kay. She recognized him, flew
to embrace him, and cried out, her arms firmly holding him the
while, "Kay, sweet little Kay! Have I then found you at last?"

But he sat quite still, numb and cold. Then little Gerda shed burning tears, and they fell on his bosom. The drops penetrated to his heart and thawed the lumps of ice, consuming the splinters of the looking glass. Kay looked at her as she sang the hymn:

"The rose in the valley is blooming so sweet,
   And angels descend there the children to greet."

At that Kay burst into tears. He wept so much that the splinter rolled out of his eye, and he recognized Gerda, and shouted, "Gerda, sweet little Gerda! Where have you been so long? And where have I been?" He looked around him. "How cold it is here!" said he. "How empty and cold!" And he held fast by Gerda, who laughed and wept for joy. It was so beautiful that even the blocks of ice danced about for joy. When they were tired and laid themselves down, they formed exactly the letters that the Snow Queen had told Kay to find out. So now he was his own master, and he would have the whole world and a pair of new skates into the bargain.

Gerda kissed his cheeks, and they grew quite blooming. She kissed his eyes, and they shone like her own. She kissed his hands and feet, and he was again well and merry. The Snow Queen might come back as soon as she liked. His freedom was written in shining pieces of ice.

Kay and Gerda took each other by the hand and wandered out of the big castle. They talked of their old grandmothers, and of the roses upon the roof. Wherever they went, the winds quieted, and the sun burst forth. When they reached the bush with the red berries, they found the reindeer waiting for them. He had brought another young reindeer with him, whose udder was filled with milk, which she gave to the children, and kissed them. The reindeer carried Kay and Gerda first to the Finland woman, where they warmed themselves in her hot room and learned what they were to do on their journey home—and then to the Lapland woman, who made some new clothes for them and repaired their sleds.

The reindeer and his young friend leaped along beside them and accompanied them to the boundary of the country where the first vegetation peeped forth. Here Kay and Gerda took leave of the Lapland woman. "Farewell! Farewell!" they all said. Then the first green buds appeared and the first little birds began to chirp. Out of the wood came a young damsel with a bright red cap on her head. She was armed with pistols and riding on a magnificent horse, which Gerda knew had belonged to her golden carriage. It was the little robber maiden, who, tired of being at home, had determined to make a journey to the north or in another direction, if that did not please her. She recognized Gerda immediately, and Gerda knew her, too. It was a joyful meeting.

"You are a fine fellow for tramping about," said she to little Kay. "I wonder if you deserve someone running from one end of the world to the other for your sake?"

But Gerda patted the bandit on the cheek, and inquired for the prince and princess.

"They are gone abroad," said the other.

"But the raven?" asked little Gerda.

"Oh! The raven is dead," she answered. "His tame sweetheart is a widow and wears a bit of black wool around her leg. She grieves most piteously, but it's all mere talk and stuff! Now tell me what you've been doing and how you managed to catch him."

Gerda and Kay told their stories.

"Well, there it is," said the robber maiden. She took their hands and promised that if she should some day pass through the town where they lived, she would come and visit them. Then away she rode. Kay and Gerda took each other's hand. It was lovely spring weather with an abundance of flowers and of green. Church bells rang, and the children recognized the high towers and the large town. It was where they lived. They entered and hastened up to Grandmother's room, where everything was standing as before. The clock said, *"tick-tock!"* and the finger moved around, but as they entered, they realized that they were now grown up. The blooming roses under the roof hung in at the open window. There stood their little children's chairs, and Kay and Gerda sat down on them, holding each other by the hand. They both had forgotten the cold empty splendor of the Snow Queen, as though it had been a dream. Grandmother sat in the bright sunshine and read aloud from the Bible: "Unless ye become as little children, ye cannot enter the kingdom of heaven."

Kay and Gerda looked in each other's eyes, and all at once they understood the old hymn:

"The rose in the valley is blooming so sweet,
And angels descend there the children to greet."

There they sat, the two adults. Grown up, and yet they were children, children at least at heart. It was summer time. Summer, glorious summer!

The Ugly Duckling

It was lovely summer weather in the country, and the golden corn, the green oats, and the haystacks piled up in the meadows looked beautiful. The stork walking about on his long red legs chattered in the Egyptian language, which he had learned from his mother. The cornfields and meadows were surrounded by large forests in the midst of which were deep pools.

It was, indeed, delightful to walk about in the country. In a sunny spot stood a pleasant old farmhouse close by a deep river, and from the house down to the waterside grew great burdock leaves so high that under the tallest of them a little child could stand upright. The spot was as wild as the center of a thick wood.

In this snug retreat sat a duck on her nest, watching for her young brood to hatch. She was beginning to get tired of her task, for the little ones were a long time coming out of their shells, and she seldom had any visitors. The other ducks preferred to swim about in the river than to climb the slippery banks and sit under a burdock leaf to gossip with her.

At length one shell cracked, and then another, and from each egg came a living creature that lifted its head and cried, *"Peep, peep."*

"Quack, quack," said the mother, and then they all quacked as well as they could and looked about them on every side at the large green leaves. Their mother allowed them to look as much as they liked, because green is good for the eyes.

"How large the world is," said the young ducks, when they found how much more room they now had than while they were inside the eggshell.

"Do you think this is the whole world?" asked the mother. "Wait till you have seen the garden. It stretches far beyond that to the parson's field, but I have never ventured to such a distance. Is everyone here?" she continued, rising. "No, I declare, the largest egg lies there still. I wonder how long this will take, I am quite tired of it." And she seated herself again on the nest.

"Well, how are you getting on?" asked an old duck, who paid her a visit.

"One egg is not hatched yet," said the duck. "It will not break. But just look at all the others, are they not the prettiest little ducklings you ever saw? They are the image of their father, who is so unkind, he never comes to see me."

"Let me see the egg that will not break," said the old duck. "I have no doubt it is a turkey's egg. I was persuaded to hatch some once, and after all my care and trouble with the young ones, they were afraid of the water. I quacked and clucked, but all to no purpose. I could not get them to venture in. Let me look at the egg. Yes, that is a turkey's egg. Take my advice, leave it where it is and teach the other children to swim."

"I think I will sit on it a little while longer," said the duck. "As I have sat so long already, a few days will be nothing."

"Please yourself," said the old duck, and she went away.

At last the large egg broke, and the hatchling crept forth crying, *"Peep, peep."* It was very large and ugly. The mother duck stared at it and said to herself, "It is very large and not at all like the others! I wonder if it really is a turkey. We shall soon find out, however, when we go to the water. It must go in, if I have to push it myself."

On the next day the weather was delightful, and the sun shone brightly on the green burdock leaves, so the mother duck took her young brood down to the water and jumped in with a splash. *"Quack, quack!"* cried she, and one after another the little ducklings jumped in. The water closed over their heads, but they came up again in an instant and swam about quite prettily with their legs paddling under them as easily as possible. The ugly duckling was in the water swimming with the rest.

Oh, thought the mother, *that is not a turkey. How well he uses his legs and how upright he holds himself! He is my own child, and he is not so very ugly after all if you look at him properly.* "Quack, quack! Come with me now, I will take you into grand society and introduce you to the farmyard, but you must keep close to me or you may be trodden upon. And, above all, beware of the cat."

When they reached the farmyard, there was a great disturbance. Two families of ducks were fighting over an eel's head, which, in the end, was carried off by the cat.

"See, children, that is the way of the world," said the mother duck, whetting her beak, for she would have liked the eel's head herself. "Come now, use your legs, and let me see how well you can behave. You must bow your heads prettily to that old duck yonder. She is the highest born of them all and has Spanish blood. Therefore, she is well off. Don't you see she has a red flag tied to her leg, which is something very grand and a great honor for a duck. It shows that everyone is anxious not to lose her, as she can be recognized both by man and beast. Come now, don't turn your toes, a well-bred duckling spreads his feet wide apart, just like his father and mother, in this way. Now bend your neck and say 'quack.'"

The ducklings did as they were bid, but the other ducks stared and said, "Look, here comes another brood, as if there were not enough of us already! And what a strange-looking duckling one of them is. We don't want him here." And then one of the ducks flew out and bit him in the neck.

"Let him alone," said his mother. "He is not doing any harm."

"Yes, but he is so big and ugly," said the spiteful duck, "and therefore he should be turned out."

"The others are very pretty children," said the old duck, with the tag on her leg, "all but that one. I wish you could improve him a little."

"That is impossible, your grace," replied the mother. "He is not pretty, but he has a very good disposition and swims as well or even better than the others. I think he will grow up pretty and perhaps be smaller. He has remained too long in the egg, and therefore his figure is not properly formed." Then she stroked his neck and smoothed the feathers, saying, "Plus, he's a drake, and therefore not of so much consequence. I think he will grow up strong and able to take care of himself."

"The other ducklings are graceful enough," said the old

duck. "Now make yourself at home, and if you can find an eel's head, you can bring it to me."

And so they made themselves comfortable. But the poor duckling, who had crept out of his shell last of all and looked so ugly, was bitten and pushed and made fun of, not only by the ducks, but by all the birds. "He is too big," they all said. The turkey cock, who had been born into the world with spurs and fancied himself really an emperor, puffed himself out like a vessel in full sail, flew at the duckling and became quite red in the head with passion, so that the poor little thing did not know where to go and was quite miserable because he was so ugly and laughed at by the whole farmyard. So it went on from day to day till it got worse and worse. The poor duckling was driven about by everyone. Even his brothers and sisters were unkind to him and would say, "Ah, you ugly creature, I wish the cat would get you." His mother said she wished he had never been born. The ducks pecked him, the chickens beat him, and the girl who fed the poultry kicked him with her feet.

At last he ran away, frightening the little birds in the hedge as he flew over the fence. *They are afraid of me because I am ugly*, he thought. So he closed his eyes and flew still farther until he came out on a large swamp inhabited by wild ducks. Here he remained the whole night, feeling very tired and sorrowful.

In the morning, when the wild ducks rose in the air, they stared at their new comrade. "What sort of a duck are you?" they all said, coming around him.

He bowed to them and was as polite as he could be, but he did not reply to their question. "You are exceedingly ugly," said the wild ducks, "but that will not matter if you do not want to marry one of our family."

Poor thing! He had no thoughts of marriage. All he wanted was permission to lie among the rushes and drink some of the water in the swamp. After he had been there two days, there came two wild geese, or rather goslings, for they had not been out of the egg long and were very saucy. "Listen, friend," said one of them to the duckling, "you are so ugly that we like you very well. Will you go with us and become a bird of passage? Not far from here is another swamp where there are some pretty wild geese, all unmarried. It is a chance for you to get a wife. You may get lucky, ugly as you are."

Just then were two loud bangs, and the two wild geese fell dead among the rushes, and the water was tinged with blood. *"Bang, bang,"* echoed far and wide in the distance, and whole flocks of wild geese rose up from the rushes. The sound continued from every direction, for the sportsmen surrounded the swamp, and some were even seated on branches of trees, overlooking the rushes. The blue smoke from the guns rose like clouds over the dark trees, and as it floated away across the water, a number of sporting dogs bounded in among the rushes, which bent beneath them wherever they went. How they terrified the poor duckling! He turned away his head to hide it under his wing, and at the same moment a large terrible dog passed quite near him. His jaws were open, his tongue hung from his mouth, and his eyes glared fearfully. He thrust his nose close to the duckling, showing his sharp teeth, and then, *"splash, splash,"* he went into the water without touching him, "Oh," sighed the duckling, "how thankful I am for being so ugly. Even a dog will not bite me."

And so he lay quite still while the shot rattled through the rushes, and gun after gun was fired over him.

It was late in the day before all became quiet, but even

then the poor young thing did not dare to move. He waited quietly for several hours, and then, after looking carefully around him, hastened away from the swamp as fast as he could. He ran over fields and meadows till a storm arose, and he could hardly move in the wind.

Toward evening, he reached a poor little cottage that seemed ready to fall and only remained standing because it could not decide on which side to fall first. The storm continued so violently that the duckling could go no farther. He sat down by the cottage, and then he noticed that the door was not quite closed in consequence of one of the hinges having given way. There was, therefore, a narrow opening near the bottom large enough for him to slip through, which he did very quietly, and got a shelter for the night.

As he soon discovered, a woman, a tomcat, and a hen lived in this cottage. The tomcat, whom the mistress called, "My little son," was a great favorite. He could raise his back, and purr, and could even throw out sparks from his fur if it were stroked the wrong way. The hen had very short legs, so she was called "Chickie short legs." She laid good eggs, and her mistress loved her as if she had been her own child. In the morning, they discovered the strange visitor, and the tomcat began to purr, and the hen to cluck.

"What is that noise about?" said the old woman, looking around the room, but her sight was not very good. Therefore, when she saw the duckling she thought it must be a fat duck that had strayed from home. "Oh, what a prize!" she exclaimed, "I hope it is not a drake, for then I shall have some duck's eggs. I must wait and see."

So the duckling was allowed to remain on trial for three weeks, but there were no eggs. Now the tomcat was the master of the house, and the hen was mistress, and they always said, "We and the world," for they believed themselves to be half the world, and the better half, too. The duckling thought that others might hold a different opinion on the subject, but the hen would not listen to such doubts.

"Can you lay eggs?" she asked.

"No."

"Then have the goodness to hold your tongue."

"Can you raise your back, or purr, or throw out sparks?" said the tomcat.

"No."

"Then you have no right to express an opinion when sensible people are speaking."

So the duckling sat in a corner, feeling very low-spirited, till the sunshine and the fresh air came into the room through the open door, and then he began to feel such a great longing for a swim on the water that he could not help telling the hen.

"What an absurd idea," said the hen. "You have nothing else to do, therefore you have foolish fancies. If you could purr or lay eggs, they would pass away."

"But it is so delightful to swim about on the water," said the duckling, "and so refreshing to feel it close over your head, while you dive down to the bottom."

"Delightful, indeed!" said the hen. "Why you must be crazy! Ask the cat; he is the cleverest animal I know. Ask him how he would like to swim about on the water, or to dive under it, for I will not speak of my own opinion. Ask our mistress, the old woman—there is no one in the world more clever than she is. Do you think she would like to swim, or to let the water close over her head?"

"You don't understand me," said the duckling.

"We don't understand you? Who can understand you, I wonder? Do you consider yourself more clever than the cat or the old woman? I will say nothing of myself. Don't imagine such nonsense, child, and thank your good fortune that you have been welcomed here. Are you not in a warm room, and in society from which you may learn something? But you are a chatterer, and your company is not very agreeable. Believe me, I speak only for your own good. I may tell you unpleasant truths, but that is a proof of my friendship. I advise you, therefore, to lay eggs and learn to purr as quickly as possible."

"I believe I must go out into the world again," said the duckling.

"Yes, do," said the hen.

So the duckling left the cottage and soon found water on which he could swim and dive, but all the other animals still avoided him because of his ugly appearance.

Autumn came, and the leaves in the forest turned to orange and gold. Then, as winter approached, the wind caught them as they fell and whirled them in the cold air. The clouds, heavy with hail and snowflakes, hung low in the sky, and the raven stood on the ferns crying, *"Caw, caw."* It made one shiver with cold to look at him. All this was very sad for the poor little duckling.

One evening, just as the sun set amid radiant clouds, there came a large flock of beautiful birds out of the bushes. The duckling had never seen birds like them before. They were swans. They curved their graceful necks, while their soft plumage shown with dazzling whiteness. They uttered a singular cry as they spread their glorious wings and flew away from those cold regions to warmer countries across the sea. As they mounted higher and higher in the air, the ugly little duckling felt quite a strange sensation as he watched them. He whirled himself in the water like a wheel, stretched out his neck toward them, and uttered a cry so strange that it frightened him. He would never forget those beautiful, happy birds. When at last they were out of his sight, he dived under the water and rose again almost beside himself with excitement. He didn't know the names of these birds, nor where they had flown, but he felt toward them as he had never felt for any other bird in the world. He was not envious of their beauty—how could he imagine being as lovely as they? Poor ugly creature, he would have been happy with only a tiny bit of encouragement from the ducks.

The winter grew colder and colder. The duckling had to swim about on the water to keep it from freezing, but every night the space on which he swam became smaller and smaller. At length it froze so hard that the ice in the water crackled as he moved, and the duckling had to paddle with his legs as hard as he could to keep the space from closing up. He became exhausted at last, and lay still and helpless, frozen fast in the ice.

Early in the morning, a peasant who was passing by saw what had happened. He broke the ice in pieces with his wooden shoe and carried the duckling home to his wife. The warmth revived the poor little creature. But when the children wanted to play with him, the duckling thought they would do him some harm, so he started up in terror, fluttered into the milk pan, and splashed the milk about the room. Then the woman clapped her hands, which frightened him still more. He flew first into the butter cask, then into the meal tub, and out again. What a condition he was in! The woman screamed and struck at him with the tongs. The children laughed and shouted, and tumbled over each other in their efforts to catch him. Luckily, the door stood open and the poor creature could just manage to slip out among the bushes. He lay down quite exhausted in the newly fallen snow.

It would be very sad, were I to relate all the misery and privations that the poor little duckling endured during the hard winter, but when it had passed, he found himself lying one morning in a marsh, among the rushes. He felt the warm sun shining and heard the lark singing, and saw that all around was beautiful spring. Then the young bird felt that his wings were strong as he flapped them against his sides and rose high into the air. They bore him onward until, before he knew it, he found himself in a large garden. The apple trees were in full blossom, and the fragrant elders bent their long green branches down to the stream that wound around a smooth lawn. Everything looked beautiful in the freshness of early spring. From a thicket close by came three beautiful white swans rustling their feathers and swimming lightly over the smooth water. The duckling remembered the lovely birds and felt more strangely unhappy than ever.

"I will fly to those royal birds," he exclaimed, "and they will kill me, because I am so ugly and dare to approach them. But it does not matter: better be killed by them than pecked by the ducks, beaten by the hens, pushed about by the maiden who feeds the poultry, or starved with hunger in the winter."

Then he flew to the water and swam toward the beautiful swans. The moment they spied the stranger, they rushed to meet him with outstretched wings.

"Kill me," said the poor bird. And he bent his head down to the surface of the water and awaited death.

But what did he see in the clear stream below? His own image: no longer a dark, gray bird, ugly and disagreeable to look at, but a graceful and beautiful swan.

To be born in a duck's nest in a farmyard is of no consequence to a bird if it is hatched from a swan's egg.

He now felt glad at having suffered sorrow and trouble because it enabled him to enjoy so much better all the pleasure and happiness awaiting him. The great swans swam around the newcomer and stroked his neck with their beaks as a welcome.

Soon, some little children came into the garden. They threw bread and cake into the water.

"See," cried the youngest, "there is a new one." And the rest were delighted and ran to their father and mother, dancing and clapping their hands, and shouting joyously, "There is another swan come. A new one has arrived."

Then they threw more bread and cake into the water and said, "The new one is the most beautiful of all. He is so young and pretty." And the old swans bowed their heads before him.

Then he felt quite ashamed and hid his head under his wing, for he did not know what to do. He was so happy, and yet not at all proud. He had been persecuted and despised for his ugliness, and now he heard them say he was the most beautiful of all the birds. Even the elder tree bent down its bows into the water before him, and the sun shone warm and bright. Then he rustled his feathers, curved his slender neck, and cried joyfully from the depths of his heart, "I never dreamed of such happiness as this, while I was an ugly duckling."

Thumbelina

～⚬⚬～

There was once a woman who wished very much to have a little child, but she could not get her wish. At last she went to a fairy and said, "I should so very much like to have a little child. Can you tell me where I can find one?"

"Oh, that can be easily managed," said the fairy. "Here is a barleyseed of a different kind to those that grow in the farmer's fields and that the chickens eat. Put it into a flower-pot and see what will happen."

"Thank you," said the woman, and she gave the fairy twelve coins, which was the price of the barleyseed. Then she went home and planted it, and immediately there grew up a large handsome flower, something like a tulip in appearance, but with its leaves tightly closed as if it were still a bud. "It is a beautiful flower," said the woman, and she kissed the red-and-golden-colored leaves. While she did so the flower opened, and she could see that it was a real tulip. Within the flower, upon the green velvet stamens, sat a very delicate and graceful little maiden. She was scarcely half as long as a thumb, and she was called "Thumbelina," because she was so small.

A walnut shell, elegantly polished, served her for a cradle. Her bedding was formed of blue violet leaves, with a rose leaf for a cover. Here she slept at night, but during the day she amused herself on a table, where the woman had placed a plateful of water. Around this plate were wreaths of flowers with their stems in the water, and upon it floated a large tulip leaf, which served Thumbelina for a boat. Here the little maiden sat and rowed herself from side to side, with two oars made of white horsehair. It really was a very pretty sight. Thumbelina could also sing so softly and sweetly that nothing like her singing had ever before been heard.

One night, while she lay in her pretty bed, a large, ugly, wet toad crept through a broken pane of glass in the window and leaped right upon the table where Thumbelina lay sleeping under her rose-leaf quilt. "What a pretty little wife she would make for my son," said the toad, and took up the walnut shell in which little Thumbelina lay asleep, and jumped through the window with it into the garden.

The toad lived with her son in the swampy bank of a broad stream in the garden. He was even uglier than his mother, and when he saw the pretty little maiden in her elegant bed, he could only cry, *"Croak, croak, croak."*

"Don't speak so loud, or she will wake," said the mother toad, "and then she might run away, for she is as light as swan's down. We will place her on one of the water lily leaves out in the stream. It will be like an island to her, she is so light and small, and then she cannot escape. While she is there, we will make haste and prepare the room under the marsh, in which you are to live when you are married."

Far out in the stream grew a number of water lilies with broad green leaves, which seemed to float on the top of the water. The largest of these leaves was farther away than the rest, and the old toad swam out to it with the walnut shell, in which little Thumbelina lay still asleep. The tiny little creature woke very early in the morning and began to cry bitterly when she found where she was, for she could see nothing but water on every side of the large green leaf, and no way of reaching the land. Meanwhile, the old toad was very busy under the marsh, decorating her room with rushes and wild yellow flowers to make it look pretty for her new daughter-in-law. Then she swam out with her ugly son to the leaf on which she had placed poor little Thumbelina. She wanted to fetch the pretty bed that she might put it in the bridal chamber to be ready for her. The old toad bowed low to her in the water and said, "Here is my son, he will be your husband, and you will live happily in the marsh by the stream."

"Croak, croak, croak," was all her son could say for himself, so the mother toad took up the elegant little bed and swam away with it, leaving Thumbelina all alone on the green leaf, where she sat and wept. She could not bear to think of living with the old toad and having her ugly son for a husband. The little fishes, who swam about in the water beneath, had seen the toad and heard what she said, so they lifted their heads above the water to look at the little maiden. As soon as they caught sight of her, they saw she was very pretty, and it made them very sorry to think that she must go and live with the ugly toads. "No, it must never be!" they decided. They assembled together in the water around the green stalk that held the leaf on which the little maiden stood and gnawed away at the root with their teeth. Then the leaf floated down the stream, carrying Thumbelina far away out of reach of land.

* * *

Thumbelina sailed past many towns, and the little birds in the bushes saw her and sang, "What a lovely little creature." The leaf floated farther and farther till it brought her to other lands. A graceful little white butterfly constantly fluttered around her, and at last alighted on the leaf. Thumbelina pleased him, and she was glad of it, for now the toad could not possibly reach her. The country through which she sailed was beautiful, and the sun shone upon the water till it glittered like liquid gold. She took the ribbon from around her waist and tied one end of it around the butterfly, and the other end of the ribbon she fastened to the leaf, which now glided on much faster than ever, taking little Thumbelina with it. But then a large beetle flew by. The moment he caught sight of Thumbelina, he seized her around her delicate waist with his claws and flew with her into a tree. The green leaf floated away on the brook, and the butterfly flew with it for he was fastened to it, and could not get away.

Oh, how frightened little Thumbelina felt when the beetle flew with her to the tree! But mostly she was sorry for the beautiful white butterfly that she had fastened to the leaf, for if he could not free himself he would die of hunger. But the beetle did not trouble himself at all about the matter. He seated himself by her side on a large green leaf, gave her some honey from the flowers to eat, and told her she was very pretty, although not in the least like a beetle. When the other beetles met Thumbelina, they turned up their feelers and said, "She has only two legs! How ugly that looks." "She has no feelers," said others. "Her waist is quite slim. Pooh! She is like a human being."

"Oh! She is ugly," said all the lady beetles, although Thumbelina was very pretty. Then the beetle who had run

away with her believed all the others when they said she was
ugly and would have nothing more to say to her, and told her
she might go where she liked. Then he flew down with her
from the tree and placed her on a daisy, and she wept at the
thought that she was so ugly that even the beetles would have
nothing to say to her. And all the while she was really the
loveliest creature that one could imagine, as tender and delicate as a beautiful rose leaf.

During the whole summer poor little Thumbelina lived
quite alone in the wide forest. She wove herself a bed with
blades of grass and hung it up under a broad leaf to protect
herself from the rain. She sucked the honey from the flowers
for food and drank the dew from their leaves every morning.
So passed away the summer and the autumn, and then came
the winter—the long, cold winter. All the birds who had sung
to her so sweetly had flown away, and the trees and the flowers had withered. The large clover leaf under the shelter of
which she had lived was now rolled together and shriveled up,
nothing remained but a yellow withered stalk. She felt dreadfully cold, for her clothes were torn. She was herself so frail
and delicate that poor little Thumbelina was nearly frozen to
death. It began to snow, too, and the snowflakes, as they fell
upon her, were like a whole shovelful falling upon one of us,
for we are tall, but she was only an inch high. Then she
wrapped herself up in a dry leaf, but it cracked in the middle
and could not keep her warm, and she shivered with cold.

Near the wood in which she had been living lay a corn-
field, but the corn had been cut for a long time. Nothing
remained but the bare dry stubble standing up out of the
frozen ground. It was to her like struggling through a large

wood. Oh! How she shivered with the cold. She came at last to
the door of a field mouse, who had a little den under the corn
stubble. There dwelled the field mouse in warmth and
comfort, with a whole roomful of corn, a kitchen, and a
beautiful dining room. Poor little Thumbelina stood before the
door just like a little beggar girl and begged for a small piece
of barleycorn, for she had been without a morsel to eat for
two days.

"You poor little creature," said the field mouse, who was
really a good old field mouse. "Come into my warm room and
dine with me." She was very pleased with Thumbelina, so she
said, "You are quite welcome to stay with me all the winter, if
you like. But you must keep my rooms clean and neat and tell
me stories, for I shall like to hear them very much." And
Thumbelina did all the field mouse asked her and found
herself very comfortable.

"We shall have a visitor soon," said the field mouse one
day. "My neighbor pays me a visit once a week. He is better
off than I am. He has large rooms and wears a beautiful black
velvet coat. If you could only have him for a husband, you
would be well provided for indeed. But he is blind, so you
must tell him some of your prettiest stories."

But Thumbelina did not feel at all interested about this
neighbor, for he was a mole. However, he came and paid his
visit dressed in his black velvet coat.

"He is very rich and learned, and his house is twenty
times larger than mine," said the field mouse.

He was rich and learned, no doubt, but he always spoke
dismissively of the sun and the pretty flowers, because he had
never seen them. Thumbelina had to sing to him, "Lady bug,
lady bug, fly away home," and many other pretty songs. And

the mole fell in love with her because she had such a sweet voice, but he said nothing yet, for he was very cautious. A short time before, the mole had dug a long passage under the earth, which led from the dwelling of the field mouse to his own, and here the mouse had permission to walk with Thumbelina whenever she liked. But he warned them not to be alarmed at the sight of a dead bird that lay in the passage. It was a perfect bird, with a beak and feathers, and could not have been dead long, and was lying underground just where the mole had made his passage.

The mole took a piece of rotting wood in his mouth that glittered like fire in the dark. Then he went before them to light them through the long, dark passage. When they came to the spot where the dead bird lay, the mole pushed his broad nose through the ceiling, the earth gave way so that there was a large hole, and the daylight shone into the passage. In the middle of the floor lay a dead swallow, his beautiful wings pulled close to his sides, his feet and his head drawn up under his feathers. The poor bird had evidently died of the cold. It made little Thumbelina very sad to see it, she did so love the little birds. All the summer they had sung and twittered for her so beautifully. But the mole pushed it aside with his crooked legs and said, "He will sing no more now. How miserable it must be to be born a little bird! I am thankful that none of my children will ever be birds, for they can do nothing but cry, 'Tweet, tweet,' and always die of hunger in the winter."

"Yes, you may well say that, as a clever man!" exclaimed the field mouse, "What is the use of his twittering, for when winter comes he must either starve or be frozen to death. Still, birds are very high bred."

Thumbelina said nothing, but when the two others had turned their backs on the bird, she stooped down and stroked aside the soft feathers that covered the head and kissed the closed eyelids. "Perhaps this was the one who sang to me so sweetly in the summer," she said, "and how much pleasure it gave me, you dear, pretty bird."

The mole stopped up the hole through which the daylight shone, and then accompanied the ladies home. But during the night Thumbelina could not sleep; so she got out of bed and wove a large, beautiful carpet of hay. Then she carried it to the dead bird and spread it over him; with some down from the flowers that she had found in the field mouse's room. It was as soft as wool, and she spread some of it on each side of the bird, so that he might lie warmly in the cold earth. "Farewell, you pretty little bird," said she, "farewell. Thank you for your delightful singing during the summer, when all the trees were green and the warm sun shone upon us." Then she laid her head on the bird's breast, but she was alarmed immediately, for it seemed as if something inside the bird went *"thump, thump."* It was the bird's heart. He was not really dead, only numb with the cold, and the warmth had restored him to life. (In autumn, all the swallows fly away into warm countries, but if one happens to linger, the cold seizes it, it becomes frozen and falls down as if dead. It remains where it fell, and the cold snow covers it.)

Thumbelina trembled very much. She was quite frightened, for the bird was large, a great deal larger than herself—she was only an inch high. But she took courage, laid the wool more thickly over the poor swallow, and then took a leaf that she had used for her own blanket, and laid it over the poor bird's head. The next morning she again stole out to see him. He was alive but very weak. He could only open his eyes for a moment to look at Thumbelina, who stood by holding a piece of decayed wood in her hand, for she had no other lantern. "Thank you, pretty little maiden," said the sick swallow. "I have been so nicely warmed that I shall soon regain my strength and be able to fly about again in the warm sunshine."

"Oh," said she, "it is cold outside now. It snows and freezes. Stay in your warm bed. I will take care of you."

Then she brought the swallow some water in a flower leaf, and after he had drank, he told her that he had wounded one of his wings in a thornbush and could not fly as fast as the others, who were soon far away on their journey to warm countries. Then at last he had fallen to the earth and could remember no more, nor how he came to be where she had found him. The whole winter the swallow remained underground, and Thumbelina nursed him with care and love. Neither the mole nor the field mouse knew anything about it, for Thumbelina knew they did not like swallows.

At last springtime came, and the sun warmed the earth. Then the swallow bade farewell to Thumbelina, and she opened the hole in the ceiling that the mole had made. The sun shone in upon them so beautifully that the swallow asked her if she would go with him. She could sit on his back, he said, and he would fly away with her into the green woods. But Thumbelina knew it would make the field mouse very grieved if she left her in that manner, so she said, "No, I cannot."

"Farewell, then, farewell, you good, pretty little maiden," said the swallow, and he flew out into the sunshine. Thumbelina looked after him, and the tears rose in her eyes. She was very fond of the poor swallow.

"*Tweet, tweet,*" sang the bird, as he flew out into the green woods, and Thumbelina felt very sad. She was not allowed to go out into the warm sunshine. The corn that had been sown in the field over the house of the field mouse had grown up high into the air and formed a thick wood to Thumbelina, who was only an inch in height.

"You are going to be married, Thumbelina," said the field mouse. "My neighbor has asked for you. What good fortune for a poor child like you. Now we will prepare your wedding clothes. They must be both woolen and linen. Nothing must be wanting when you are the mole's wife."

Thumbelina had to turn the spindle, and the field mouse hired four spiders, who were to weave day and night. Every evening the mole visited her and was continually speaking of the time when the summer would be over. Then he would keep his wedding day with Thumbelina, but now the heat of the sun was so great that it burned the earth and made it quite hard, like a stone. As soon as the summer was over, the wedding should take place. But Thumbelina was not at all pleased, for she did not like the tiresome mole. Every morning when the sun rose, and every evening when it went down, she would creep out the door. When the wind blew aside the ears of corn so that she could see the blue sky, she thought how beautiful and bright it seemed out there and wished so much to see her dear swallow again. But he never returned, for by this time he had flown far away into the lovely green forest.

When autumn arrived, Thumbelina had her outfit quite ready. The field mouse said to her, "In four weeks the wedding must take place." Then Thumbelina wept and said she would not marry the disagreeable mole.

"Nonsense," replied the field mouse. "Now don't be obstinate, or I shall bite you with my white teeth. He is a very handsome mole. The queen herself does not wear more beautiful velvets and furs. His kitchen and cellars are quite full. You ought to be very thankful for such good fortune."

So the wedding day was fixed, on which the mole was to fetch Thumbelina away to live with him deep under the earth and never again to see the warm sun because he did not like it. The poor child was very unhappy at the thought of saying farewell to the beautiful sun, and as the field mouse had given her permission to stand at the door, she went to look at it once more.

"Farewell, bright sun!" she cried, stretching out her arm toward it. Then she walked a short distance from the house, for the corn had been cut, and only the dry stubble remained in the fields. "Farewell, farewell," she repeated, twining her arm around a little red flower that grew just by her side. "Greet the little swallow for me, if you should see him again."

Suddenly, directly above her, she heard, *"Tweet, tweet."* She looked up, and there was the swallow himself flying close by. As soon as he spied Thumbelina, he was delighted. She told him how unwilling she felt to marry the ugly mole and to live always beneath the earth and never to see the bright sun anymore. And as she told him she wept.

"Cold winter is coming," said the swallow, "and I am going to fly away into warmer countries. Will you go with me? You can sit on my back and fasten yourself on with your sash. Then we can fly away from the ugly mole and his gloomy rooms—far away, over the mountains into warmer countries, where the sun shines more brightly than here, where it is always summer, and the flowers bloom in greater beauty. Fly now with me, dear little Thumbelina. You saved my life when I lay frozen in that dark passage."

"Yes, I will go with you," said Thumbelina. She seated herself on the bird's back, with her feet on his outstretched wings, and tied her ribbon to one of his strongest feathers.

Then the swallow rose in the air and flew over forest and over sea, high above the highest mountains covered with eternal snow. Thumbelina would have been frozen in the cold air, but she crept under the bird's warm feathers, keeping her little head uncovered so that she might admire the beautiful lands over which they passed. At length they reached the warm countries where the sun shines brightly, and the sky seems so much higher above the earth. Here, on the hedges and by the wayside, grew purple, green, and white grapes. Lemons and oranges hung from trees in the woods, and the air was fragrant with myrtles and orange blossoms. Beautiful children ran along the country lanes, playing with large gay butterflies, and as the swallow flew farther and farther, every place appeared still more lovely.

At last they came to a blue lake, and by the side of it, shaded by trees of the deepest green, stood a palace of dazzling white marble, built in the olden times. Vines clustered around its lofty pillars, and at the top were many swallows' nests. One of these was the home of the swallow who carried Thumbelina.

"This is my house," said the swallow, "but it would not do for you to live there—you would not be comfortable. You must choose for yourself one of those lovely flowers, and I will put you down upon it, and then you shall have everything that you can wish to make you happy."

"That will be delightful," she said, and clapped her little hands for joy.

A large marble pillar lay on the ground, which, in falling, had been broken into three pieces. Between these pieces grew the most beautiful large white flowers, so the swallow flew down with Thumbelina and placed her on one of the broad leaves. But how surprised she was to see in the middle of the flower a tiny little man, as white and transparent as if he had been made of crystal! He had a gold crown on his head and delicate wings at his shoulders, and was not much larger than Thumbelina herself. He was the angel of the flower, for a tiny man and a tiny woman dwell in every flower. And this was the king of them all.

"Oh, how beautiful he is!" whispered Thumbelina to the swallow.

The little prince was at first quite frightened at the bird, who was like a giant compared to such a delicate little creature as himself. But when he saw Thumbelina, he was delighted, and thought her the prettiest little maiden he had ever seen. He took the gold crown from his head, placed it on hers, and asked her name and if she would be his wife and queen over all the flowers.

This certainly was a very different sort of husband to the son of a toad or the mole with his black velvet and fur, so she said yes to the handsome prince. Then all the flowers opened, and out of each came a little lady or a tiny lord, all so pretty it was quite a pleasure to look at them. Each of them brought Thumbelina a present, but the best gift was a pair of beautiful wings, which had belonged to a large white fly. They fastened them to Thumbelina's shoulders, so that she might fly from flower to flower. Then there was much rejoicing, and the little swallow who sat above them in his nest was asked to sing a wedding song, which he did as well as he could. But in his heart he felt sad for he was very fond of Thumbelina and would have liked never to part from her again.

"You must not be called Thumbelina anymore," said the spirit of the flowers to her. "It is an ugly name, and you are so very pretty. We will call you Maya."

"Farewell, farewell," said the swallow, with a heavy heart as he left the warm countries to fly back into Denmark. There he had a nest over the window of a house in which dwelled the writer of fairy tales. The swallow sang, *"Tweet, tweet,"* and from his song came the whole story.

The Red Shoes

There was once a little girl who was very pretty and delicate. She was so poor that in summer she was forced to run about with bare feet and in winter wear very large wooden shoes, which made her little insteps quite red.

In the middle of the village lived old Dame Shoemaker; she sat and sewed together a little pair of shoes out of old red strips of cloth as well as she could. They were very clumsy, but it was a kind thought and she wanted the little girl to have them. The little girl was called Karen.

On the very day her mother was buried, Karen received the red shoes and wore them for the first time. They were certainly not intended for mourning, but she had no others, and with stockingless feet she followed the poor straw coffin in them.

Suddenly a large old carriage drove up bearing an equally large old lady. She looked at the little girl, felt compassion for her, and said to the clergyman, "Here, let me have the little girl. I will adopt her!"

Karen believed all this happened on account of the red shoes, but the old lady thought they were horrible, and had them burned. Karen herself was given clean new clothes, she learned to read and sew, and people said she was a pretty little thing. But the looking glass said: "You are more than pretty, you are beautiful!"

Now the queen once traveled through the land, and she had her little daughter, the princess, with her. People streamed to the castle, and Karen was there also. The little princess stood in her fine white dress in a window and let herself be stared at. She had neither a train nor a golden crown, but splendid red morocco shoes. They were certainly far more handsome than those Dame Shoemaker had made for little Karen. Nothing in the world is quite like red shoes.

Eventually Karen was old enough to be confirmed. She had new clothes and was to get new shoes also. The rich shoemaker in the city took the measure of her little foot. This took place in a room at his house, where there were large glass cases filled with elegant shoes and brilliant boots. They all looked charming, but the old lady could not see well, and so had no pleasure in them. In the midst of the shoes stood a pair of red ones, just like those the princess had worn. How beautiful they were! The shoemaker said they had been made for the child of a count, but had not fitted.

"That must be patent leather!" said the old lady. "They shine so!"

"Yes, they shine!" said Karen. They fit her and were bought, but the old lady knew nothing about their being red, else she would never have allowed Karen to have gone in red shoes to be confirmed. Yet that is what happened.

Everybody looked at Karen's feet. When she stepped

through the chancel door, it seemed to her as if even the old figures on the tombs, those portraits of old preachers and preachers' wives, with stiff ruffs and long black dresses, fixed their eyes on her red shoes. She could think only of the shoes as the clergyman laid his hand upon her head and spoke of the holy baptism, of the covenant with God, and how she should be now a matured Christian. The organ pealed solemnly, the sweet children's voices rang out, and the old music directors sang, but Karen only thought of her red shoes.

In the afternoon, the old lady heard from everyone that the shoes had been red. She said that it was very wrong of Karen, that it was not at all becoming, and that in the future Karen should only go in black shoes to church, even when she was older.

The next Sunday there was the sacrament, and Karen looked at the black shoes, looked at the red ones—looked at them again, and put on the red shoes.

The sun shone gloriously. Karen and the old lady walked along the path through the corn. It was rather dusty there.

At the church door stood an old soldier with a crutch and a wonderfully long beard that was more red than white. He bowed to the ground and asked the old lady whether he might dust her shoes. And Karen stretched out her little foot.

"Just look at those beautiful dancing shoes!" said the soldier. "May they sit firm when you dance," and he put his hand out toward the soles.

The old lady gave the old soldier alms and went into the church with Karen.

Once again, all the people in the church looked at Karen's red shoes. As Karen knelt before the altar and raised the cup to her lips, she only thought of the red shoes. The shoes seemed to be floating in the cup. She forgot to sing her psalm, and she forgot to recite the Lord's Prayer.

All the people went out of church, and the old lady got into her carriage. But as Karen raised her foot to get in after her, the old soldier said, "Look, what beautiful dancing shoes!" and Karen could not help dancing a step or two. But once she began her feet continued to dance, it was just as though the shoes had power over them. She danced around the corner of the church, and she could not leave off. The coachman was obliged to run after and grab hold of her. He lifted her in the carriage, but her feet continued to dance so that she kicked the old lady dreadfully. Finally she got the shoes off, and then her legs had peace.

When they got home, the shoes were put away in a closet, but Karen could not avoid looking at them.

The old lady got sick, and it was said she could not recover. She must be nursed and waited upon, and there was no one whose duty it was so much as Karen's. But there was a great ball in the city, to which Karen was invited. She looked at the old lady, who could not recover. She looked at the red shoes, and she thought there could be no sin in it. She put on the red shoes, and that seemed okay, but then she went to the ball and began to dance.

When she wanted to dance to the right, the shoes would dance to the left, and when she wanted to dance up the room, the shoes danced back again, down the steps, into the street, and out of the city gate. She danced—was forced to dance—straight out into the gloomy wood.

Karen saw light up among the trees ahead of her. She fancied it must be the moon, for it had a face, but it was the old soldier with the red beard. He sat there, nodded his head, and said, "Look, what beautiful dancing shoes!"

Karen was terrified and wanted to fling off the red shoes, but they clung fast. She pulled down her stockings, but the shoes seemed to have grown to her feet. So she danced—she had to dance—over fields and meadows, in rain and sunshine, by night and day. It was the scariest at night.

She danced into the churchyard, but the dead did not dance—they had something better to do than to dance. She wanted to seat herself on a poor man's grave, where the bitter tansy grew, but for her there was neither peace nor rest and she danced on toward the open church door. There she saw an angel standing in long, white robes. He had wings that reached from his shoulders to the earth. His countenance was severe and grave. And in his hand he held a sword, broad and glittering.

"You shall dance!" said he. "Dance in your red shoes till you are pale and cold! Till your skin shrivels up and you are a skeleton! You shall dance from door to door! And where proud, vain children dwell, you will knock, that they may hear you and tremble! You shall dance!"

"Mercy!" cried Karen. But she did not hear the angel's reply, for the shoes carried her through the gate into the fields, across roads and bridges, and she had to keep dancing and dancing.

One morning she danced past a door she recognized. She heard a psalm from within. A coffin, decked with flowers, was carried out. Then she knew that the old lady was dead and felt that she was abandoned by all and condemned by the angel.

She danced—she had to dance—through the gloomy night. The shoes carried her over stick and stone and she was torn till she bled. She danced over the heath till she came to a little house. Here, she knew, dwelled the executioner. She tapped with her fingers at the window and said, "Come out! Come out! I cannot come in, for I am forced to dance!"

And the executioner said, "You do not know who I am, I fancy? I strike bad people's heads off, and my axe is always ready!"

"Don't strike my head off!" said Karen. "Then I can't repent of my sins! But strike off my feet in the red shoes!"

And then she confessed all her sins, and the executioner struck off her feet with the red shoes. But the red shoes danced away with her little feet across the field into the deep wood.

The executioner carved out little wooden feet and crutches for her and taught her the hymn criminals always sing. Then she kissed the hand that had wielded the axe and went off over the heath.

"Now I have suffered enough for the red shoes!" said she. "Now I will go into the church that people may see me!" And she hastened toward the church door. But when she came near it, the red shoes danced in front of her, and she was terrified and turned around.

The whole week she was unhappy and wept many bitter tears. But when Sunday returned, she said, "Well, now I have suffered and struggled enough! I really believe I am as good as many a one who sits in the church and holds her head high!"

Away she went boldly, but she had not got farther than the churchyard gate before she saw the red shoes dancing before her. She was frightened and turned back, and repented of her sins from her heart.

She went to the parsonage and begged that they would take her into service. She would be very industrious, she said, and would do everything she could. She did not care about the wages, only she wished to have a home and be with good people. The clergyman's wife felt sorry for her and took her into service, and she was industrious and thoughtful. She sat still and listened when the clergyman read the Bible in the evenings. All the children liked her very much, but when they spoke of fancy clothes, and grandeur and beauty, she shook her head.

The following Sunday, when the family was going to church, they asked her whether she would go with them, but she glanced sorrowfully, with tears in her eyes, at her crutches. The family went on to church, but she went alone into her little chamber. There was only room in it for a bed and chair. Here she sat down with her prayer book, and while she read with a pious mind, the wind bore the strains of the organ toward her. She raised her tearful countenance and said, "O God, help me!"

Just then the sun shone clearly, and straight before her stood an angel in white robes, the same she had seen that night at the church door. He no longer carried the sharp sword, but in its stead a splendid green bouquet of roses. He touched the ceiling with the bouquet, and the ceiling rose high, and where he had touched it there gleamed a golden star. He touched the walls, and they widened out, and she saw the organ that was playing. She saw the old pictures of the preachers and the preachers' wives and the congregation sitting in cushioned seats and singing out of their prayer books. For the church itself had come to the poor girl in her narrow chamber, or else she had come into the church. She sat in the pew with the clergyman's family. When they had ended the psalm and looked up, they nodded and said, "It is right that you have come!"

"It was through mercy!" she said.

The organ pealed, and the children's voices in the choir sounded sweet and soft! The clear sunshine streamed warmly through the window into the pew where Karen sat. Her heart was so full of sunshine, peace, and joy that it burst. Her soul flew on the sunshine to God, and there no one asked about the red shoes.

The Little Match Girl

It was most terribly cold. Snow fell and it was nearly dark on the last evening of the year. In this cold and darkness, a poor little girl, bareheaded and with naked feet, walked along the street. When she left home she had had slippers on, it is true, but what was the good of that? They were very large slippers, which her mother had worn until then. So large were they that the poor little thing lost them as she scuffled away across the street when two carriages rolled by dreadfully fast.

One slipper was nowhere to be found; the other had been laid hold of by an urchin, and off he ran with it. He thought it would do capitally for a cradle when he some day or other should have children himself. So the little maiden walked on with her tiny naked feet, which were quite red and blue from cold. She carried a quantity of matches in an old apron, and she held a bundle of them in her hand. Nobody had bought anything from her the whole day. No one had given her a single coin.

She crept along trembling with cold and hunger—a very

picture of sorrow, the poor little thing!

The flakes of snow covered her long, fair hair, which fell in beautiful curls around her neck, but of that, of course, she never once thought now. From all the windows the candles were gleaming, and it smelled deliciously of roast goose, for it was New Year's Eve. Of that she was thinking.

In a corner formed by two houses, of which one stuck out more than the other, she seated herself down and huddled tight. Her little feet she had drawn close up to her, but she grew colder and colder. She would not venture to go home, for she had not sold any matches and could not bring any money. From her father she would certainly get blows, and at home it was cold too, for above her she had only the roof, through which the wind whistled, even though the largest cracks were stopped up with straw and rags.

Her little hands were almost numb with cold. Oh! A match might give her a world of comfort, if she only dared take a single one out of the bundle, draw it against the wall, and warm her fingers by it. She drew one out. *"Rischt!"* How it blazed and burned!

It made a warm, bright flame like a candle, as she held her hands over it. It was a wonderful light. It seemed really to the little maiden as though she were sitting before a large iron stove, with burnished brass feet and a brass ornament at top. The fire burned with such blessed heat; it warmed so delightfully. The little girl had already stretched out her feet to warm them, too, but the small flame went out and the stove vanished. She had only the remains of the burned-out match in her hand.

She rubbed another against the wall. It burned brightly,

and where the light fell on the wall it became transparent like a veil, so that she could see into the room. On the table was spread a snow white tablecloth. Upon it was a splendid porcelain table service, and a roast goose steaming deliciously with its stuffing of apple and dried plums. What was still more amazing was that the goose hopped down from the dish and waddled over to the poor little girl with knife and fork in its breast. Then, the match went out, and nothing but the thick, cold, damp wall was left behind.

She lighted another match. Now she was sitting under the most magnificent Christmas tree. It was still larger and more decorated than the one which she had seen through the glass door in the rich merchant's house. Thousands of lights were burning on the green branches, and gaily colored pictures, such as she had seen in the shop windows, looked down upon her. The little maiden stretched out her hands toward them when—the match went out. The lights of the Christmas tree rose higher and higher until she saw them as stars in heaven. One fell down and formed a long trail of fire.

"Someone has just died!" said the little girl, for her old grandmother, the only person who had loved her and who was now dead, had told her that when a star falls a soul ascends to God.

She drew another match against the wall. It was again light, and in the luster there stood her old grandmother, bright and radiant, mild, and with an expression of love.

"Grandmother!" cried the little one. "Oh, take me with you! You'll go away when the match burns out. You'll vanish like the warm stove, like the delicious roast goose and like the magnificent Christmas tree!" She rubbed the whole bundle of matches quickly against the wall, for she wanted to be quite sure of keeping her grandmother near her. And the matches gave such a brilliant light that it was brighter than at noon. Never formerly had the grandmother been so beautiful and so tall. She took the little maiden in her arms, and both flew in brightness and in joy so high, so very high. Above there was neither cold, nor hunger, nor anxiety—they were with God.

But at the cold hour of dawn, in the nook of the house, sat the poor girl, with rosy cheeks and with a smiling mouth, leaning against the wall. She was dead—frozen to death on the last evening of the old year. Stiff and stark sat the child there with her matches, of which one bundle had been burned. "She wanted to warm herself," people said. No one had the slightest suspicion of what beautiful things she had seen. No one even dreamed of the splendor in which, with her grandmother, she had entered on the joys of a new year.

Little Claus and Big Claus

In a village there once lived two men who had the same name. They were both called Claus. One of them had four horses, but the other had only one. To distinguish them, people called the owner of the four horses, "Big Claus," and he who had only one, "Little Claus." Now we shall hear what happened to them, for this is a true story.

All week long, Little Claus had to plough for Big Claus and lend him his one horse. In return, every Sunday, Big Claus lent him all his four horses. Then how Little Claus would smack his whip over all five horses, because they were as good as his own on that one day. The sun shone brightly, and the church bells were ringing merrily as the people passed by, dressed in their best clothes, with their prayer books under their arms. They were going to hear the clergyman preach. They looked at Little Claus ploughing with his five horses, and he was so proud that he smacked his whip and said, "Gee-up, my five horses."

"You must not say that," said Big Claus, "for only one of them belongs to you." But Little Claus soon forgot what he ought to say, and when anyone passed he would call out, "Gee-up, my five horses!"

"I must beg you not to say that again," said Big Claus, "for if you do, I shall hit your horse on the head, so that he will drop dead on the spot, and that will be the end of him."

"I promise you I will not say it anymore," said the other. But as soon as people came by, nodding to him and wishing him "Good day," he became so pleased and thought how grand it looked to have five horses ploughing in his field that he cried out again, "Gee-up, all my horses!"

"I'll gee-up your horses for you," said Big Claus. Seizing a hammer, he struck the one horse of Little Claus on the head, and he fell dead instantly.

"Oh, now I have no horse at all," said Little Claus, weeping. After a while he took off the dead horse's skin and hung the hide to dry in the wind. Then he put the dry skin into a bag and, placing it over his shoulder, went out into the next town to sell it.

He had a very long way to go and had to pass through a dark, gloomy forest. Presently a storm arose, and he lost his way. Before he could find the right path, evening came on, and it was still a long way to the town and too far to return home before night.

Near the road stood a large farmhouse. The shutters outside the windows were closed, but light shone through the crevices at the top. *Perhaps they will let me stay here for the night*, thought Little Claus, so he went up to the door and knocked.

The farmer's wife opened the door; but when she heard what he wanted, she told him to go away, as her husband would not allow her to admit strangers.

"Then I shall be obliged to sleep out here," said Little Claus to himself, as the farmer's wife shut the door in his face.

Near to the farmhouse stood a large haystack, and between it and the house was a small shed with a thatched roof. "I can lie down up there," said Little Claus, as he saw the roof. "It will make a great bed, but I hope the stork will not fly down and bite my legs," for on it stood a stork, whose nest was in the roof. Little Claus climbed to the roof of the shed. While he turned himself to get comfortable, he discovered that the wooden shutters, which were closed, did not reach to the tops of the windows of the farmhouse, so that he could see into a room, in which a large table was laid out with wine, roast meat, and a splendid fish. The farmer's wife and the sexton were sitting at the table together. She filled his glass and helped him plenteously to fish, which appeared to be his favorite dish. *If I could only have some, too*, thought Little Claus. Then, as he stretched his neck toward the window, he spied a large, beautiful pie—indeed they had a glorious feast before them.

At this moment he heard someone riding down the road toward the farmhouse. It was the farmer returning home. He was a good man, but still he had a very strange prejudice—he could not bear the sight of a sexton. If one appeared before him, he would go into a terrible rage. In consequence of this dislike, the sexton had gone to visit the farmer's wife during her husband's absence from home, and the good woman had placed before him the best she had in the house to eat. When she heard the farmer coming she was frightened and begged the sexton to hide himself in a large empty chest that stood in the room. He did so, for he knew her husband could not endure the sight of a sexton. The woman then quickly put away the wine and hid all the rest of the nice things in the oven, for if her husband had seen them he would have asked what they were brought out for.

"Oh, dear," sighed Little Claus from the top of the shed, as he saw all the good things disappear.

"Is anyone up there?" asked the farmer, looking up and discovering Little Claus. "Why are you lying up there? Come down, and come into the house with me." So Little Claus came down and told the farmer how he had lost his way and begged for a night's lodging.

"All right," said the farmer, "but we must have something to eat first."

The woman received them both very kindly, laid the cloth on a large table, and placed before them a dish of porridge. The farmer was very hungry and ate his porridge with a good appetite, but Little Claus could not help thinking of the nice roast meat, fish, and pies, which he knew were in the oven. Under the table at his feet lay the sack containing the horse's skin, which he intended to sell at the next town. Now Little Claus did not relish the porridge at all, so he trod with his foot on the sack under the table, and the dry skin squeaked quite loud. "Hush!" said Little Claus to his sack, at the same time treading upon it again till it squeaked louder than before.

"Hallo! What have you got in your sack?" asked the farmer.

"Oh, it is a troll," said Little Claus, "and he says we need not eat porridge, for he has conjured the oven full of roast meat, fish, and pie."

"Wonderful!" cried the farmer, starting up and opening the oven door; and there lay all the nice things hidden by the farmer's wife, but which he supposed had been conjured there by the troll under the table. The woman dared not say anything, so she placed the things before them, and they both ate of the fish, the meat, and the pastry.

Then Little Claus trod again upon his sack, and it squeaked as before. "What does he say now?" asked the farmer.

"He says," replied Little Claus, "that there are three bottles of wine for us, standing in the corner by the oven."

So the woman was obliged to bring out the wine also, which she had hidden, and the farmer drank it till he became quite merry. He would have liked such a troll as Little Claus carried in his sack. "Could he conjure up the evil one?" asked the farmer. "I should like to see him now, while I am so merry."

"Oh, yes!" replied Little Claus. "My conjuror can do anything I ask him, can you not?" he asked, treading at the same time on the sack till it squeaked. "Do you hear? He answers yes, but he fears that we shall not like to look at him."

"Oh, I am not afraid. What will he be like?"

"Well, he is very much like a sexton."

"Ha!" said the farmer. "Then he must be ugly. Do you know I cannot endure the sight of a sexton? However, that doesn't matter. I shall know who it is, so I shall not mind. Now then, I have got up my courage, but don't let him come too near me."

"Stop, I must ask the troll," said Little Claus, so he trod on the bag and stooped his ear down to listen.

"What does he say?"

"He says that you must go and open that large chest that stands in the corner, and you will see the evil one crouching down inside. But you must hold the lid firmly, that he may not slip out."

"Will you come and help me hold it?" said the farmer, going toward the chest in which his wife had hidden the sexton, who now lay inside very much frightened. The farmer opened the lid a very little way and peeped in.

"Oh!" cried he, springing backward. "I saw him, and he is exactly like our sexton. How dreadful it is!" So after that he needed a drink again, and they sat and drank till far into the night.

"You must sell your troll to me," said the farmer. "Ask as much as you like, I will pay it. Indeed I would give you a whole bushel of gold right away."

"No, indeed, I cannot," said Little Claus. "Only think how much profit I could make out of this troll."

"But I should like to have him," said the farmer, still continuing his entreaties.

"Well," said Little Claus at length, "you have been so good as to give me a night's lodging, I will not refuse you. You shall have the troll for a bushel of money, but I will have it quite full to the top."

"So you shall," said the farmer, "but you must take away the chest as well. I would not have it in the house another hour. There is no knowing if the sexton is still in there."

So Little Claus gave the farmer the sack containing the dried horse's skin and received in exchange a bushel of money—full measure. The farmer also gave him a wheelbarrow on which to carry away the chest and the gold.

"Farewell," said Little Claus, as he went off with his money and the great chest, in which the sexton lay still concealed. On one side of the forest was a broad, deep river. The water flowed so rapidly that very few were able to swim against the stream. A new bridge had lately been built across it, and in the middle of this bridge Little Claus stopped and said, loud enough to be heard by the sexton, "Now what shall I do with this stupid chest. It is as heavy as if it were full of stones. I shall be tired if I roll it any farther, so I may as well throw it in the river. If it swims after me to my house, well and good, and if not, it will not much matter."

So he seized the chest in his hand and lifted it up a little, as if he were going to throw it into the water.

"No, leave it alone!" cried the sexton from within the chest. "Let me out first."

"Oh!" exclaimed Little Claus, pretending to be frightened. "He is in there still, is he? I must throw him into the river, that he may be drowned."

"Oh, no! Oh, no!" cried the sexton. "I will give you a whole bushel full of money if you will let me go."

"Why, that is another matter," said Little Claus, opening the chest. The sexton crept out, pushed the empty chest into the water, and went to his house where he measured out a whole bushel full of gold for Little Claus, who had already received one from the farmer. Little Claus now had a whole barrow full of gold.

"I have been well paid for my horse," said he to himself when he reached home, entered his own room, and emptied all his money into a heap on the floor. "How vexed Big Claus will be when he finds out how rich I have become all through my one horse. But I shall not tell him exactly how it all happened." Then he sent a boy to Big Claus to borrow a bushel measure.

What can he want that for? thought Big Claus. He was so curious that he smeared the bottom of the measure with tar so that some of whatever was put into it would stick to it. And so it happened, for when the measure returned, three new silver coins were sticking to it.

"What does this mean?" said Big Claus. He ran off directly to Little Claus and asked, "Where did you get so much money?"

"Oh, for my horse's skin, I sold it yesterday."

"It was certainly well paid for then," said Big Claus. He ran home to his house, seized a hatchet, knocked all his four horses on the head, flayed off their skins, and took them to the town to sell. "Skins, skins, who'll buy skins?" he cried, as he went through the streets. All the shoemakers and tanners came running and asked how much he wanted for them.

"A bushel of money for each," replied Big Claus.

"Are you mad?" they all cried. "Do you think we have money to spend by the bushel?"

"Skins, skins!" he cried again. "Who'll buy skins?" But to all who inquired the price, his answer was "a bushel of money."

"He is making fools of us," they decided. Then the shoemakers took their straps and the tanners their leather aprons, and they began to beat Big Claus.

"Skins, skins!" they cried, mocking him. "Yes, we'll mark your skin for you, till it is black and blue."

"Out of the town with him," said they. And Big Claus was obliged to run as fast as he could; he had never before been so thoroughly beaten.

"Ah," said he, as he came to his house. "Little Claus shall pay me for this. I'm going to kill him."

Meanwhile, Little Claus's old grandmother died. She had been cross, unkind, and really spiteful to him, but he was very sorry and took the dead woman and laid her in his warm bed to see if he could bring her to life again. There he determined that she should lie the whole night, while he seated himself in a chair in a corner of the room as he had often done before. During the night, as he sat there, the door opened, and in came Big Claus with a hatchet. He knew well where Little Claus's bed stood, so he went right up to it and struck the old grandmother on the head, thinking it must be Little Claus.

"There!" cried he. "Now you cannot make a fool of me again." And then he went home.

That is a very wicked man, thought Little Claus. *He meant to kill me. It is a good thing for my old grandmother that she was already dead, or he would have taken her life.* Then, he dressed his old grandmother in her best clothes, borrowed a horse of his neighbor, and harnessed it to a cart. Then he placed the old woman on the backseat, so that she might not fall out as he drove, and rode away through the wood. By sunrise they reached a large inn, where Little Claus stopped and went to get something to eat. The landlord was a rich man and a good man, too, but as quick-tempered as if he had been made of pepper and snuff.

"Good morning," said he to Little Claus. "You are come early today."

"Yes," said Little Claus. "I am going to the town with my old grandmother. She is sitting at the back of the wagon, but I cannot bring her into the room. Will you take her a glass of mead? But you must speak very loud, for she cannot hear well."

"Yes, certainly I will," replied the landlord. Pouring out a glass of mead, he carried it out to the dead grandmother, who sat upright in the cart. "Here is a glass of mead from your grandson," said the landlord. The dead woman did not answer a word, but sat quite still. "Do you not hear?" cried the landlord as loud as he could. "Here is a glass of mead from your grandson."

Again and again he bawled it out, but as she did not stir he flew into a passion and threw the glass of mead in her face. It struck her on the nose, and she fell backward out of the cart, for she was only seated there, not tied in.

"Hallo!" cried Little Claus, rushing out of the door and seizing hold of the landlord by the throat. "You have killed my grandmother. See, here is a great hole in her forehead."

"Oh, how unfortunate," said the landlord, wringing his hands. "This all comes of my fiery temper. Dear Little Claus, I will give you a bushel of money. I will bury your grandmother as if she were my own. Only keep silent or else they will cut off my head, and that would be disagreeable."

So it happened that Little Claus received another bushel of money, and the landlord buried his old grandmother as if she had been his own. When Little Claus reached home again, he immediately sent a boy to Big Claus, requesting him to lend him a bushel measure. *How is this?* thought Big Claus. *Did I not kill him? I must go and see for myself.* So he went to

Little Claus and took the bushel measure with him. "How did you get all this money?" asked Big Claus, staring with wide open eyes at his neighbor's treasures.

"You killed my grandmother instead of me," said Little Claus, "so I have sold her for a bushel of money."

"That is a good price at all events," said Big Claus. So he went home, took a hatchet, and killed his old grandmother with one blow. Then, he placed her on a cart, drove into the town to the apothecary, and asked him if he would buy a dead body.

"Whose is it, and where did you get it?" asked the apothecary.

"It is my grandmother," he replied. "I killed her so that I could get a bushel of money for her."

"Heaven preserve us!" cried the apothecary. "You are out of your mind. Don't say such things, or you will lose your head." And then he talked to him seriously about the wicked deed he had done and told him that such a wicked man would surely be punished. Big Claus got so frightened that he rushed out of the shop, jumped into the cart and drove home quickly. The apothecary and all the people thought him mad and let him go.

"You shall pay for this," said Big Claus, as soon as he got into the high road, "That you shall, Little Claus." So as soon as he reached home he took the largest sack he could find and went over to Little Claus. "You have played me another trick," he said. "First, I killed all my horses, and then my old grandmother, and it is all your fault. But you shall not make a fool of me anymore." So he took hold of Little Claus around the waist and pushed him into the sack, which he took on his shoulders, saying, "Now I'm going to drown you in the river."

He had a long way to go before he reached the river, and Little Claus was not a very light weight to carry. The road led by the church, and as they passed he could hear the organ playing and the people singing beautifully. Big Claus put down the sack close to the church door and thought he might as well go in and hear a psalm before he went any farther. Little Claus could not possibly get out of the sack, and all the people were in church, so in he went.

"Oh dear, oh dear," sighed Little Claus in the sack, as he turned and twisted about. But he found he could not loosen the string with which it was tied. After a while an old cattle driver with snowy hair passed by, carrying a large staff in his hand, with which he drove a large herd of cows and oxen before him. They stumbled against the sack where Little Claus was stuck, and turned it over. "Oh dear," sighed Little Claus. "I am very young, yet I am soon going to heaven."

"And I, poor fellow," said the herder, "I who am so old already cannot get there."

"Open the sack," cried Little Claus. "Creep into it instead of me, and you will soon be there."

"With all my heart," replied the herder, opening the sack, from which sprung Little Claus as quickly as possible. "Will you take care of my cattle?" said the old man, as he crept into the bag.

"Yes," said Little Claus, and he tied up the sack and then walked off with all the cows and oxen.

When Big Claus came out of church, he took up the sack and placed it on his shoulders. It appeared to have become lighter, for the old herder was not half so heavy as Little Claus.

"How light he seems now. It must be because I have been to a church." Big Claus walked on to the river, which was deep and broad, and threw the sack containing the old herder into the water, believing it to be Little Claus. "There you can stay!" he exclaimed. "You will play me no more tricks now." Then he turned to go home, but when he came to a place where two roads crossed, there was Little Claus driving the cattle. "How is this?" said Big Claus. "Did I not drown you just now?"

"Yes," said Little Claus. "You threw me into the river about half an hour ago."

"But wherever did you get all these fine beasts?" asked Big Claus.

"These beasts are sea cattle," replied Little Claus. "I'll tell you the whole story, and thank you for drowning me. I am above you now, I am really very rich. I was frightened, to be sure, while I lay tied up in the sack. The wind whistled in my ears when you threw me into the river from the bridge, and I sank to the bottom immediately. But I did not hurt myself, for I fell upon beautifully soft grass that grows down there. In a moment, the sack opened, and the sweetest little maiden came toward me. She had snow-white robes and a wreath of green leaves on her wet hair. She took me by the hand and said, 'So you are come, Little Claus, and here are some cattle for you to begin with. About a mile farther on the road, there is another herd for you.' Then I saw that the river formed a great highway for the people who live in the sea. They were walking and driving here and there from the sea to the land at the spot where the river terminates. The bed of the river was covered with the loveliest flowers and sweet fresh grass. The fish swam past me as rapidly as the birds do here in the air. How handsome all the people were, and what fine cattle were grazing on the hills and in the valleys!"

"But why did you come up again," said Big Claus, "if it was all so beautiful down there? I should not have done so."

"Well," said Little Claus, "it was good policy on my part. You heard me say just now that I was told by the sea maiden to go a mile farther on the road, and I should find a whole herd of cattle. By the road she meant the river, for she could not travel any other way. But I knew the winding of the river and how it bends sometimes to the right and sometimes to the left. It seemed a long way, so I chose a shorter one. By coming up to the land and then driving across the fields back again to the river, I shall save half a mile and get all my cattle more quickly."

"What a lucky fellow you are!" exclaimed Big Claus. "Do you think I should get any sea cattle if I went down to the bottom of the river?"

"Yes, I think so," said Little Claus, "but I cannot carry you there in a sack, you are too heavy. However, if you will go there first and then creep into a sack, I will throw you in with the greatest pleasure."

"Thank you," said Big Claus. "But remember, if I do not get any sea cattle down there, I shall come up again and give you a good thrashing."

"No, now, don't be too fierce about it!" said Little Claus, as they walked on toward the river. When they approached it, the cattle, who were very thirsty, saw the stream and ran down to drink.

"See what a hurry they are in," said Little Claus. "They are longing to get down again."

"Come, help me, make haste," said Big Claus, "or you'll get beaten." So he crept into a large sack, which had been lying across the back of one of the oxen.

"Put in a stone," said Big Claus, "or I may not sink."

"Oh, there's not much fear of that," he replied. Still he put a large stone into the bag and then tied it tightly and gave it a push.

"Plump!" In went Big Claus, and he immediately sank to the bottom of the river.

"I'm afraid he will not find any cattle," said Little Claus, and then he drove his own beasts homeward.

The Flying Trunk

There was once a merchant who was so rich that he could have paved the whole street with gold and would even then still have had enough for a small alley. But he did not do so. He knew the value of money better than to use it in this way. So clever was he, that every shilling he put out brought him a crown, and so he continued till he died.

His son inherited his wealth, and he lived a merry life with it. He went to a masquerade every night, made kites out of five-pound notes, and threw pieces of gold into the sea instead of stones when he played ducks and drakes. In this manner he soon lost all his money. At last he had nothing left but a pair of slippers, an old dressing gown, and four shillings. All his friends deserted him, for they could not walk with him in the streets. But one of them who was very good-natured sent him an old trunk with this message, "Pack up!"

"Yes," he said, "it is all very well to say 'pack up,'" but he had nothing left to pack up, therefore he sat himself in the trunk.

It was a very wonderful trunk. No sooner did anyone press

on the lock than the trunk could fly. As soon as the merchant's son shut the lid and pressed the lock, the trunk flew away up the chimney, right up into the clouds.

Whenever the bottom of the trunk creaked, he was in a great fright, for if the trunk fell to pieces he would have fallen out and made a tremendous somersault over the trees. However, he got safely in his trunk to the land of Turkey. He hid the trunk in the wood under some dry leaves, and then went into the town. He could do so without embarrassment, for the Turks' clothing was very similar to his dressing gown and slippers.

On his way to town, he happened to meet a nurse with a little child. "I say, nurse!" cried he. "What castle is that near the town, with the windows placed so high?"

"The king's daughter lives there," she replied. "It has been prophesied that she will be very unhappy about a lover, and therefore no one is allowed to visit her, unless the king and queen are present."

"Thank you," said the merchant's son. He went back to the wood, seated himself in his trunk, flew up to the roof of the castle, and crept through the window into the princess's room. She lay on the sofa asleep, and she was so beautiful that the merchant's son could not help kissing her. Then she awoke and was very much frightened, but he told her he was a Turkish angel who had come down through the air just to see her, which pleased her very much.

He sat down by her side and talked to her. He said her eyes were like beautiful dark lakes, in which the thoughts swam about like little mermaids, and he told her that her forehead was a snowy mountain, which contained splendid halls full of pictures. And then he told her about the stork who brings the beautiful children from the rivers. These were delightful stories, and when he asked the princess if she would marry him, she consented immediately.

"But you must come on Saturday," she said, "for then the king and queen will take tea with me. They will be very proud when they find that I am going to marry a Turkish angel, but you must think of some very pretty stories to tell them, for my parents like to hear stories better than anything. My mother prefers tales that are deep and moral, but my father likes something funny, to make him laugh."

"Very well," he replied. "I shall bring you no other marriage portion than a story," and so they parted. But the princess gave him a sword that was studded with gold coins, and these he could use.

He flew away to the town and bought a new dressing gown. Afterward, he returned to the wood, where he composed a story, so as to be ready for Saturday, which was no easy matter. It was ready, however, by Saturday when he went to see the princess. The king and queen and the whole court were at tea with the princess, and he was received with great politeness.

"Will you tell us a story?" said the queen. "One that is instructive and full of deep learning."

"Yes, but with something in it to laugh at," said the king.

"Certainly," he replied, and commenced at once, asking them to listen attentively. "There was once a bundle of matches that were exceedingly proud of their high descent. Their family tree, that is, the large pine tree from which they had been cut, was at one time a large, old tree in the forest. As the matches lay between a tinderbox and an old iron saucepan, they talked about their youthful days. 'Ah! Then we grew on the green boughs, and were as green as they. Every morning and evening we were fed with diamond drops of dew. Whenever the sun shone, we felt its warm rays, and the little birds would tell stories to us as they sang. We knew that we were rich, for the other trees only wore their green dress in summer, but our family could wear green in both summer and winter. But then the woodcutter came, and like a great revolution, and our family fell under the axe. The head of the house obtained a situation as mainmast in a very fine ship and can sail around the world when he will. The other branches of the family were taken to different places, and our job now is to kindle a light for common people. This is how such highborn people as we came to be in a kitchen.'

"'Mine has been a very different fate,' said the iron pot, which stood by the matches. 'From my first entrance into the world I have been used to cooking and scouring. I am the most important member of this house, when anything solid or useful is required. My only pleasure is to be made clean and shining after dinner, and to sit in my place and have a little sensible conversation with my neighbors. All of us, except the water bucket, which is sometimes taken into the courtyard, live here together within these four walls. We get our news from the market basket, but he sometimes tells us very unpleasant things about the people and the government. Yes, and one day an old pot was so alarmed that he fell down and was broken to pieces. That basket is a liberal, I can tell you.'

"'You are talking too much,' said the tinderbox, and the steel struck against the flint till some sparks flew out, crying, 'We want a merry evening, don't we?'

"'Yes, of course,' said the matches, 'let us talk about those who are the most aristocratic.'

"'No, I don't like to be always talking of what we are,' remarked the saucepan. 'Let us think of some other amusement. I will begin. We will tell an experience we've had. That will be very easy and interesting as well. On the Baltic Sea, near the Danish shore—'

"'What a pretty commencement!' said the plates. 'We shall all like that story, I am sure.'

"'Yes, well in my youth, I lived with a quiet family, where the furniture was polished, the floors scoured, and clean curtains put up every fortnight.'

"'What an interesting way you have of telling a story,' said the carpet broom. 'It is easy to see that you have been a great deal in women's society. Something so pure runs through what you say.'

"'That is quite true,' said the water bucket. He made a happy jump and splashed some water on the floor.

"The saucepan went on with his story, and the end was as good as the beginning.

"The plates rattled with pleasure, and the carpet broom brought some green parsley out of the dust hole and crowned the saucepan since he knew it would vex the others. He thought, *If I crown him today, he will crown me tomorrow.*

"'Now, let us have a dance,' said the fire tongs. And then how they danced and kicked their legs in the air. The chair cushion in the corner burst with laughter when she saw it.

"'Shall I be crowned now?' asked the fire tongs, so the broom found another wreath for the tongs.

"'They are all such commoners,' thought the matches.

"The tea urn was now asked to sing, but she said she had a cold and could not sing without boiling water. They all thought this was affectation because she did not wish to sing except in the parlor, when she was on the table with the grand people.

"In the window sat an old quill pen, with which the maid generally wrote. There was nothing remarkable about the pen, except that it had been dipped too deeply in the ink, but it was proud of that.

"'If the tea urn won't sing,' said the pen, 'she can stay silent. There is a nightingale in a cage outside the window who can sing. She has not been taught much, certainly, but we need not be too critical of her this evening.'

"'I think it highly improper,' said the tea kettle, who was the official kitchen singer and half-brother to the tea urn, 'Is it patriotic that a rich foreign bird should be listened to here? Let the market basket decide what is right.'

"'I certainly am annoyed,' said the basket, 'inwardly vexed, more than anyone can imagine. Are we spending the evening properly? Would it not be more sensible to put the house in order? If everyone would take his proper place I would lead the game. This would be quite different.'

"'Let us all make noise,' they all said. At the same moment the door opened, and the maid came in. Then no one moved. They all remained quite still. Yet, at the same time, there was not a single pot among them who did not have a high opinion of himself, and of what he could do if he chose.

"*If I had been in charge*, they each thought, *we might have spent a very pleasant evening.*

"The maid took the matches and lighted them. Dear me, how they sputtered and blazed up!

"*Now then*, the matches thought, *everyone will see that we*

are the most important. How we shine; what a light we give!
But while they spoke their light went out."

"What a delightful story," said the queen. "I feel as if I
were really in the kitchen and could see the matches. Yes, you
shall marry our daughter."

"Certainly," said the king, "You, son, shall have our
daughter." The king said "son" to him because he was going
to be one of the family. The wedding day was fixed, and on the
evening before the whole city was illuminated. Cakes and
sweetmeats were thrown among the people. The street boys
stood on tiptoe and shouted "Hurrah!" and whistled between
their fingers. Altogether it was a very splendid affair.

"I will give them another treat," said the merchant's son.
So he went and bought rockets and crackers and all sorts of
fireworks that could be thought of, packed them in his trunk,
and flew up with it into the air. What a whizzing and popping
they made as they went off! The Turks, when they saw such a
sight in the air, jumped so high that their slippers flew about
their ears. It was easy to believe after this that the princess
was really going to marry a Turkish angel.

As soon as the merchant's son had come down in his flying trunk to the wood after the fireworks, he thought, "I will go
back into the town now, and hear what they think of the enter-
tainment." It was very natural that he should wish to know.
And what strange things people did say, to be sure! Everyone
whom he questioned had a different tale to tell, although they
all thought it had been beautiful.

"I saw the Turkish angel myself," said one. "He had eyes
like glittering stars and a head like foaming water."

"He flew in a mantle of fire," cried another, "and lovely

little cherubs peeped out from the folds!"

He heard many more fine things about himself. After this he went back to the forest to rest himself in his trunk but it had disappeared! A spark from the fireworks had set it on fire. It was burned to ashes! So the merchant's son could not fly anymore, nor go to meet his bride. She stood all day on the roof waiting for him. And most likely she is waiting there still, while he wanders through the world telling fairy tales that are never as amusing as the one he related about the matches.

The Storks

On the last house in a little village the storks had built a nest. The mother stork sat in it with her four young ones, who stretched out their necks and pointed their black beaks, which had not yet turned red like those of the parent birds. A little way off, on the edge of the roof, stood the father stork, quite upright and stiff. Not liking to be completely idle, he drew up one leg and stood on the other, so still that it seemed almost as if he were carved in wood. *It must look very grand,* thought he, *for my wife to have a sentry guarding her nest. People don't know that I am her husband. They will think I am a servant who has been commanded to stand here, which is quite aristocratic.* So he continued standing on one leg.

In the street below were a number of children at play, and when they caught sight of the storks, one of the boldest among the boys began to sing a song about them, and very soon he was joined by the rest. These are the words of the song, but each only sang what he could remember of them in his own way.

> "Stork, stork, fly away,
> Stand not on one leg, I pray,
> See your wife is in her nest,
> With her little ones at rest.
> They will hang one,
> And roast another;
> They will shoot a third,
> And roast his brother."

"Just hear what those boys are singing," said the young storks. "They say we shall be hanged and roasted."

"Never mind what they say. You need not listen," said the mother. "They can do no harm."

But the boys went on singing and pointing at the storks, and mocking at them, except one of the boys whose name was Peter. He said it was a shame to make fun of animals and would not join with them at all.

The mother stork comforted her young ones and told them not to mind. "See," she said, "How quiet your father stands, although he is only on one leg."

"But we are very much frightened," said the young storks, and they drew back their heads into the nest.

The next day when the children were playing together, they saw the storks and sang the song again—

> "They will hang one,
> And roast another."

"Shall we be hanged and roasted?" asked the young storks.

"No, certainly not," said the mother. "I will teach you to

fly, and when you have learned, we will fly into the meadows and pay a visit to the frogs, who will bow themselves to us in the water, and cry *'Croak, croak,'* and then we shall eat them up. That will be fun."

"And what next?" asked the young storks.

"Then," replied the mother, "all the storks in the country will assemble together, and go through their autumn maneuvers. It is very important for all of you to know how to fly properly. If any birds can't, the general will thrust them through with his beak and kill them. Therefore, you must take pains and learn, so as to be ready when the drilling begins."

"Then we may be killed after all, as the boys say. Listen! they are singing again."

"Listen to me and not to them," said the mother stork. "After the great review is over, we shall fly away to warm countries far from here, where there are mountains and forests. To Egypt, where we shall see three-cornered houses built of stone, with pointed tops that reach nearly to the clouds. They are called pyramids and are older than a stork could imagine. In that country, there is a river that overflows its banks, and then goes back, leaving nothing but mire. There we can walk about and eat frogs in abundance."

"Oh, oh!" cried the young storks.

"Yes, it is a delightful place. There is nothing to do all day long but eat. While we are so well off out there, in this country there will not be a single green leaf on the trees, and the weather will be so cold that the clouds will freeze and fall on the earth in little white rags." The mother stork meant snow, but she could not explain it in any other way.

"Will the naughty boys freeze and fall in pieces, too?" asked the young storks.

"No, they will not freeze and fall into pieces," said the mother, "but they will be very cold and be obliged to sit all day in a dark, gloomy room, while we shall be flying about in foreign lands, where there are blooming flowers and warm sunshine."

Time passed on, and the young storks grew so large that they could stand upright in the nest and look about them. Every day, the father brought them beautiful frogs, little snakes, and all kinds of stork dainties that he could find. And then, how they laughed at the tricks he would perform to amuse them. He would lay his head quite around over his tail and clatter with his beak, as if it had been a rattle, and then he would tell them stories all about the marshes they would see someday.

"Come," said the mother one day. "Now you must learn to fly." All the four young ones had to come out on the top of the roof. Oh, how they tottered at first, and were obliged to balance themselves with their wings or they would have fallen to the ground below.

"Look at me," said the mother. "You must hold your heads in this way and place your feet so. Once, twice, once, twice— that is it. Now you will be able to take care of yourselves in the world."

Then she flew a little distance from them, and the young ones made a spring to follow her, but down they fell with a bump, for their bodies were still too heavy.

"I don't want to fly," said one of the young storks, creeping back into the nest. "I don't care about going to warm countries."

"Would you like to stay here and freeze when the winter comes?" said the mother, "or till the boys come to hang you, or to roast you? Well then, I'll call them."

"Oh no, no," said the young stork, jumping out on the roof with the others. Now they were all attentive, and by the third day could fly a little. Then they began to fancy they could soar, so they tried to do so, resting on their wings, but they soon found themselves falling and had to flap their wings as quickly as possible. The boys came again in the street singing their song—

"Stork, stork, fly away."

"Shall we fly down, and pick their eyes out?" asked the young storks.

"No, leave them alone," said the mother. "Pay attention to me. That is much more important. Now then. One-two-three. Now to the right. One-two-three. Now to the left, around the chimney. There now, that was very good. That last flap of the wings was so easy and graceful that I shall give you permission to fly with me tomorrow to the marshes. There will be a number of very superior storks there with their families, and I expect you to show them that my children are the best brought up of any who may be present. You must strut about proudly—it will look well and make you respected."

"But may we not punish those naughty boys?" asked the young storks.

"No, let them scream away as much as they like. You can fly from them now up high amid the clouds and will be in the land of the pyramids when they are freezing and there is not a green leaf on the trees or an apple to eat."

"We will revenge ourselves," whispered the young storks to each other, as they again joined the exercising.

Of all the boys in the street who sang the mocking song about the storks, not one was so determined to go on with it as he who first began it. Yet he was a little fellow not more than six years old. To the young storks he appeared at least a hundred, for he was so much bigger than their father and mother. To be sure, storks cannot be expected to know how old children and grown-up people are. So they determined to have their revenge on this boy, because he began the song first and would keep on with it. The young storks were very angry and grew worse as they grew older, so at last their mother was obliged to promise that they should be revenged, but not until the day of their departure.

"We must see first how you acquit yourselves at the grand review," said she. "If you get on badly there, the general will thrust his beak through you, and you will be killed as the boys said, although not exactly in the same manner. So we must wait and see."

"You shall see," said the young birds, and then they took such pains and practiced so hard every day that at last it was quite a pleasure to see them fly so lightly and prettily.

As soon as the autumn arrived, all the storks began to assemble together before taking their departure for warm countries during the winter. Then the review commenced. They flew over forests and villages to show what they could do, for they had a long journey before them. The young storks performed their part so well that they received a mark of honor, with frogs and snakes as a prize. These prizes were the best part of the affair, for they could eat the frogs and snakes, which they very quickly did.

"Now let us have our revenge!" they cried.

"Yes, certainly!" cried the mother stork. "I have thought

of the best way to be revenged. I know the pond in which all the little children lie, waiting till the storks come to take them to their parents. The prettiest little babies lie there dreaming more sweetly than they will ever dream in the time to come. All parents are glad to have a little child, and children are so pleased with a little brother or sister. Now we will fly to the pond and fetch a little baby for each of the children who did not sing that naughty song to make fun of the storks."

"But the naughty boy, who began the song first, what shall we do to him?" cried the young storks.

"There lies in the pond a little dead baby who has dreamed itself to death," said the mother. "We will take it to the naughty boy, and he will cry because we have brought him a little dead brother. But you have not forgotten the good boy who said it was a shame to laugh at animals. We will take him a little brother and sister, too, because he was good. He is called Peter, and you shall all be called Peter in the future."

So they all did what their mother had arranged, and from that day to this, all storks have been called Peter.

The Bell

❦

In the evening, when the sun was setting, a strange wondrous
tone would be heard in the narrow streets of a large town. It
was like the sound of a church bell, but it was only heard for
a moment, for the rolling of the carriages and the voices of the
multitude made too great a noise. People would say, "The
evening bell is sounding; the sun is setting."

People who were walking outside the town, where the
houses were farther apart, with gardens or little fields between
them, could see the evening sky even better and heard the
sound of the bell much more distinctly. It was as if the tones
came from some church buried in the depths of the still forest.
People looked in that direction and their minds were solemn.

A long time passed, and people began to say to each other,
"I wonder if there is a church out in the wood? The bell has a
tone that is wondrously sweet. Let us go there and examine the
matter more closely."

So the rich people drove out, and the poor walked, but the
way seemed strangely long to them. When they came to a
clump of willows that grew on the outskirts of the forest, they

sat down and looked up at the long branches, and fancied they were really in the heart of the green forest. The confectioner of the town came out and set up his booth there. Soon after came another confectioner, who hung a bell over his stand as a sign or ornament, but it had no clapper, and it was tarred over to preserve it from the rain.

When all the people returned home, they said it had been very romantic and that it was quite a different sort of thing to a picnic or tea party. There were three persons who said they had walked all the way to the end of the forest and that they had always heard the wonderful sounds of the bell, but it had seemed to them as if it had come from the town. One wrote a whole poem about it and said that the bell sounded like the voice of a mother to a good dear child and that no melody was sweeter than the tones of the bell.

The king of the country heard about the bell and proclaimed that he who could discover the source of the lovely sounds should have the title of "Universal Bellringer," even if it were not really a bell.

After the proclamation, many people went to the wood to try to win the title, but only one returned with any sort of explanation. The truth was that nobody went far enough into the wood, even the man who claimed he had discovered the cause. He said that the sound proceeded from a very large owl in a hollow tree, a sort of learned owl that continually knocked its head against the branches. But whether the sound came from his head or from the hollow tree, no one could say with certainty. Even so, he got the place of "Universal Bellringer" and wrote yearly a short treatise entitled "On the Owl," but no one was any wiser than before.

It was confirmation day. The clergyman had spoken so

touchingly that the children who were confirmed had been greatly moved. It was an eventful day for them; from children they become grown-ups all at once. It was as if their infant souls would now fly into persons with more understanding. The sun was shining gloriously. The children who had been confirmed were walking together out of the town when from the wood they heard the sound of the unknown bell with wonderful distinctness.

They all immediately felt a wish to go into the wood and find the bell, all except three. One of them had to go home to try on a ball dress, for the ball was the reason she had been confirmed this time, otherwise she would have had to wait another year. The other was a poor boy, who had borrowed his coat and boots from the innkeeper's son to be confirmed in, and he was to give them back by a certain hour. The third said that he never went to a strange place if his parents were not with him—that he had always been a good boy till now and would still be so now that he was confirmed, and that one ought not to laugh at him for it. The others, however, did make fun of him, which was very wrong of them.

There were three, therefore, who did not go. The others hastened on. The sun shone, the birds sang, and the children sang, too. Each held the other by the hand, for as yet they had none of them any high office and were all of equal rank in the eye of God.

But two of the youngest soon grew tired, and both returned to town. Two other little girls sat down to weave garlands, so they did not go either. When the others reached the willow tree, where the confectioner was, they said, "Now we are there! In reality the bell does not exist. It is only a fancy that people have taken into their heads!"

But at that moment the bell sounded deep in the wood, so clear and solemnly that five or six determined to go farther into the wood. It was so thick, and the foliage so dense, that it was quite tiring to proceed. Woodroof and anemonies grew almost too high. Blooming morning glories and blackberry bushes hung in long garlands from tree to tree, where the nightingale sang and the sunbeams were playing. It was very beautiful, but it was a bad place for girls to go, because their clothes would get so torn.

Large blocks of stone lay overgrown with moss of every color. A fresh spring bubbled forth and made a strange gurgling sound.

"That surely cannot be the bell," said one of the children, lying down and listening. "This must be looked into." So he remained and let the others go on without him.

They came to a little house made of branches and the bark of trees. A large wild apple tree bent over it, as if it would shower down all its blessings on the roof, where roses were blooming. The long stems twined around the gable, on which there hung a small bell.

Was it that which people had heard? Yes, everybody was unanimous on the subject, except one, who said that the bell was too small and too fine to be heard at so great a distance, and besides it was very different tones to those that could move a human heart in such a manner. It was a king's son who spoke, and the others said, "Such people always think they are wiser than everybody else."

They stopped and let him go on alone. As he went, his breast was filled more and more with the solitude of the forest, but he could still hear the little bell with which the others were so satisfied. Now and then, when the wind blew, he could also hear the people singing who were sitting at tea where the confectioner had his tent.

But the deep sound of the bell rose above the rest. It was almost as if an organ were accompanying it, and the tones came from the left, the side where the heart is placed.

Suddenly, there was a rustling in the bushes, and a little boy appeared before the king's son, a boy in wooden shoes and with so short a jacket that one could see what long wrists he had. Both knew each other. The boy was the same child who could not come because he had to go home and return his jacket and boots to the innkeeper's son. This he had done, and was now going on in wooden shoes and in his humble dress, for the bell sounded with so deep a tone, and with such strange power, that proceed he must.

"Why, then, we can go together," said the king's son. But the poor child that had been confirmed was quite ashamed. He looked at his wooden shoes, pulled at the short sleeves of his jacket, and said that he was afraid he could not walk so fast. Besides, he thought that the bell must be looked for to the right, for that was the place where all sorts of beautiful things were to be found.

"Then I guess we won't go together," said the king's son, nodding at the same time to the poor boy, who went into the darkest, thickest part of the wood, where thorns tore his humble dress and scratched his face and hands and feet till they bled. The king's son got some scratches, too, but the sun shone on his path. It is him that we will follow, for he was an excellent and resolute youth.

"I must and will find the bell," said he, "even if I am obliged to go to the end of the world."

Above him, the ugly apes sat upon the trees and grinned.

"Shall we thrash him?" said they. "Shall we thrash him? He is the son of a king!"

But on he went, without being disheartened, deeper and deeper into the wood, where the most wonderful flowers were growing. There stood white lilies with blood-red stamens, sky-blue tulips, which shone as they waved in the winds, and apple trees, the apples of which looked exactly like large soapbubbles. Only think how the trees must have sparkled in the sunshine! Around the beautiful green meadows, where the deer were playing in the grass, grew magnificent oaks and beeches. If the bark of one of the trees was cracked, grass and long creeping plants grew in the crevices. And there were large calm lakes there, too, in which white swans swam and beat the air with their wings. The king's son often stood still and listened. He thought the bell sounded from the depths of these still lakes, but then he was convinced again that the tone proceeded not from there, but farther off, from out of the depths of the forest.

The sun was setting and the atmosphere glowed like fire. It was still in the woods, so very still. The boy fell on his knees, sung his evening hymn, and said to himself: "I cannot find what I seek. The sun is going down, and night is coming—the dark, dark night. Yet perhaps I may be able once more to see the round red sun before it entirely disappears. I will climb up those rocks over there."

Seizing hold of the creeping plants and the roots of trees, he climbed up the moist stones where the water snakes were writhing and the toads were croaking. He reached the summit just before the sun had completely gone down. How magnificent was the sight from this height!

The sea—the great, the glorious sea that dashed its long waves against the coast—was stretched out before him. And farther out, where sea and sky meet, stood the sun like a large shining altar, all melted together in the most glowing colors. The wood and the sea sang a song of rejoicing, and his heart sang with the rest. All nature was a vast holy church, in which the trees and the buoyant clouds were the pillars, flowers and grass the velvet carpeting, and heaven itself the large cupola. The red colors above faded away as the sun vanished, but a million stars were lighted like a million shining lamps. The king's son spread out his arms toward heaven, and wood, and sea.

At that moment, coming from a path to the right, appeared, in his wooden shoes and jacket, the poor boy who had been confirmed that day. He had followed his own path and had reached the spot just as quickly as the son of the king. They ran toward each other and stood together hand in hand in the vast church of nature and of poetry, while over them sounded the invisible holy bell. Blessed spirits floated around them and lifted up their voices in a rejoicing hallelujah!

The Wild Swans

Far away in the land where the swallows fly in winter dwelled a king who had eleven sons and one daughter, Eliza. The eleven brothers were princes, and each went to school with a star on his chest and a sword by his side. They wrote with diamond pencils on gold slates and learned their lessons so quickly and read so easily that everyone knew right away they were princes. Their sister, Eliza, sat on a little stool of plateglass and had a book full of pictures, which had cost as much as half a kingdom. Oh, these children were indeed happy, but it was not to remain so always.

Their father, who was king of the country, married a very wicked queen who did not love the poor children at all. They knew this from the very first day after the wedding. In the palace there were great festivities, and the children played at receiving company. But instead of having, as usual, all the cakes and apples that were left, the new queen gave them some sand in a teacup and told them to pretend it was cake.

The next week, she sent little Eliza into the country to a

peasant and his wife, and then she told the king so many untrue things about the young princes that he no longer cared for them.

"Go out into the world and get your own living," said the queen. "Fly like great birds, who have no voice." But she could not make them ugly as she wished, for they were turned into eleven beautiful wild swans. Then, with a strange cry, they flew through the windows of the palace, over the park, to the forest beyond.

It was early morning when they passed the peasant's cottage, where their sister, Eliza, lay asleep in her room. They hovered over the roof, twisted their long necks and flapped their wings, but no one heard or saw them. At last they had to fly away, high up in the clouds. Over the wide world they flew till they came to a thick, dark wood, which stretched far away to the seashore.

At the peasant's house, poor little Eliza played alone with a green leaf, for she had no other playthings. She pierced a hole through the leaf and looked through it at the sun, and it was as if she saw her brothers' clear eyes. When the warm sun shone on her cheeks, she thought of all the kisses they had given her.

One day passed just like another. Sometimes the winds rustled through the leaves of the rosebush and would whisper to the roses, "Who can be more beautiful than you!" But the roses would shake their heads, and say, "Eliza is." When the old woman sat at the cottage door on Sunday and read her hymnbook, the wind would flutter the leaves and say to the book, "Who can be more pious than you?" and then the hymnbook would answer, "Eliza." The roses and the hymnbook told the truth.

At fifteen Eliza returned home, but when the queen saw how beautiful she was, she became full of spite and hatred toward her. Willingly would she have turned her into a swan like her brothers, but she did not dare to do so yet, because the king wished to see his daughter.

Early one morning the queen went into the bathroom. It was built of marble and had soft cushions trimmed with the most beautiful tapestry. She took three toads with her, kissed them, and said to one, "When Eliza comes to the bath, seat yourself upon her head that she may become as stupid as you are." Then she said to another, "Place yourself on her forehead that she may become as ugly as you are and that her father may not know her." "Rest on her heart," she whispered to the third, "then she will have evil inclinations and be tormented."

She put the toads into the clear water, which turned green immediately. Then the queen called Eliza and helped her to undress and get into the bath. As Eliza dipped her head under the water, one of the toads sat on her hair, a second on her forehead, and a third on her breast, but she did not seem to notice them. When she rose out of the water, there were three red poppies floating upon it. If the toads had not been been poisonous and kissed by the witch, they would have been changed into red roses. At all events they became flowers, because they had rested on Eliza's head and on her heart. She was too good and too innocent for witchcraft to have any power over her.

When the wicked queen saw this, she rubbed Eliza's face with walnut juice, so that she was quite brown. Then she tangled her beautiful hair and smeared it with disgusting ointment, till it was quite impossible to recognize the beautiful princess.

When her father saw her, he was much shocked and

declared she was not his daughter. No one but the watchdog and the swallows knew her, and they were only poor animals and could say nothing.

Then poor Eliza wept and thought of her eleven brothers, who were all away. Sorrowfully, she stole away from the palace and walked the whole day over fields and moors till she came to the great forest. She knew not in what direction to go, but she was so unhappy and longed so for her brothers, who had been, like herself, driven out into the world, that she was determined to seek them.

She had been but a short time in the wood when night came on, and she quite lost the path. She lay down on the soft moss, offered up her evening prayer, and leaned her head against the stump of a tree. All of nature was still, and the soft, mild air fanned her forehead. The light of hundreds of glow-worms shone amid the grass and the moss, like green fire. If she touched a twig with her hand ever so lightly, the brilliant insects fell down around her, like shooting stars.

All night long she dreamed of her brothers. She and they were children again, playing together. She saw them writing with their diamond pencils on golden slates, while she looked at the beautiful picture book that had cost half a kingdom. They were not writing lines and letters, as they used to do, but descriptions of the noble deeds they had performed and of all they had discovered and seen. In the picture book, too, everything was living. The birds sang, and the people came out of the book and spoke to Eliza and her brothers, but, as the leaves turned over, they darted back again to their places, that all might be in order.

When she awoke, the sun was high in the heavens, yet she could not see it, for the lofty trees spread their branches thickly over her head. But its beams were glancing through the leaves here and there, like a golden mist. There was a sweet fragrance from the fresh greenery, and the birds almost perched upon her shoulders. She heard water rippling from a number of springs, all flowing into a lake with golden sand on the bottom. Bushes grew thickly around the lake, and at one spot an opening had been made by deer, through which Eliza went down to the water. The lake was so clear that, had not the wind rustled the branches of the trees and the bushes so that they moved, they would have appeared as if painted in the depths of the lake, for every leaf was reflected in the water whether it stood in the shade or the sunshine.

As soon as Eliza saw her own face reflected in the water, she was quite terrified at finding it so different and ugly. But when she wetted her little hand and rubbed her eyes and forehead, her skin gleamed forth once more. After she had undressed and dipped herself in the fresh water, a more beautiful king's daughter could not be found in the wide world.

As soon as Eliza had dressed herself again and braided her long hair, she went to the bubbling spring and drank some water out of the hollow of her hand. Then she wandered far into the forest, not knowing where she was going. She thought of her brothers and felt sure that God would not forsake her. It is a divine power that makes the wild apples grow in the wood to satisfy the hungry, and this same power now led her to one of these trees, which was so loaded with fruit that the boughs bent beneath the weight. Here she held her noontime meal, propped up the branches, and then headed into the gloomiest depths of the forest. It was so still that she could hear the sound of her own footsteps, as well as the rustling of every withered leaf that she crushed under her feet. Not a bird was to be seen, not a sunbeam could penetrate through the large, dark boughs of the trees. Their lofty trunks stood so close together that when she looked in front of her it seemed as if she were enclosed within a fence. Such solitude she had never known before.

The night was very dark. Not a single glowworm glittered in the moss. Sorrowfully she laid herself down to sleep. After a while, it seemed to her as if the branches of the trees parted over her head and that the mild eyes of angels looked down upon her.

When Eliza awoke in the morning, she knew not whether she had dreamed this or if it had really happened. Then she continued her wandering, but she had not gone many steps forward when she met an old woman with berries in her basket who gave her a few to eat. Eliza asked her if she had seen eleven princes riding through the forest.

"No," replied the old woman, "but yesterday I saw eleven swans with gold crowns on their heads, swimming on the river close by."

She led Eliza a little distance farther to a sloping bank, and at the foot of it wound a little river. The trees on its banks stretched their long leafy branches across the water toward each other. Wherever the limbs were too short to meet naturally, the roots had torn themselves away from the ground, so that the branches might mingle their foliage as they hung over the water.

Eliza bade the old woman farewell and walked along the flowing river till she reached the shore of the open sea.

There, before the young maiden's eyes, lay the glorious ocean, but not a sail appeared on its surface, not even a boat could be seen. How was she to go farther? She noticed how the countless pebbles on the seashore had been smoothed and rounded by the action of the water. Glass, iron, stones, everything that lay on the beach had taken its shape from the same power and felt as smooth, or even smoother than her own delicate hand. "The water rolls on without weariness," she said, "till all that is hard becomes smooth, so will I be unwearied in my task. Thanks for your lessons, bright rolling waves. My heart tells me you will lead me to my dear brothers."

On some foam-covered seaweed lay eleven white swan feathers, which she gathered up and placed together. Drops of water lay upon them; whether they were dewdrops or tears no one could say. Lonely as it was on the seashore, she did not feel it, for the ever-moving sea showed more changes in a few hours than the most varying lake could produce during a whole year. If a black heavy cloud arose, it was as if the sea said, "I can look dark and angry, too." And then the wind blew, and the waves turned to white foam as they rolled. When the wind slept, and the clouds glowed with the red sunlight, then the sea looked like a rose leaf. But however quietly its white glassy surface rested, there was still a motion on the shore, as its waves rose and fell like the chest of a sleeping child.

When the sun was about to set, Eliza saw eleven white swans with golden crowns on their heads flying toward the land, one behind the other like a long white ribbon. Then she went down the slope from the shore and hid herself behind the bushes. The swans alighted quite close to her and flapped their great white wings.

As soon as the sun had disappeared under the water, the feathers of the swans fell off, and eleven beautiful princes,

Eliza's brothers, stood revealed. She uttered a loud cry, for, although they were very much changed, she knew them immediately. She sprang into their arms and called them each by name. Then, how happy the princes were at meeting their little sister again, for they recognized her, although she had grown so tall and beautiful. They laughed, and they wept, and very soon learned how wickedly their stepmother had acted to them all.

"We brothers," said the eldest, "fly about as wild swans so long as the sun is in the sky, but as soon as it sinks behind the hills, we recover our human shape. Therefore, we must always be near solid ground before sunset. If we were flying among the clouds at the time we recovered our natural shape as men, we would plunge into the sea. We do not live here, but in a land just as fair that lies on the other side of the ocean across a long distance. There is no island in our passage upon which we can pass the night, nothing but a little rock rising out of the sea, upon which we can scarcely stand with safety, even closely crowded together. If the sea is rough, the foam dashes over us, still we thank God even for this rock. We have passed whole nights upon it, or we should never be able to visit our beloved fatherland, for our flight across the sea takes two of the longest days of the year.

"We have permission to visit our homeland once in every year and to remain eleven days, during which we fly across the forest to look once more at the palace where our father lives and where we were born, and at the church where our mother lies buried. Here it feels as if even the trees and bushes are related to us. The wild horses leap over the plains as we saw in our childhood. The charcoal burners sing the old songs, to which we danced as children. This is our fatherland, to which we are drawn by loving ties; and here we have found you, our dear little sister. Two days longer we can remain here, and then must we fly away to a beautiful land that is not our home. How can we take you with us? We have neither ship nor boat."

"How can I break this spell?" said their sister. They talked nearly the whole night, only sleeping for a few hours.

Eliza was awakened by the rustling of the swans' wings as they soared above her. Her brothers were again changed to swans, and they flew in circles wider and wider, till they were far away. But one of them, the youngest swan, remained behind and laid his head in his sister's lap, while she stroked his wings. They stayed together the whole day. Toward evening, the rest came back, and as the sun went down they resumed their human forms.

"Tomorrow," said one, "we shall fly away, not to return again till a whole year has passed. But we cannot leave you here. Have you courage to go with us? If my arm is strong enough to carry you through the wood, wouldn't all our wings be strong enough to fly with you over the sea?"

"Yes, take me with you," said Eliza. Then they spent the whole night in weaving a net with the pliant willow and rushes. It was very large and strong. Eliza laid herself down on the net, and when the sun rose and her brothers again became wild swans, they took up the net with their beaks and flew up to the clouds with their dear sister, who still slept. The sunbeams fell on her face, so one of the swans soared over her head to shade her with his wings.

They were far from the land when Eliza woke. She thought she must still be dreaming. It seemed so strange to her to feel herself being carried so high in the air over the sea. By her side lay a branch full of beautiful ripe berries and a bundle of sweet roots. The youngest of her brothers had gathered them for her and placed them by her side. She smiled her thanks to him. She knew he was the one who hovered over her to shade her with his wings.

They were now so high that a large ship beneath them looked like a white seagull skimming the waves. A great cloud floating behind them appeared like a vast mountain, and on it Eliza saw her own shadow and those of the eleven swans, looking gigantic in size. Altogether it formed a more beautiful picture than she had ever seen. But as the sun rose higher, and the clouds were left behind, the shadowy picture vanished away.

The whole day they flew through the air like a winged arrow, yet more slowly than usual, for they had their sister to carry. The weather seemed inclined to be stormy, and Eliza watched the sinking sun with great anxiety, for the little rock in the ocean was not yet in sight. It appeared to her as if the swans were making great efforts with their wings. Alas! She was the cause of their not advancing more quickly. When the sun set, they would change to men, fall into the sea, and be drowned. Then she offered a prayer from her inmost heart, but still the rock did not appear. Dark clouds came nearer, the gusts of wind told of a coming storm, while from a thick, heavy mass of clouds the lightning burst forth flash after flash.

The sun had reached the edge of the sea, when the swans darted down so swiftly that Eliza's heart trembled. She believed they were falling, but they again soared onward. Finally she caught sight of the rock just below them, and by this time the sun was half hidden by the waves. The rock did not seem any larger than a seal's head poking out of the water.

The sun set so rapidly that at the moment their feet touched the rock, it was no bigger than a star, and at last disappeared like the last spark in a piece of burned paper. Then she saw her brothers standing closely around her with their arms linked together. There was just room enough for all of them.

The sea dashed against the rock and covered them with spray. The heavens were lighted up with continual flashes, and peal after peal of thunder rolled. But the sister and brothers sat holding each other's hands and singing hymns, from which they gained hope and courage.

In the early dawn the air became calm and still, and at sunrise the swans flew away from the rock with Eliza. The sea was still rough, and from their high position in the air, the white foam on the dark green waves looked like millions of swans swimming on the water.

As the sun rose higher, Eliza saw before her, floating on the air, a range of mountains with shining masses of ice on their summits. In the center rose a castle apparently a mile long, with rows of columns rising one above another, while, around it, palm trees waved and garish flowers bloomed as large as mill wheels. She asked if this was the land to which they were hurrying. The swans shook their heads, for what she beheld were the beautiful ever-changing cloud palaces of the *fata morgana*, into which no mortal can enter.

Eliza was still gazing at the scene when the mountains, forests, and castles melted away and twenty stately churches rose in their stead, with high towers and pointed gothic windows. Eliza even fancied she could hear the tones of the organ, but it was the music of the murmuring sea that she heard. As they drew nearer to the churches, they in turn changed into a fleet of ships, which seemed to be sailing beneath her. But as she looked again, she found it was only a sea mist gliding over the ocean. So there continued to pass before her eyes a constant change of scene, till at last she saw the real land to which they were bound, with its blue mountains, its cedar forests, and its cities and palaces. Long before the sun went down, she sat on a rock in front of a large cave, on the floor of which the overgrown yet delicate green creeping plants looked like an embroidered carpet.

"I wonder what you will dream of tonight," said the youngest brother, as he showed his sister her bedroom.

"Heaven grant that I may dream how to save you," she replied. And this thought took such hold upon her mind that she prayed earnestly to God for help, and even in her sleep she continued to pray. Then it appeared to her as if she were flying high in the air, toward the cloudy palace of the *fata morgana*, and a fairy came out to meet her, radiant and beautiful in appearance, and yet very much like the old woman who had given her berries in the wood and who had told her of the swans with golden crowns on their heads.

"Your brothers can be saved," said she, "if you have enough courage and perseverance. True, water is softer than your own delicate hands, and yet it polishes stones into shapes. It feels no pain as your fingers would feel. It has no soul and cannot suffer such agony and torment as you will have to endure. Do you see the stinging nettle that I hold in my hand? Quantities of the same sort grow around the cave in which you sleep, but none will be of any use to you unless they grow upon the graves in a churchyard. These you must gather even while they burn blisters on your hands. Break them to pieces with your hands and feet, and they will become flax, from which you must spin and weave eleven coats with long sleeves. If these are then thrown over the eleven swans, the spell will be broken. But remember that from the moment you commence your task until it is finished, even should it occupy years of your life, you must not speak. The first word you utter will pierce through the hearts of your brothers like a deadly dagger. Their lives hang upon your tongue. Remember all I have told you."

As she finished speaking, she touched Eliza's hand lightly with the nettle, and a pain as of burning fire awoke her.

It was broad daylight, and close by where she had been sleeping lay a nettle on a grave like the one she had seen in her dream. She fell on her knees and offered her thanks to God. Then she went forth from the cave to begin her work with her delicate hands. She groped in among the ugly nettles, which burned great blisters on her hands and arms, but she determined to bear it gladly if she could only release her dear brothers. So she bruised the nettles with her bare feet and spun the flax.

At sunset her brothers returned and were very much frightened when they found her mute. They believed it to be some new sorcery of their wicked stepmother. But when they saw her hands they understood what she was doing on their behalf. The youngest brother wept, and where his tears fell the pain ceased and the burning blisters vanished.

She kept to her work all night, for she could not rest till she had released her dear brothers. During the whole of the following day, while her brothers were gone, she sat in solitude, but never before had the time flown so quickly.

One coat was already finished and she had begun the second, when she heard a huntsman's horn and was struck with fear. The sound came nearer and nearer. She heard dogs barking and fled in terror into the cave. She hastily bound together the nettles she had gathered into a bundle and sat upon them.

Suddenly a huge dog came bounding toward her out of the ravine, and then another and another. They barked loudly, ran away, and then came back again. In a very few minutes all the huntsmen stood before the cave, and the handsomest of them was the king of the country. He went toward her, for he had never seen a more beautiful maiden.

"How did you come here, my sweet child?" he asked. But Eliza shook her head. She dared not speak, at the cost of her brothers' lives. And she hid her hands under her apron, so that the king might not see how she must be suffering.

"Come with me," he said. "You cannot remain here. If you are as good as you are beautiful, I will dress you in silk and velvet, I will place a golden crown upon your head, and you shall dwell, and rule, and make your home in my richest castle." And then he lifted her on his horse. She wept and wrung her hands, but the king said, "I wish only for your happiness. A time will come when you will thank me for this." And then he galloped away over the mountains, holding her before him on his horse, and the hunters followed behind them.

As the sun went down, they approached a beautiful city with churches and cupolas. On arriving at the castle the king led Eliza into marble halls, where large fountains played, and where the walls and the ceilings were covered with rich paintings. But she had no eyes for all these glorious sights; she could only mourn and weep. Patiently she allowed the women to array her in royal robes, to weave pearls in her hair, and to draw soft gloves over her blistered fingers. As she stood before them in all her rich dress, she looked so dazzlingly beautiful that the court bowed low in her presence.

Then the king declared his intention of making her his bride, but the archbishop shook his head and whispered that the fair young maiden was only a witch who had blinded the king's eyes and bewitched his heart. But the king would not listen to this. He ordered the music to sound, the daintiest dishes to be served, and the loveliest maidens to dance. Afterward he led Eliza through fragrant gardens and lofty halls, but not a smile appeared on her lips or sparkled in her eyes. She looked the very picture of grief.

Then the king opened the door of a little chamber in which she was to sleep. It was adorned with rich green tapestry and resembled the cave in which he had found her. On the floor lay the bundle of flax that she had spun from the nettles, and under the ceiling hung the coat she had made. These things had been brought away from the cave as curiosities by one of the huntsmen.

"Here you can dream yourself back again in the old home in the cave," said the king. "Here is the work with which you employed yourself. It will amuse you now in the midst of all this splendor to think of that time."

When Eliza saw all these things which lay so near her heart, a smile played around her mouth, and the crimson blood rushed to her cheeks. She thought of her brothers, and their release made her so joyful that she kissed the king's hand. Then he pressed her to his heart. Very soon the joyous church bells announced the marriage feast and that the beautiful mute girl out of the wood was to be made the queen of the country.

The archbishop whispered wicked words in the king's ear, but they did not sink into his heart. The marriage was still to take place, and the archbishop himself had to place the crown on the bride's head. In his wicked spite, he pressed the narrow circlet so tightly on her forehead that it caused her pain.

But a heavier weight encircled her heart—sorrow for her brothers—and she felt not bodily pain. Her mouth was closed for of course a single word would cost the lives of her brothers. But she loved the kind, handsome king who did everything to make her happy. She loved him with all her heart, and her eyes beamed with the love she dared not speak. Oh! If she had only been able to confide in him and tell him of her grief. But silent she must remain till her task was finished. Therefore, at night she crept away into her little chamber, which had been decked out to look like the cave, and quickly wove one coat after another. But when she began the seventh she found she had no more flax.

She knew that the nettles she wanted to use grew in the churchyard and that she must pluck them herself. How should she get out there?

What is the pain in my fingers to the torment that my heart endures? thought she. *I must ask it, I shall not be denied help from heaven.*

Then with a trembling heart, as if she were about to perform a wicked deed, she crept into the garden in the broad moonlight and passed through the narrow walks and the deserted streets till she reached the churchyard. There she saw on one of the broad tombstones a group of ghouls. These hideous creatures took off their rags, as if they intended to bathe, and then, clawing open the fresh graves with their long, skinny fingers, pulled out the dead bodies and ate the flesh! Eliza had to pass close by them, and they fixed their wicked glances upon her, but she prayed silently while she gathered the burning nettles, and then carried them home with her to the castle.

One person only had seen her, and that was the archbishop—he was awake while everybody was asleep. Now he thought his opinion was evidently correct. All was not right with the queen. She was a witch, and had bewitched the king and all the people.

Secretly he told the king what he had seen and what he feared, and as the hard words came from his tongue, the carved images of the saints shook their heads as if they would say, "It is not so. Eliza is innocent." But the archbishop interpreted it in another way. He believed that they spoke against her and were shaking their heads at her wickedness. Two large tears rolled down the king's cheeks, and he went home with doubt in his heart, and at night he pretended to sleep, but there came no real sleep to his eyes, for he saw Eliza get up every night and disappear in her own chamber.

From day to day his brow became darker, and Eliza saw it and did not understand the reason, but it alarmed her and made her heart tremble for her brothers. Her hot tears glittered like pearls on the regal velvet and diamonds, while all who saw her were wishing they could be queens.

In the meantime she had almost finished her task. Only one coat was wanting, but she had no flax left, not a single nettle. Once more only, and for the last time, must she venture to the churchyard and pluck a few handfuls. She thought with terror of the solitary walk and of the horrible ghouls, but her will was firm, as well as her trust in Providence.

Eliza went, and the king and the archbishop followed her. They saw her vanish through the wicket gate into the churchyard, and when they came nearer they saw the ghouls sitting on the tombstone, as Eliza had seen them. The king turned away his head, for he thought she was with them—she whose head had rested on his breast that very evening.

"The people must judge her," said he, and she was very quickly condemned by everyone to suffer death by fire.

Away from the gorgeous regal halls she was led to a dark, dreary cell, where the wind whistled through the iron bars. Instead of the velvet and silk dresses, they gave her the coats of mail that she had woven to cover her and the bundle of nettles for a pillow, but nothing they could give her would have pleased her more. She continued her task with joy and prayed for help, while the boys in the streets sang jeering songs about her and not a soul comforted her with a kind word.

Toward evening, she heard the flutter of a swan's wing the bars of her cell. It was her youngest brother—he had found his sister, and she sobbed for joy, although she knew that very likely this would be the last night she would have to live. But still she could hope, for her task was almost finished, and her brothers were here.

Then the archbishop arrived to be with her during her last hours, as he had promised the king. But she shook her head and begged him, by looks and gestures, not to stay, for in this night she knew she must finish her task. Otherwise all her pain and tears and sleepless nights would have been suffered in vain. The archbishop withdrew, uttering bitter words against her, but poor Eliza knew that she was innocent and diligently continued her work.

Little mice ran about the floor. They dragged the nettles to her feet to help as well as they could. A thrush sat outside the grating of the window and sang to her the whole night long, as sweetly as possible, to keep up her spirits.

It was still twilight, and at least an hour before sunrise, when the eleven brothers stood at the castle gate and demanded to be brought before the king. They were told it could not be, it was yet almost morning, and as the king slept they dared not disturb him. They threatened; they entreated. Then the guard appeared, and even the king himself, inquiring what all the noise meant. At this moment the sun rose. The eleven brothers were seen no more, but eleven wild swans flew away over the castle.

All the people came streaming forth from the gates of the city to see the witch burned. An old horse drew the cart on which she sat. They had dressed her in a garment of coarse sackcloth. Her lovely hair hung loose on her shoulders, her cheeks were deadly pale, her lips moved silently, while her fingers still worked at the green flax. Even on the way to her death, she would not give up her task. The ten coats lay at her feet. She was working hard at the eleventh, while the mob jeered at her and said, "Look at the witch, how she mutters! She has no hymnbook in her hand. She sits there with her ugly sorcery. Let us tear it in a thousand pieces."

And then they pressed toward her and would have destroyed the coats, but at the same moment eleven wild swans flew over her and alighted on the cart. Then they flapped their large wings, and the crowd drew back in alarm.

"It is a sign from heaven that she is innocent," whispered many of them, but they didn't dare to say it aloud.

As the executioner seized her by the hand to lift her out of the cart, she hastily threw the eleven coats of mail over the swans, and they immediately became eleven handsome princes. But the youngest had a swan's wing instead of an arm, for she had not been able to finish the last sleeve of the coat.

"Now I may speak!" she exclaimed. "I am innocent."

Then the people, who saw what happened, bowed to her as before a saint, but she sank lifeless in her brothers' arms, overcome with suspense, anguish, and pain.

"Yes, she is innocent," said the eldest brother. Then he told them all that had taken place, and while he spoke there rose in the air a fragrance as from millions of roses. Every piece of firewood in the pile had taken root and grown branches. Soon a thick hedge appeared, large and high and covered with roses. On top bloomed a white and shining flower that glittered like a star. This flower the king plucked and placed on Eliza's chest. She awoke with peace and happiness in her heart.

All the church bells rang by themselves, and the birds came flying in great flocks. A marriage procession returned to the castle, such as no king had ever before seen.

The Fir Tree

Deep in the forest, where the warm sun and the fresh air made a sweet resting place, there stood a pretty little fir tree. Though it had a lovely home, it was not a happy tree. It wished so much to be tall like its companions, the pines and firs that grew around it. The sun shone, and the soft air fluttered its leaves, and the little peasant children passed by prattling merrily, but the fir tree didn't care. Sometimes the children would bring a large basket of raspberries or strawberries, wreathed on a straw, seat themselves near the fir tree, and say, "Is it not a pretty little tree?" which made it feel more unhappy than before. And yet all this while the tree grew a notch taller every year, for by the number of joints in the stem of a fir tree we can discover its age.

Still, as it grew, it complained, "Oh! How I wish I were as tall as the other trees; then I would spread out my branches on every side, and my top would overlook the wide world. I should have the birds building their nests on my boughs, and when the wind blew, I should bow with stately dignity like my tall companions."

The tree was so discontented that it took no pleasure in

the warm sunshine, the birds, or the rosy clouds that floated over it morning and evening.

Sometimes, in winter, when the snow lay white and glittering on the ground, a hare would come springing along and jump right over the little tree, and then how mortified it would feel! Two winters passed, and when the third arrived, the tree had grown so tall that the hare was obliged to run around it. Yet the tree remained unsatisfied and would exclaim, "Oh, if I could but keep on growing tall and old! There is nothing else worth caring for in the world!"

In the autumn, as usual, the woodcutters came and cut down several of the tallest trees, and the young fir tree, which was not yet grown to its full height, shuddered as the noble trees fell to the earth with a crash. After the branches were lopped off, the trunks looked so slender and bare that they could scarcely be recognized. Then they were placed upon wagons and drawn by horses out of the forest. *Where were they going? What would become of them?* The young fir tree wished very much to know, so in the spring, when the swallows and the storks came, it asked, "Do you know where those trees were taken? Did you see them?"

The swallows knew nothing, but the stork, after a little reflection, nodded his head and said, "Yes, I think I do. I met several new ships when I flew from Egypt, and they had fine masts that smelled like fir. I think these must have been the trees. I assure you they were stately, very stately."

"Oh, how I wish I were tall enough to go on the sea," said the fir tree. "What is the sea, and what does it look like?"

"It would take too much time to explain," said the stork, flying quickly away.

"Rejoice in your youth," said the sunbeam. "Rejoice in

your fresh growth, and the young life that is in you."

And the wind kissed the tree, and the dew watered it with tears, but the fir tree paid no attention.

Christmastime drew near, and many young trees were cut down, some even smaller and younger than the fir tree who enjoyed neither rest nor peace with longing to leave its forest home. These young trees, which were chosen for their beauty, kept their branches, and were also laid on wagons and drawn by horses out of the forest.

"Where are they going?" asked the fir tree. "They are not taller than I am—indeed, one is much shorter. And why aren't the branches cut off? Where are they going?"

"We know, we know," sang the sparrows. "We have looked in at the windows of the houses in the town, and we know what is done with them. They are dressed up in the most splendid manner. We have seen them standing in the middle of a warm room and adorned with all sorts of beautiful things—honey cakes, gilded apples, playthings, and many hundreds of wax candles."

"And then," asked the fir tree, trembling through all its branches, "and then what happens?"

"We did not see anymore," said the sparrows, "but this was enough for us."

I wonder whether anything so brilliant will ever happen to me, thought the fir tree. *It would be much better than crossing the sea. I long for it almost with pain. Oh! When will Christmas be here? I am now as tall and well grown as the trees that were taken away last year. If only I were laid in a wagon or standing in the warm room with all that brightness and splendor around me! Something better and more beautiful must*

come after, or the trees would not be so decked out. Yes, what
follows must be grander and more splendid. What can it be? I
am weary with longing. I scarcely know how I feel.

"Rejoice with us," said the air and the sunlight. "Enjoy
your own bright life in the fresh air."

But the tree would not rejoice, although it grew taller
every day. In winter and summer, its dark green foliage might
be seen in the forest, while passersby would say, "What a
beautiful tree!"

A short time before Christmas, the discontented fir tree
was the first to fall. As the axe cut through the stem, the tree
fell with a groan to the earth, conscious of pain and faintness
and forgetting all its anticipations of happiness, in sorrow at
leaving its home in the forest. It knew that it would never
again see its dear old companions, the trees, nor the
little bushes and many colored flowers that had grown by
its side, perhaps not even the birds. Nor was the journey at
all pleasant.

The tree did not recover itself until the wagon was being
unpacked in the courtyard of a house. It heard a man say, "We
only want one, and this is the prettiest." Then two servants in
grand livery carried the fir tree into a large and beautiful
apartment. On the walls hung pictures, and near the great
stove stood large china vases, with lions on the lids. There
were rocking chairs, silken sofas, large tables covered with
pictures, books, and playthings, worth a great deal of
money—at least, the children said so.

Then the fir tree was placed in a large tub, full of sand,
but green cloth hung all around it so that no one could see it
was a tub, and it stood on a very handsome carpet. How the fir

tree trembled! What was going to happen to him now? Some young ladies came, and the servants helped them to adorn the tree. On one branch they hung little bags cut out of colored paper, and each bag was filled with sweetmeats. From other branches hung gilded apples and walnuts, as if they had grown there. And above and all around, were hundreds of red, blue, and white candles, which were fastened on the branches. Dolls, exactly like real babies, were placed under the green leaves—the tree had never seen such things before—and at the very top was fastened a glittering star made of tinsel. Oh, it was very beautiful!

"This evening," they all exclaimed, "how bright it will be!"

Oh, that the evening were come, thought the tree, *and the candles lighted! Then I shall know what else is going to happen. Will the trees of the forest come to see me? I wonder if the sparrows will peep in at the windows as they fly. Shall I grow faster here, and keep on all these ornaments summer and winter?*

But guessing was of very little use. It made his bark ache, and this pain is as bad for a slender fir tree as a headache is for us. At last the candles were lighted, and then what a glistening blaze of light the tree presented! It trembled so with joy in all its branches that one of the candles fell among the green leaves and burned some of them. "Help! Help!" exclaimed the young ladies, but there was no danger, for they quickly extinguished the fire. After this, the tree tried not to tremble at all, although the fire frightened him. He was anxious not to hurt any of the beautiful ornaments, even while their brilliancy dazzled him.

And then the folding doors were thrown open, and a troop

of children rushed in as if they intended to upset the tree. They were followed more silently by their elders. For a moment the little ones stood silent with awe, and then they shouted for joy till the room rang, and they danced merrily around the tree, while one present after another was taken from it.

What are they doing? What will happen next? thought the fir. At last the candles burned down to the branches and were put out. Then the children received permission to plunder the tree.

Oh, how they rushed upon it till the branches cracked, and had it not been fastened with the glistening star to the ceiling, it would have been knocked over. The children then danced about with their pretty toys, and no one noticed the tree, except the children's maid who came and peeped among the branches to see if an apple or a fig had been forgotten.

"A story, a story!" cried the children, pulling a little fat man toward the tree.

"Now we shall be in the green shade," said the man, as he seated himself under it, "and the tree will have the pleasure of hearing also, but I shall only tell one story. What shall it be? 'Ivede-Avede,' or 'Humpty Dumpty,' who fell down stairs, but soon got up again and at last married a princess."

"'Ivede-Avede!'" cried some. "'Humpty Dumpty!'" cried others, and there was a fine shouting and crying out. But the fir tree remained quite still and thought to himself, *Shall I have anything to do with all this?* But he had already amused them as much as they wished. Then the old man told them the story of Humpty Dumpty, how he fell down stairs and was raised up again, and married a princess. And the children clapped their hands and cried, "Tell another, tell another," for they wanted to hear the story of Ivede-Avede. After this the fir tree became quite silent and thoughtful. Never had the birds in the forest told such tales as "Humpty Dumpty," who fell down stairs and yet married a princess.

Ah! Yes, so it must happen in the world, thought the fir tree. He believed it all, because it was told by such a nice man. *Ah! Well*, he thought, *who knows? Perhaps I may fall down, too, and marry a princess*. And he looked forward joyfully to the next evening, expecting to be again decked out with lights and playthings, gold, and fruit. *Tomorrow I will not tremble*, thought he; *I will enjoy all my splendor, and I shall hear the story of "Humpty Dumpty" again, and perhaps "Ivede-Avede."* And the tree remained quiet and thoughtful all night.

In the morning the servants and the housemaid came in. *Now*, thought the fir, *all my splendor is going to begin again*. But they dragged him out of the room and upstairs to the attic, and threw him on the floor in a dark corner where no daylight shone, and there they left him. *What does this mean?* thought the tree, *what am I to do here? I can hear nothing in a place like this*. He had time enough to think, for days and nights passed and no one came near him, and when at last somebody did come, it was only to put away large boxes in a corner. So the tree was completely hidden from sight as if it had never existed.

It is winter now, thought the tree. *The ground is hard and covered with snow, so that people cannot plant me. I shall be sheltered here, I imagine, until spring comes. How thoughtful and kind everybody is to me! Still I wish this place were not so dark, as well as lonely, with not even a little hare to look at. How pleasant it was out in the forest while the snow lay on the ground, when the hare would run by, yes, and jump over me, too, although I did not like it then. It is terribly lonely here.*

"*Squeak, squeak,*" said a little mouse, creeping cautiously toward the tree. Then came another, and they both sniffed at the fir tree and crept between the branches.

"Oh, it is very cold," said the little mouse, "or else we would be so comfortable here, wouldn't we, you old fir tree?"

"I am not old," said the fir tree. "There are many who are older than I am."

"Where do you come from? And what do you know?" asked the mice, who were full of curiosity. "Have you seen the most beautiful places in the world, and can you tell us all about them? And have you been in the storeroom, where cheeses lie on the shelf and hams hang from the ceiling? One can run about on tallow candles there, and go in thin and come out fat."

"I know nothing of that place," said the fir tree, "but I know the wood where the sun shines and the birds sing." And then the tree told the little mice all about its youth. They had never heard such an account in their lives, and after they had listened to it attentively, they said, "What a number of things you have seen! You must have been very happy."

"Happy!" exclaimed the fir tree, and then as he reflected upon what he had been telling them, he said, "Ah, yes! After all those were happy days." But when he went on and related all about Christmas Eve and how he had been dressed up with cakes and lights, the mice said, "How happy you must have been, you old fir tree."

"I am not old at all," replied the tree. "I only came from the forest this winter, though I have currently suspended my growth."

"What splendid stories you can tell," said the little mice. The next night four other mice came with them to hear what the tree had to tell. The more he talked, the more he remembered, and then he thought to himself, *Those were happy days, but they may come again. Humpty Dumpty fell down stairs, and yet he married the princess. Perhaps I may marry a princess, too.* And the fir tree thought of the pretty little birch tree that grew in the forest. To him she was a real and beautiful princess.

"Who is Humpty Dumpty?" asked the little mice. And then the tree told the whole story. He could remember every single word, and the little mice were so delighted with it that they were ready to jump to the top of the tree. The next night a great many more mice made their appearance, and on Sunday two rats came with them. But they said it was not a pretty story at all, and the little mice were sad, for it made them also think less of it.

"Do you know only one story?" asked the rats.

"Only one," replied the fir tree. "I heard it on the happiest evening of my life, but I did not know I was so happy at the time."

"We think it is a very miserable story," said the rats. "Don't you know any story about bacon, or candles in the storeroom?"

"No," replied the tree.

"Many thanks to you then," replied the rats, and they marched off.

The little mice also kept away after this, and the tree sighed, and thought, *It was very pleasant when the merry little mice sat around me and listened while I talked. Now that is all passed, too. However, I shall know I am happy when someone comes to take me out of this place.*

But would this ever happen? Yes, one morning people came to clear out the attic, the boxes were packed away, and the tree was pulled out of the corner and thrown roughly on the floor. Finally the servant dragged it out onto the staircase where the daylight shone.

Now life is beginning again, thought the tree, rejoicing in the sunshine and fresh air. Then it was carried downstairs and taken into the courtyard so quickly that it forgot to think of itself and could only look about, there was so much to be seen. The courtyard was close to a garden, where everything looked blooming. Fresh and fragrant roses hung over the little palings. The linden trees were in blossom, while the swallows flew here and there, crying, *"Twit, twit, twit,* my love is coming." But it was not the fir tree they meant.

"Now I shall live," cried the tree, joyfully spreading out its branches. But alas! They were all withered and yellow, and it lay in a corner among weeds and nettles. The star of gold paper still stuck in the top of the tree and glittered bravely in the sunshine.

In the same courtyard two of the merry children were playing who had danced around the tree at Christmas and had been so happy. The youngest saw the gilded star, and ran and pulled it off the tree.

"Look what is sticking to the ugly old fir tree," said the child, treading on the branches till they crackled under his boots.

The tree saw all the fresh bright flowers in the garden, and then looked at itself and wished it had remained in the dark corner of the attic. It thought of its fresh youth in the forest, of the merry Christmas evening, and of the little mice who had listened to the story of "Humpty Dumpty."

"It's all in the past!" said the old tree. "Oh, had I but enjoyed myself while I could have done so! But now it is too late."

Then a servant came and chopped the tree into small pieces, until it lay in a heap on the ground. The pieces were placed in a fire under the copper kettle, and they quickly blazed up brightly, while the tree sighed so deeply that each sigh was like a pistol shot. Then the children who were at play came and seated themselves in front of the fire, looked at it, and cried, *"Pop, pop!"* But at each "pop," which was a deep sigh, the tree was thinking of a summer day in the forest, and of Christmas evening, and of "Humpty Dumpty," the only story it had ever heard or knew how to tell, until at last it was consumed.

The children still played in the garden, and the youngest wore the golden star on his breast, with which the tree had been adorned during the happiest evening of its existence. Now all was past—the tree's life, and the story also, for all stories must come to an end at last.

The Traveling Companion

Poor John was very sad, for his father was so ill, he had no hope of recovery. John sat alone with the sick man in their little room where the lamp had nearly burned out, for it was late in the night.

"You have been a good son, John," said the sick father, "and God will help you along in the world." He looked at him as he spoke, with mild, earnest eyes, drew a deep sigh, and died so peacefully that it appeared as if he still slept.

John wept bitterly. He had no one in the whole world now. Neither father, mother, brother, nor sister. Poor John! He knelt down by the bed, kissed his dead father's hand, and wept many, many bitter tears. But at last his eyes closed, and he fell asleep with his head resting against the hard bedpost.

Then he dreamed a strange dream. He thought he saw the sun shining upon him, and his father alive and well, and even heard him laughing as he used to do when he was very happy. A beautiful girl, with a golden crown on her head and long, shining hair, gave him her hand, and his father said, "See what a bride you have won. She is the loveliest maiden on the whole earth." Then he awoke, and all the beautiful things vanished before his eyes, his father lay dead on the bed, and he was all alone. Poor John!

During the following week the dead man was buried. The son walked behind the coffin that contained his father, whom he so dearly loved and would never again behold. He heard the earth fall on the coffin lid and watched it till only a corner remained in sight, and at last that also disappeared. He felt as if his heart would break with its weight of sorrow, till those who stood around the grave sang a psalm. The sweet, holy tones brought tears into his eyes, which relieved him. The sun shone brightly down on the green trees, as if it would say, "You must not be so sorrowful, John. Do you see the beautiful blue sky above you? Your father is up there, and he prays that you may do well in the future."

"I will always be good," said John, "and then I shall go to be with my father in heaven. What joy it will be when we see each other again! How much I shall have to tell him, and how many things he will be able to explain to me and teach me as he once did on earth. Oh, what joy it will be!"

He pictured it all so plainly to himself that he smiled even while the tears ran down his cheeks. The little birds in the chestnut trees twittered, *"Tweet, tweet."* They were happy even though they had seen the funeral because they knew that the dead man was now in heaven and that he had wings much larger and more beautiful than their own. They knew he was happy now, because he had been good here on earth, and they were glad of it.

John saw them fly away out of the green trees into the wide

world, and he longed to follow them. But first he cut out a large wooden cross to place on his father's grave. When he brought it there in the evening, he found the grave decked out with sand and flowers. Strangers had done this, they who had known the good old father who was now dead and who had loved him very much.

Early the next morning, John packed up his little bundle of clothes and placed all his money, which consisted of fifty dollars and a few pieces of silver, in his money belt. With this he was determined to try his fortune in the world. But first he went into the churchyard. By his father's grave, he offered up a prayer and said, "Farewell."

As he passed through the fields, all the flowers looked fresh and beautiful in the warm sunshine and nodded in the wind, as if they wished to say, "Welcome to the green wood, where all is fresh and bright."

Then John turned to have one more look at the old church, in which he had been christened in his infancy, and where his father had taken him every Sunday to hear the service and join in singing the psalms. As he looked at the old bell tower, he saw the ringer standing at one of the narrow openings, with his little pointed red cap on his head and shading his eyes from the sun with his bent arm. John nodded farewell to him, and the little ringer waved his red cap, laid his hand on his heart, and kissed his hand to him a great many times to show that he felt kindly toward him and wished him a prosperous journey.

John continued his journey and thought of all the wonderful things he would see in the large, beautiful world till he found himself farther away from home than ever he had been before. He did not even know the names of the places he passed through and could scarcely understand the language of the people he met.

The first night he slept on a haystack out in the fields, for there was no other bed for him. But it seemed to him so nice and comfortable that even a king need not wish for a better. The field, the brook, and the haystack, with the blue sky above, formed a beautiful bedroom. The green grass, with the little red and white flowers, was his carpet. The elder bushes and the hedges of wild roses looked like decorations on the walls. And for a bath he could use the clear, fresh water of the brook, while the rushes bowed their heads to him to wish him good morning and good evening. The moon, like a large lamp, hung high up in the blue ceiling, and he had no fear of its setting fire to his curtains. John slept here quite safely all night. When he awoke, the sun was up, and all the little birds were singing around him, "Good morning, good morning. Are you not up yet?"

It was Sunday, and the bells were ringing for church. As the people went in, John followed them. He heard God's word, joined in singing the psalms, and listened to the preacher. It seemed to him just as if he were in his own church, where he had been christened and had sung the psalms with his father.

Out in the churchyard were several graves, and on some of them the grass had grown very high. John thought of his father's grave, which he knew would someday look like these, now that he was not there to weed and attend to it. Then he set to work, pulled up the high grass, raised the wooden crosses that had fallen down, and replaced the wreaths that had been blown away from their places by the wind, thinking all the time, "Perhaps someone is doing the same for my father's grave, as I am not there to do it."

Outside the church door stood an old beggar, leaning on his crutch. John gave him his silver coins, and then he continued his journey, feeling lighter and happier than ever. Toward evening, the weather became very stormy, and he hastened on as quickly as he could to get shelter. It was quite dark by the time he reached a little lonely church that stood on a hill. "I will go in here," he said, "and sit down in a corner, for I am quite tired and want rest."

So he went in and seated himself. Then he folded his hands and offered up his evening prayer, and was soon fast asleep and dreaming, while the thunder rolled and the lightning flashed without. When he awoke, it was still night, but the storm had ceased, and the moon shone in upon him through the windows. Then he saw an open coffin standing in the center of the church, which contained a dead man, waiting for burial.

John was not at all timid. He had a good conscience, and he knew also that the dead can never hurt any one. It is living, wicked people who do harm to others. Two such wicked people stood by the dead man, who had been brought to the church to be buried. Their evil intentions were to throw the poor dead body outside the church door and not let him rest in his coffin.

"Why do you want to do this?" asked John, when he saw what they were going to do. "It is very wicked. Leave him to rest in peace, for heaven's sake."

"Nonsense," replied the two evil men. "He has cheated us. He owed us money that he could not pay. Now that he is dead we shall not get a penny, so we mean to have our revenge and let him lie like a dog outside the church door."

"I have only fifty dollars," said John. "It is all I possess in the world, but I will give it to you if you will promise me faithfully to leave the dead man in peace. I shall be able to get on without the money. I have strong and healthy limbs, and God will always help me."

"Why, of course," said the horrid men. "If you will pay his debt we will both promise not to touch him. You may depend upon that." Then they took the money he offered them, laughed at him for his good nature, and went their way.

John laid the dead body back in the coffin, folded the hands, and took leave of it. He went away contentedly through the great forest. All around him he could see the prettiest little elves dancing in the moonlight that shone through the trees. They were not disturbed by his appearance, for they knew he was good and harmless. It is only wicked people who are never allowed to see fairies.

Some of the fairies were not taller than the breadth of a finger, and wore golden combs in their long, yellow hair. They were rocking themselves two together on the large dewdrops with which the leaves and the high grass were sprinkled. Sometimes the dewdrops would roll away, and then they fell down between the stems of the long grass and caused a great deal of laughing and noise among the other little people. It was quite charming to watch them at play. Then they sang songs, and John remembered that he had learned those pretty songs when he was a little boy.

Large speckled spiders with silver crowns on their heads were busy spinning suspension bridges and palaces from one hedge to another, and when the tiny drops fell upon them, they glittered in the moonlight like shining glass. This continued till sunrise. Then the little elves crept into the flowerbuds, and the wind took the bridges and palaces and fluttered them in the air like cobwebs.

Just as John was leaving the wood, a strong man's voice called after him, "Hallo, comrade, where are you traveling?"

"Into the wide world," he replied. "I am only a poor lad. I have neither father nor mother, but God will help me."

"I am going into the wide world also," replied the stranger. "Shall we keep each other company?"

"With all my heart," said John, and so they went on together. Soon they began to like each other very much, for they were both good people. But John soon found that the stranger was much wiser than himself. He had traveled all over the world and could describe almost everything.

The sun was high in the heavens when they seated themselves under a large tree to eat their breakfast. At the same moment an old woman came toward them. She was very old and almost bent double. She leaned upon a stick and carried on her back a bundle of firewood, which she had collected in the forest. Her apron was tied around it, and John saw three great stems of fern and some willow twigs peeping out. Just as she came close up to them, her foot slipped and she fell to the ground screaming loudly. Poor old woman, she had broken her leg!

John suggested that they carry the old woman home to her cottage, but the stranger opened his knapsack and took out a box in which he said he had a salve that would quickly make her leg well and strong again, so that she would be able to walk home herself as if her leg had never been broken. All that he asked in return was the three fern stems that she carried in her apron.

"That is rather too high a price," said the old woman, nodding her head quite strangely. She did not seem at all inclined to part with the fern stems. However, it was not very agreeable to lie there with a broken leg, so she gave them to him. Such was the power of the ointment that no sooner had he rubbed her leg with it than the old mother rose up and walked even better than she had done before. Clearly this wonderful ointment could not be bought at a chemist's.

"What can you want with those three fern rods?" asked John of his fellow traveler.

"Oh, they will make fine brooms," said he, "and I like them because I have strange whims sometimes." Then they walked on together for a long distance.

"How dark the sky is becoming," said John. "Look at those thick, heavy clouds."

"Those are not clouds," replied his fellow traveler. "They are mountains—large lofty mountains—on the tops of which we should be above the clouds in the pure, free air. Believe me, it is delightful to climb so high. Tomorrow we shall be there."

But the mountains were not so near as they appeared. They had to travel a whole day, and pass through black forests and piles of rock as large as a town before they reached them. The journey was so tiring that John and his fellow traveler stopped to rest at a roadside inn, so that they might gain strength for their journey on the morrow.

In the large public room of the inn a great many persons were assembled to see a comedy performed with puppets. The showman had just set up his little theater, and the people were sitting around the room to watch the performance. Right in front, in the very best place, sat a stout butcher, with a great bulldog by his side who seemed very much inclined to bite. He sat staring with wide eyes, and so indeed did everyone else in the room.

Then the play began. It was a pretty piece, with a king and a queen in it, who sat on beautiful thrones, and had gold crowns on their heads. The trains to their dresses were very long, according to the fashion. The prettiest of wooden dolls, with glass eyes and large mustaches, stood at the doors, and opened and shut them, so that the fresh air might come into the room.

It was a very pleasant play, not at all mournful. But just as the queen stood up and walked across the stage, the great bulldog, who should have been held back by his master, made a spring forward and caught the queen in his teeth by her slender waist, so that it snapped in two. This was a very dreadful disaster.

The poor man who was exhibiting the dolls was much frightened and quite sad about his queen. She was the prettiest doll he had, and the bulldog had broken her head and shoulders off.

After all the people were gone away, the stranger, who came with John, said that he could soon set her to rights. And then he brought out his box and rubbed the doll with some of the salve with which he had cured the old woman when she broke her leg. As soon as this was done the doll's back became quite right again; her head and shoulders were fixed on, and, even better she could now move her limbs herself. There was no longer any need to pull the wires, for the doll acted just like a living creature, except that she could not speak. The man to whom the show belonged was quite delighted at having a doll who could dance by herself without being pulled by the wires. None of the other dolls could do this.

During the night, when all the people at the inn were gone to bed, someone was heard to sigh deeply and painfully. The sighing continued for so long a time that everyone got up to see what could be the matter. The showman went at once to his little theater and found that it proceeded from the dolls, who all lay on the floor sighing piteously and staring with their glass eyes. They all wanted to be rubbed with the ointment, so that, like the queen, they might be able to move by themselves. The queen threw herself on her knees, took off her beautiful crown, and held it in her hand, as if to say, "Take this from me, but do rub my husband and his courtiers."

The poor man who owned the theater could scarcely refrain from weeping. He was so sorry that he could not help them. He spoke to John's comrade and promised him all the money he would make at the next evening's performance if he would only rub the ointment on four or five of his dolls. But the fellow traveler said he did not require anything in return, except the sword that the showman wore by his side. As soon as he received the sword he anointed six of the dolls with the ointment, and they were able immediately to dance so gracefully that all the living girls in the room could not help joining in the dance. The coachman danced with the cook, and the waiters with the chambermaids, and all the strangers joined. Even the tongs and the fire shovel made an attempt, but they fell down after the first jump. So after all it was a very merry night.

The next morning John and his companion left the inn to continue their journey through the great pine forests and over the high mountains. They arrived at last at such a great height that towns and villages lay beneath them, and the church steeples looked like little specks between the green trees.

They could see for miles around, far away to places they had never visited, and John saw more of the beautiful world than he had ever known before. The sun shone brightly in the blue firmament above, and through the clear mountain air came the sound of the huntsman's horn. The soft, sweet notes brought tears into his eyes, and he could not help exclaiming, "How good and loving God is to give us all this beauty and loveliness in the world to make us happy!"

His fellow traveler stood by with folded hands, gazing on the dark wood and the towns bathed in the warm sunshine. At this moment there sounded over their heads sweet music. They looked up and saw a large white swan floating in the air and singing as never a bird sang before. But the song soon became weaker and weaker, the bird's head drooped, and he sunk slowly down and lay dead at their feet.

"It is a beautiful bird," said the traveler, "and these large white wings are worth a great deal of money. I will take them with me. You see now that a sword will be very useful."

So he cut off the wings of the dead swan with one blow and carried them away with him.

They continued their journey over the mountains for many miles, till at length they reached a large city containing hundreds of towers that shone in the sunshine like silver. In the midst of the city stood a splendid marble palace, roofed with pure red gold, in which lived the king. John and his companion did not want to go into the town immediately, so they stopped at an inn outside the town to change their clothes, for they wished to appear respectable as they walked through the streets. The landlord told them that the king was a very good man, who never injured anyone: but as to his daughter, "Heaven defend us!"

She was indeed a wicked princess. She possessed beauty enough—nobody could be more elegant or prettier than she was. But what good was that? She was a wicked witch who was responsible for many noble young princes losing their lives. Anyone was at liberty to offer her his hand. Were he a prince or a beggar, it mattered not to her. She would ask him to guess three things that she had just thought of, and if he succeeded, he would marry her and be king over all the land when her father died. But if he could not guess these three things, then she ordered him to be hanged or to have his head cut off.

The old king, her father, was very much grieved at her conduct, but he could not prevent her from being so wicked, because he once said he would have nothing more to do with her lovers. She might do as she pleased. Every prince who came and tried the three guesses so that he might marry the princess had failed and had been hanged or beheaded. They had all been warned and could have left her alone, if they wanted. The old king became at last so distressed at all these dreadful circumstances that for a whole day every year he and his soldiers knelt and prayed that the princess might become good, but she continued as wicked as ever. As a sign of mourning, the old women who drank brandy would color it quite black before they drank it—what more could they do?

"What a horrible princess!" said John. "She ought to be flogged. If I were the old king, I would have her punished in some way."

Just then they heard the people outside shouting, "Hurrah!" Looking out, they saw the princess passing by. She was really so beautiful that everybody forgot her wickedness and shouted "Hurrah!" Twelve lovely maidens in white silk dresses, holding golden tulips in their hands, rode by her side on coal black horses. The princess herself had a snow-white steed, decked with diamonds and rubies. Her dress was of cloth of gold, and the whip she held in her hand looked like a sunbeam. The golden crown on her head glittered like the stars of heaven, and her mantle was formed of thousands of butterflies' wings sewn together. Yet she herself was more beautiful than all.

When John saw her, his face became as red as a drop of blood, and he could scarcely utter a word. The princess looked exactly like the beautiful lady with the golden crown, of whom he had dreamed on the night his father died. She appeared to him so lovely that he could not help loving her.

It could not be true, he thought, *that she was really a wicked witch who ordered people to be hanged or beheaded if they could not guess her thoughts. Everyone has permission to go and ask her hand, even the poorest beggar.* "I shall pay a visit to the palace," he said. "I must go, for I cannot help myself."

Everyone advised him not to attempt it, for he would be sure to share the same fate as the rest. His fellow traveler also tried to persuade him against it, but John felt sure he would succeed. He brushed his shoes and his coat, washed his face and his hands, combed his soft flaxen hair, and then went out alone into the town and walked to the palace.

"Come in," said the king, as John knocked at the door. John opened it, and the old king, in a dressing gown and embroidered slippers, came toward him. He had the crown on his head, and carried his scepter in one hand and the orb in the other. "Wait a bit," said he, and he placed the orb under his arm so that he could offer the other hand to John. But when he found that John was another suitor, he began to weep so violently that both the scepter and the orb fell to the floor, and he was obliged to wipe his eyes with his dressing gown. Poor old king!

"Let her alone," he said. "You will fare as badly as all the others. Come, I will show you." Then he led him out into the princess's pleasure gardens, and there he saw a frightful sight. On every tree hung three or four king's sons who had wooed the princess, but had not been able to guess the riddles she gave them. Their skeletons rattled in every breeze, so that the terrified birds never dared to venture into the garden. All the flowers were supported by human bones instead of sticks, and human skulls in the flowerpots grinned horribly. It was really a horrible garden for a princess. "Do you see all this?" said the old king. "Your fate will be the same as those who are here; therefore, do not attempt it. You really make me very unhappy—I take these things to heart so very much."

John kissed the good old king's hand and said he was sure it would be all right; for he was quite infatuated with the beautiful princess. Then the princess herself came riding into the palace yard with all her ladies, and he wished her "Good morning." She looked wonderfully fair and lovely when she offered her hand to John, and he loved her more than ever. How could she be a wicked witch, as all the people asserted?

He accompanied her into the hall. The little pages offered them gingerbread nuts and sweetmeats, but the old king was so unhappy he could eat nothing, and besides, gingerbread nuts were too hard for his teeth.

It was decided that John should come to the palace the next day, when the judges and the whole of the counselors would be present, to see if he could guess the first riddle. If he succeeded, he would have to come a second time, but if not, he would lose his life. No one had ever been able to guess even one of the riddles.

However, John was not at all worried about the result of his trial. On the contrary, he was very merry. He thought only of the beautiful princess and believed that in some way he should have help, but how he knew not and did not like to think about it. He danced along the high road as he went back to the inn, where he had left his fellow traveler waiting for him. John could not refrain from telling him how gracious the princess had been and how beautiful she looked. He longed for the next day so much that he might go to the palace and try his luck at guessing the riddles. But his comrade shook his head and looked very mournful.

"I do so wish you to do well," said he. "We might have continued together much longer, and now I am likely to lose you; poor dear John! I could shed tears, but I will not make you unhappy on the last night we may be together. We will be merry, really merry this evening. Tomorrow, after you are gone, I shall be able to weep undisturbed."

It was very quickly known among the inhabitants of the town that another suitor had arrived for the princess, and there was great sorrow in consequence. The theater remained closed, the women who sold sweetmeats tied black crepe around the sugar sticks, and the king and the priests were on their knees in the church. There was a great lamentation, for no one expected John to succeed better than those who had been suitors before.

In the evening John's comrade prepared a large bowl of punch, and said, "Now let us be merry, and drink to the health of the princess." But after drinking two glasses, John became so sleepy that he could not keep his eyes open and fell fast asleep. Then his fellow traveler lifted him gently out of his chair and laid him on the bed. As soon as it was completely dark, he took the two large wings that he had cut from the dead swan and tied them firmly to his own shoulders. Then he put into his pocket the largest of the three bundles of sticks that he had obtained from the old woman who had fallen and broken her leg. After this he opened the window and flew away over the town, straight toward the palace, and seated himself in a corner under the window that looked into the bedroom of the princess.

The town was perfectly still when the clocks struck a quarter to twelve. Presently the window opened, and the princess, who wore large black wings on her shoulders and a long white mantle, flew away over the city toward a high mountain. The traveler, who had made himself invisible so that she could not possibly see him, flew after her through the air and whipped the princess with his rod so that the blood came whenever he struck her. Ah, it was a strange flight through the air! The wind caught her mantle, so that it spread out on all sides like the large sail of a ship, and the moon shone through it.

"How it hails, to be sure!" said the princess, at each blow she received from the rod. And it was just what she deserved.

At last she reached the side of the mountain, and knocked. The mountain opened with a noise like the roll of thunder, and the princess went in. The traveler followed her. No one could see him, as he was still invisible. They went through a long, wide passage. A thousand gleaming spiders ran here and there on the walls, causing them to glitter as if they were illuminated with fire. They next entered a large hall built of silver and gold. Large red and blue flowers shone on the walls, looking like sunflowers in size, but no one would dare to pluck them, for the stems were hideous poisonous snakes and the flowers were flames of fire darting out of their jaws. Shining glowworms covered the ceiling, and sky blue bats flapped their transparent wings.

Altogether the place had a frightful appearance. In the middle of the floor stood a throne supported by four skeleton horses, whose harnesses had been made by fiery red spiders. The throne itself was made of milk white glass, and the cushions were little black mice, each biting the other's tail. Over it hung a canopy of rose-colored spider's webs, spotted with the prettiest little green flies, which sparkled like precious stones.

On the throne sat an old magician with a crown on his ugly head and a scepter in his hand. He kissed the princess on the forehead, seated her by his side on the splendid throne, and then the music commenced. Great black grasshoppers played the mouth organ, and the owl struck herself on the body instead of a drum. It was a ridiculous concert. Little black goblins with lights in their caps danced about the hall. But no one could see the traveler, but he had placed himself just behind the throne where he could see and hear everything.

The courtiers who came in looked noble and grand. but anyone with common sense could see they really were only broomsticks, with cabbages for heads. The magician had given them life and dressed them in embroidered robes. This worked very well, as they were only wanted for show.

After there had been a little dancing, the princess told the magician that she had a new suitor and asked him what she should have the suitor guess when he came to the castle the next morning.

"Listen to what I say," said the magician. "You must choose something very easy; he is less likely to guess it then. Think of one of your shoes, he will never imagine it is that. Then cut his head off, and mind you do not forget to bring his eyes with you tomorrow night, that I may eat them."

The princess curtsied low and said she would not forget the eyes.

The magician then opened the mountain and she flew home again, but the traveler followed and flogged her so much with the rod that she sighed quite deeply about the heavy hailstorm and made as much haste as she could to get back to her bedroom through the window. The traveler then returned to the inn where John still slept, took off his wings, and laid down on the bed, for he was very tired. Early in the morning John awoke, and when his fellow traveler got up, he said that he had a very wonderful dream about the princess and her shoe. He therefore advised John to ask her if she had not thought of her shoe. Of course the traveler knew this from what the magician in the mountain had said.

"I may as well say that as anything," said John. "Perhaps your dream may come true. Still I will say farewell, for if I guess wrong I shall never see you again."

Then they embraced each other, and John went into the town and walked to the palace. The great hall was full of people, and the judges sat in armchairs, with eiderdown cushions to rest their heads upon because they had so much to think of. The old king stood near, wiping his eyes with his white pocket handkerchief. When the princess entered, she looked even more beautiful than she had appeared the day before and greeted everyone present most gracefully. To John she gave her hand and said, "Good morning to you."

Now came the time for John to guess what she was thinking of. Oh, how kindly she looked at him as she spoke. But when he uttered the single word "shoe," she turned as pale as a ghost. All her wisdom could not help her, for he had guessed rightly. Oh, how pleased the old king was! It was quite amusing to see how he danced about. All the people clapped their hands, both on his account and John's, who had guessed rightly the first time. His fellow traveler was glad also when he heard how successful John had been. But John folded his hands and thanked God, who, he felt quite sure, would help him again. He knew he had to guess twice more.

The evening passed pleasantly like the one preceding. While John slept, his companion flew behind the princess to the mountain and flogged her even harder than before. This time he had taken two switches with him. No one saw him go in with her, and he heard all that was said. The princess this time was to think of a glove. The traveling companion told John as if he had again heard the answer in a dream.

The next day, therefore, John was able to guess correctly the second time, and it caused great rejoicing at the palace. The whole court jumped about as they had seen the king do the day before, but the princess lay on the sofa and would not say a single word. All now depended upon John. If he only guessed rightly the third time, he would marry the princess and reign over the kingdom after the death of the old king. But if he failed, he would lose his life, and the magician would have his beautiful blue eyes.

That evening John said his prayers and went to bed very early, and soon fell asleep calmly. But his companion tied his wings to his shoulders, took three switches, and, with his sword at his side, flew to the palace.

It was a very dark night, and so stormy that the tiles flew from the roofs of the houses and the trees in the garden upon which the skeletons hung bent themselves like reeds before the wind. The lightning flashed, and the thunder rolled in one long-continued peal all night. The window of the castle opened, and the princess flew out. She was pale as death, but she laughed at the storm as if it were not bad enough. Her white mantle fluttered in the wind like a large sail, and the traveler flogged her with the three rods till the blood trickled down. At last she could scarcely fly. She managed, however, to reach the mountain. "What a hailstorm!" she said, as she entered. "I have never been out in such weather as this."

"Yes, there may be too much of a good thing sometimes," said the magician.

Then the princess told him that John had guessed rightly the second time, and if he succeeded the next morning, he would win, and she could never come to the mountain again or practice magic as she had done, and therefore she was quite unhappy. "I will figure out something for you to think of which he will never guess, unless he is a greater conjuror than myself. But now let us be merry."

Then he took the princess by both hands, and they danced with all the little goblins and jack-o'-lanterns in the room. The red spiders sprang here and there on the walls quite as merrily, and the flowers of fire appeared as if they were throwing out sparks. The owl beat the drum, the crickets whistled, and the grasshoppers played the mouth organ. It was a very ridiculous ball. After they had danced enough, the princess was obliged to go home, for fear she should be missed at the palace. The magician offered to go with her, that they might be company to each other on the way.

Then they flew away through the bad weather, and the traveler followed them and broke his three rods across their shoulders. The magician had never been out in such a hail-storm as this. Just by the palace the magician stopped to wish the princess farewell, and to whisper in her ear, "Tomorrow think of my head."

But the traveler heard it, and just as the princess slipped through the window into her bedroom and the magician turned around to fly back to the mountain, he seized him by the long black beard and with his saber cut off the wicked conjuror's head just above the shoulders, so that he could not even see who it was. He threw the body into the sea to the fishes, and after dipping the head into the water, he tied it up in a silk handkerchief, took it with him to the inn, and then went to bed.

The next morning he gave John the handkerchief and told him not to untie it till the princess asked him what she was thinking of. There were so many people in the great hall of the palace that they stood as thick as radishes tied together in a bundle. The council sat in their armchairs with the white cushions. The old king wore new robes, and the golden crown and scepter had been polished up so that he looked quite smart. But the princess was very pale and wore a black dress as if she were going to a funeral.

"What have I thought of?" asked the princess. He immediately untied the handkerchief and was himself quite frightened when he saw the head of the ugly magician.

Everyone shuddered, for it was terrible to look at. But the princess sat like a statue and could not utter a single word. At length she rose and gave John her hand, for he had guessed rightly.

She looked at no one, but sighed deeply, and said, "You are my master now. This evening our marriage must take place."

"I am very pleased to hear it," said the old king. "It is just what I wish."

Then all the people shouted "Hurrah!" The band played music in the streets, the bells rang, and the cake women took the black crepe off the sugar sticks. There was universal joy. Three oxen, stuffed with ducks and chickens, were roasted whole in the marketplace, where everyone might help himself to a slice. The fountains spouted forth the most delicious wine, and whoever bought a loaf at the baker's received six large buns, full of raisins, as a present. In the evening the whole town was illuminated. The soldiers fired off cannons, and the boys let off crackers. There was eating and drinking, dancing and jumping everywhere. In the palace, the high-born gentlemen and beautiful ladies danced with each other. They could be heard from far away singing—

"Here are maidens, young and fair,
Dancing in the summer air;
Like two spinning wheels at play,
Pretty maidens dance away—
Dance the spring and summer through
Till the sole falls from your shoe."

But the princess was still a witch, and she could not love John. His fellow traveler had thought of that, so he gave John three feathers out of the swan's wings and a little bottle with a few drops in it. He told him to place a large bath full of water by the princess's bed and put the feathers and the drops into it. Then, at the moment she was about to get into bed, he must give her a little push, so that she might fall into the water, and then dip her three times. This would destroy the power of the magician, and she would love him very much.

John did all that his companion told him to do. The princess shrieked aloud when he dipped her under the water the first time and struggled under his hands in the form of a great black swan with fiery eyes. As she rose the second time from the water, the swan had become white with a black ring around its neck. John allowed the water to close once more over the bird, and at the same time it changed into the beautiful princess. She was more lovely even than before and thanked him, while her eyes sparkled with tears, for having broken the spell of the magician.

The next day, the king came with the whole court to offer their congratulations and stayed till quite late. Last of all came the traveling companion. He had his staff in his hand and his knapsack on his back. John kissed him many times and told him he must not go, he must remain with him, for he was the cause of all his good fortune. But the traveler shook his head and said gently and kindly, "No, my time is up now. I have only paid my debt to you. Do you remember the dead man whom the bad people wished to throw out of his coffin? You gave all you possessed that he might rest in his grave. I am that man." As he said this, he vanished.

The wedding festivities lasted a whole month. John and his princess loved each other dearly, and the old king lived to see many a happy day when he took their little children on his knees and let them play with his scepter. And John became king over the whole country.

The Nightingale

❧

In China, you know, the emperor is Chinese, and all those about him are Chinese also. The story I am going to tell you happened a great many years ago, so it is well to hear it now before it is forgotten.

The emperor's palace was the most beautiful in the world. It was built entirely of porcelain—so expensive and so delicate and brittle that whoever touched it had to be very careful. In the garden could be seen the most amazing flowers with pretty silver bells tied to them, which tinkled so that everyone who passed could not help noticing the flowers. Indeed, everything in the emperor's garden was remarkable, and it stretched so far that the gardener himself did not know where it ended. Those who traveled beyond its limits knew that there was a noble forest, with lofty trees sloping down to the deep blue sea, and the great ships sailed under the shadow of its branches. In one of these trees lived a nightingale, who sang so beautifully that even the poor fishermen, who had so many other things to do, would stop and listen. Sometimes, when they went at night to spread their nets, they would hear her sing, and say, "Oh, isn't that beautiful?" But when they returned to their fishing, they forgot the bird until the next night. Then they would hear it again and exclaim, "Oh, how beautiful is the nightingale's song!"

Travelers from every country in the world came to the city of the emperor, which they admired very much, along with the palace and gardens. But when they heard the nightingale, they all declared it to be the best of all.

When the travelers came home, they described what they had seen. Learned men wrote books describing the town, the palace, and the gardens, but they did not forget the nightingale, which was really the greatest wonder. And those who could write poetry composed beautiful verses about the nightingale who lived in a forest near the deep sea.

These books traveled all over the world, and some of them came into the hands of the emperor. He sat in his golden chair, and, as he read, he nodded his approval every moment, for it pleased him to find such beautiful descriptions of his city, his palace, and his gardens. But when he read, "The nightingale is the most beautiful of all," he exclaimed, "What is this? I know nothing of any nightingale. Is there such a bird in my empire—even in my own garden? I was never told of this—I had to learn of it from a book!"

Then he called one of his lords-in-waiting, who was so sophisticated that when anyone in an inferior rank to himself spoke to him or asked him a question, he would answer, "Pooh," which means nothing.

"There is a very wonderful bird mentioned here, called a nightingale," said the emperor. "They say it is the best thing in my large kingdom. Why have I not been told of it?"

"I have never heard the name," replied the courtier. "It has not been presented at court."

"It is my pleasure that it shall appear this evening and sing for me," said the emperor. "The whole world knows what I possess better than I do myself."

"I have never heard of it," said the courtier, "yet I will endeavor to find it."

But where was the nightingale to be found? The nobleman went upstairs and down, through halls and passages, yet none of those whom he met had heard of the bird. So he returned to the emperor and said that it must be a fable, invented by those who had written the book. "Your imperial majesty," said he, "cannot believe everything it says in books. Sometimes they are only fiction, or what is called the black art."

"But the book in which I have read this account," said the emperor, "was sent to me by the great and mighty emperor of Japan, and therefore it cannot contain a falsehood. I will hear the nightingale. It must be here this evening. It has my highest favor, and if it does not come, the whole court shall be hit in the stomach after supper is ended."

"Tsing-pe!" cried the lord-in-waiting, and again he ran up- and downstairs, through all the halls and corridors. Half the court ran with him, for they did not like the idea of being hit in the stomach. There was a great inquiry about this wonderful nightingale, whom all the world knew, but who was unknown to the court.

At last they met with a poor little girl in the kitchen, who said, "Oh, yes, I know the nightingale quite well. Indeed, it can sing. Every evening I have permission to take home to my poor sick mother the scraps from the table. She lives down by the seashore, and as I come back I feel tired, and I sit down in the wood to rest and listen to the nightingale's song. Then the tears come into my eyes, and it is just as if my mother kissed me."

"Little maiden," said the lord-in-waiting, "I will get you constant employment in the kitchen, and you shall have permission to see the emperor dine if you will lead us to the nightingale, for it is invited for this evening to the palace."

The girl went into the wood where the nightingale sang, and half the court followed her. As they went along, a cow began to moo.

"Oh," said a young courtier, "now we have found it. What wonderful power for such a small creature. I have certainly heard it before."

"No, that is only a cow lowing," said the little girl. "We are still a long way from the place."

Then some frogs began to croak in the marsh.

"Beautiful," said the young courtier again. "Now I hear it, tinkling like little church bells."

"No, those are frogs," said the little maiden, "but I think we shall soon hear it." Then the nightingale began to sing.

"Listen, listen! There it is," said the girl. "And there it sits," she added, pointing to a little gray bird who was perched on a bough.

"Is it possible?" said the lord-in-waiting, "I never imagined it would be a little, plain, simple thing like that. It must have turned pale at seeing so many grand people."

"Little nightingale," cried the girl, raising her voice, "our most gracious emperor wishes you to sing before him."

"With the greatest pleasure," said the nightingale, and began to sing most delightfully.

"It sounds like tiny glass bells," said the lord-in-waiting, "and see how its little throat works. It is surprising that we have never heard this before. She will be a great success at court."

"Shall I sing once more before the emperor?" asked the nightingale, who thought he was present.

"My excellent little nightingale," said the courtier, "I have the great pleasure of inviting you to a court festival this evening, where you will gain imperial favor by your charming song."

"My song sounds best in the green wood," said the bird, but still it came willingly when it heard the emperor's wish.

The palace was elegantly decorated for the occasion. The walls and floors of porcelain glittered in the light of a thousand lamps. Beautiful flowers, around which little bells were tied, stood in the corridors. What with the running to and fro and the draft, these bells tinkled so loudly that no one could speak to be heard.

In the center of the great hall, a golden perch had been fixed for the nightingale to sit on. The whole court was present, and the little kitchen maid had received permission to stand by the door. She had been given the title of Real Court Cook. All were in full dress, and every eye was turned to the little gray bird when the emperor nodded to it to begin.

The nightingale sang so sweetly that tears came into the emperor's eyes and then rolled down his cheeks. Its song became still more touching and went to everyone's heart. The emperor was so delighted that he declared the nightingale should have his gold slipper to wear around its neck, but the nightingale declined the honor with thanks. It had been sufficiently rewarded already. "I have seen tears in an emperor's eyes," it said, "That is my richest reward. An emperor's tears have wonderful power and are quite sufficient honor for me." Then it sang again more enchantingly than ever.

"That singing is a lovely gift," said the ladies of the court to each other. They took water in their own mouths to try to make the gurgling sounds of the nightingale when they spoke to anyone, so thay they might fancy themselves nightingales. And the footmen and chambermaids also expressed their satisfaction, which is saying a great deal, for they are very difficult to please. In fact, the nightingale's visit was most successful.

It was now to remain at court, to have its own cage, with freedom to go outside twice a day and once during the night. Twelve servants were appointed to attend the bird on these occasions, who each held it by a silken string fastened to her leg. There was certainly not much pleasure in this kind of flying.

The whole city spoke of the wonderful bird. When two people met, one said "nightin," and the other said "gale," and they understood what was meant, for nothing else was talked of. Eleven peddlers' children were named after her, but none of them could sing a note.

One day the emperor received a large packet on which was written "The Nightingale."

"Here is, no doubt, a new book about our celebrated bird," said the emperor. But instead of a book, it was a work of art. Inside the box was an artificial nightingale made to look like a living one, covered all over with diamonds, rubies, and sapphires. As soon as the artificial bird was wound up, it could sing like the real one and could move its tail up and down, which sparkled with silver and gold. Around its neck hung a piece of ribbon, on which was written "The Emperor of Japan's nightingale cannot compare with that of the Emperor of China's."

"This is very beautiful," exclaimed all who saw it, and he who had brought the artificial bird received the title of "Imperial nightingale-bringer-in-chief."

"Now they must sing together," said the court, "and what a duet it will be." But they did not get on well, for the real nightingale sang in its own natural way, but the artificial bird sang only waltzes.

"That is not a fault," said the music master. "It is quite perfect to my taste." Then the artificial bird had to sing alone and was as successful as the real bird. Besides, it was so much prettier to look at, for it sparkled like bracelets and breast pins.

It could sing the same tunes thirty-three times without being tired. The people would gladly have heard it again, but the emperor said the living nightingale ought to sing something. But where was it? No one had noticed it when it flew out the open window, back to the green woods.

"What strange conduct," said the emperor, when the nightingale's flight had been discovered. All the courtiers blamed it and said it was a very ungrateful creature.

"But we have the best bird after all," said one. Then they had the artificial bird sing again, although it was the thirty-fourth time they had listened to the same piece. Even then they had not learned it, for it was a rather difficult piece. But the music master praised the bird in the highest degree and even asserted that it was better than a real nightingale, not only in its dress and the beautiful diamonds, but also in its musical power.

"You must see, my chief lord and emperor, that with a real nightingale we can never tell what is going to be sung, but with this bird everything is settled. It can be opened and explained, so that people may understand how the waltzes are formed and why one note follows upon another."

"This is exactly what we think," everyone replied. Then the music master received permission to exhibit the bird to the people on the following Sunday, and the emperor commanded that the public should be present to hear it sing. When they heard it they were like people intoxicated; it was as if they were tipsy from drinking tea, which is quite a Chinese custom. They all said "Oh!" and held up their forefingers and nodded their approval. But a poor fisherman, who had heard the real nightingale, said, "It sounds prettily enough, and the melodies are all alike, yet there seems something wanting. I cannot exactly tell what."

After this the real nightingale was banished from the empire, and the artificial bird placed on a silk cushion close to the emperor's bed. The presents of gold and precious stones that had been received with it were around the bird. It was given the title of "Little Imperial Bedside Table Singer," and the rank of number one on the left hand, for the emperor considered the left side, on which the heart lies, as the most noble, and the heart of an emperor is in the same place as that of other people.

The music master wrote a work in twenty-five volumes about the artificial bird, which was very learned and very long, and full of the most difficult Chinese words. Yet all the people said they had read it and understood it, for fear of being thought stupid and having their bodies trampled upon.

* * *

A year passed, and the emperor, the court, and all the other Chinese people knew every little turn in the artificial bird's song, and that was why they liked it so much. They could sing with the bird, which they often did. The street boys sang, *"Zi-zi-zi, cluck, cluck, cluck,"* and the emperor himself also sang it. It was really most amusing.

One evening, when the artificial bird was singing its best, and the emperor lay in bed listening to it, the bird made a strange *"boing"* noise. Then a spring cracked. *"Whir-r-r-r"* went all the wheels, spinning around, and then the music stopped.

The emperor immediately sprang out of bed and called for his physician. But what could he do? Then they sent for a watchmaker. After a great deal of talking and examination, the bird was put into something like its old shape, but he said that it must be used very carefully, as the barrels were worn, and it would be impossible to put in new ones without injuring the music. Now there was great sorrow, as the bird could only be allowed to play once a year, and even that was dangerous for the works inside it. Then the music master made a little speech, full of difficult words, and declared that the bird was as good as ever, and, of course no one contradicted him.

Five years passed, and then a real grief came upon the land. The Chinese people were fond of their emperor, and he now lay so ill that he was not expected to live. Already a new emperor had been chosen and the people who stood in the street asked the lord-in-waiting how the old emperor was, but he only said, "Pooh!" and shook his head.

Cold and pale lay the emperor in his royal bed. The whole court thought he had died, and everyone ran away to pay homage to his successor. The chamberlains went out to have a talk on the matter, and the ladies' maids invited all of their friends for coffee. Cloth had been laid down on the halls and passages, so that not a footstep should be heard, and all was silent and still. But the emperor was not yet dead, although he lay white and stiff on his gorgeous bed with the long velvet curtains and heavy gold tassels. A window stood open, and the moon shone in upon the emperor and the artificial bird.

The poor emperor! He could scarcely breathe and felt a strange weight on his chest. He opened his eyes, and saw Death sitting there. He had put on the emperor's golden crown, and held in one hand his sword of state and in the other his beautiful banner. All around the bed and peeping through the long velvet curtains were a number of strange heads, some very ugly and others lovely and gentle looking. These were the emperor's good and bad deeds, which stared him in the face now as Death sat at his heart.

"Do you remember this?" "Do you recollect that?" they asked one after another, thus bringing to his remembrance circumstances that made the perspiration stand on his brow.

"I know nothing about it," said the emperor. "Music! Music!" he cried. "Bring the large Chinese drum that I may not hear what they say." But the voices still went on, and Death nodded at all they said.

"Music! Music!" shouted the emperor. "You little precious golden bird, sing, pray sing! I have given you gold and costly presents. I have even hung my golden slipper around your neck. Sing! Sing!" But the bird remained silent. There was no one to wind it up, and therefore it could not sing a note.

Death continued to stare at the emperor with his cold,

hollow eyes, and the room was fearfully still. Suddenly there came through the open window the sound of sweet music. Outside, on the bough of a tree, sat the living nightingale. It had heard of the emperor's illness and was therefore come to sing to him of hope and trust. And as it sang, the shadows grew paler and paler. The blood in the emperor's veins flowed more rapidly and gave life to his weak limbs. Even Death himself listened, and said, "Go on, little nightingale, go on."

"Then will you give me the beautiful golden sword and that rich banner? And will you give me the emperor's crown?" said the bird.

So Death gave up each of these treasures for a song, and the nightingale continued her singing. She sung of the quiet churchyard, where the white roses grow, where the elder tree wafts its perfume on the breeze, and the fresh, sweet grass is moistened by the mourners' tears. Then Death longed to go and see his garden, and floated out through the window in the form of a cold, white mist.

"Thanks, thanks, you heavenly little bird. I know you well. I banished you from my kingdom once, and yet you have charmed away the evil faces from my bed and banished Death from my heart with your sweet song. How can I reward you?"

"You have already rewarded me," said the nightingale. "I shall never forget that I drew tears from your eyes the first time I sang to you. These are the jewels that rejoice a singer's heart. But now sleep, and grow strong and well again. I will sing to you again."

And as it sang, the emperor fell into a sweet sleep, and how mild and refreshing that slumber was! When he awoke, strengthened and restored, the sun shone brightly through the window. But not one of his servants had returned—they all believed he was dead. Only the nightingale still sat beside him, and sang.

"You must always remain with me," said the emperor. "You shall sing only when it pleases you, and I will break the artificial bird into a thousand pieces."

"No, do not do that," replied the nightingale. "The bird did very well as long as it could. Keep it here still. I cannot live in the palace and build my nest, but let me come when I like. I will sit on a bough outside your window in the evening and sing to you, so that you may be happy and have thoughts full of joy. I will sing to you of those who are happy and those who suffer, of the good and the evil that is hidden around you. A little singing bird flies far from you and your court to the home of the fisherman and the peasant's cot. I love your heart better than your crown, and yet something holy lingers around that also. I will come, I will sing to you, but you must promise me one thing."

"Everything," said the emperor, who, having dressed himself in his imperial robes, stood with the hand that held the heavy golden sword pressed to his heart.

"I only ask one thing," it replied. "Let no one know that you have a little bird who tells you everything. It will be best to conceal it." So saying, the nightingale flew away.

The servants came back to look after the dead emperor, when, lo! there he stood and, to their astonishment, said, "Good morning."

The Darning Needle

There was once a darning needle who thought herself so fine that she fancied she must be fit for embroidery. "Hold me tight," she would say to the fingers, when they took her up. "Don't let me fall. If you do I shall never be found again, I am so very fine."

"That is your opinion, is it?" said the fingers, as they seized her around the body.

"Look, here I come with my train," said the darning needle, drawing a long thread after her, but there was no knot in the thread.

The fingers aimed the point of the needle at the cook's slipper. There was a crack in the upper leather, which had to be sewn together.

"What coarse work!" said the darning needle. "I shall never get through. I shall break! I am breaking!" And sure enough she broke. "Did I not say so?" said the darning needle. "I know I am too fine for work such as that."

"This needle is quite useless for sewing now," said the fingers, but they still held it tight. For the cook dropped some sealing wax on the needle to make a pinhead and fastened her handkerchief with it in front.

"Now I am a breast pin," said the darning needle. "I knew very well I should come to honor someday. Merit is sure to rise." And she laughed quietly to herself, for of course no one ever saw a darning needle laugh. And there she sat as proudly as if she were in a state coach and looked all around her.

"May I be allowed to ask if you are made of gold?" she inquired of a neighboring pin. "You have a very pretty appearance and a curious head, although you are rather small. You must take pains to grow, for it is not everyone who has sealing wax on them like me." As she spoke, the darning needle drew herself up so proudly that she fell out of the handkerchief right into the sink, which the cook was cleaning.

"I guess I'm going on a journey," said the needle, as she floated away with the dirty water, "I do hope I shall not be lost." But she really was lost in a gutter.

"I am too fine for this world," said the darning needle, as she lay in the gutter. "But I know who I am, and that is always some comfort." So the darning needle kept up her proud behavior and did not lose her good humor. Then there floated over her all sorts of things—chips and straws, and pieces of old newspaper.

"See how they sail," said the darning needle. "They do not know what is under them. I am here, and here I shall stick. See, there goes a chip, thinking of nothing in the world but himself, only a chip. There's a straw going by now. How he turns and twists about! Don't be thinking too much of yourself, or you may chance to run against a stone. There swims a piece of newspaper. What is written upon it has been forgotten long ago, and yet it gives itself airs. I sit here patiently and quietly. I know who I am, and won't forget it."

One day something lying close to the darning needle glittered so splendidly that she thought it was a diamond, yet it was only a piece of broken bottle. The darning needle spoke to it because it sparkled. She introduced herself as a breast pin. "I suppose you are really a diamond?" she said.

"Why yes, something of the kind," he replied. And so each believed the other to be very valuable, and then they began to talk about the world and the conceited people in it.

"I have been in a lady's workbox," said the darning needle, "and this lady was the cook. She had on each hand five fingers, and anything so conceited as these five fingers I have never seen, and yet they were only there to take me out of the box and to put me back again."

"Were they not highborn?"

"Highborn!" said the darning needle, "No indeed, but so haughty. They were five brothers, all born fingers. They kept very proudly together, although they were of different lengths. The one who stood first in the rank was named the thumb. He was short and thick, and had only one joint in his back and could therefore make but one bow. But he said that if he were cut off from a man's hand, that man would be unfit for a soldier. Sweet Tooth, his neighbor, dipped himself into anything sweet or sour, pointed to the sun and moon, and formed the letters when the fingers wrote. Longman, the middle finger, looked over the heads of all the others. Gold Band, the next finger, wore a golden circle around his waist. And little Playfellow did nothing at all and seemed proud of it. They were boasters, and boasters they will remain, and therefore I left them."

"And now we sit here and glitter," said the piece of broken bottle.

At the same moment more water streamed into the gutter so that it overflowed, and the piece of bottle was carried away.

"So he's been promoted," said the darning needle, "while I remain here. I am too fine for that but that is my pride and what do I care?" And so she sat there in her pride, and had many such thoughts as these: "I could almost fancy that I came from a sunbeam, I am so fine. It seems as if the sunbeams were always looking for me under the water. Ah! I am so fine that even my mother cannot find me. Had I still my old eye, which was broken off, I believe I should weep. But no, I would not do that, it is not genteel to cry."

One day a couple of street boys were paddling in the gutter, for they sometimes found old nails, coins, and other treasures. It was dirty work, but they took great pleasure in it. "Hallo!" cried one, as he pricked himself with the darning needle. "Here's a fellow for you."

"I am not a fellow, I am a young lady," said the darning needle, but no one heard her.

The sealing wax had come off, and she was quite black, but black makes a person look slender, so she thought herself even finer than before.

"Here comes an eggshell sailing along," said one of the boys, so they stuck the darning needle into the eggshell.

"White walls, and I am black myself," said the darning needle, "That looks well. Now I can be seen, but I hope I shall not be seasick, or I shall break again." But she was not seasick, and she did not break. "It is a good thing against seasickness to have a steel stomach and not to forget one's own importance. Now I'm fine: Delicate people can bear a great deal."

Crack went the eggshell, as a wagon passed over it. "Good heavens, how it crushes!" said the darning needle. "I shall be sick now. I am breaking!" But she did not break, although the wagon went over her as she lay at full length. And there let us leave her.

Five Peas in a Pod

There were once five peas in one pod. They were green, the shell was green, and so they believed that the whole world must be green also, which was a very natural conclusion. The shell grew, and the peas grew. They accommodated themselves to their surroundings and sat all in a row. The sun shone and warmed the shell, and the rain made it clear and transparent. It was mild and agreeable in broad daylight, and dark at night as it generally is, and the peas as they sat there grew bigger and bigger, and more thoughtful as they sat, for they felt there must be something else they should do in life.

"Are we to sit here forever?" asked one. "Shall we not become hard by sitting so long? It seems to me there must be something outside, and I feel sure of it."

And as weeks passed by, the peas became yellow, and the shell became yellow.

"All the world is turning yellow, I suppose," said they, and perhaps they were right.

Suddenly they felt the pod jerk. It was torn off by a human hand, then slipped into the pocket of a jacket in company with other full pods.

"Now we shall soon be opened," said one, just what they all wanted.

"I should like to know which of us will travel farthest," said the smallest of the five. "We shall soon see now."

"What is to happen will happen," said the largest pea.

Crack went the shell as it burst, and the five peas rolled out into the bright sunshine. There they lay in a child's hand. A little boy was holding them tightly and said they were fine peas for his peashooter. And immediately he put one in and shot it out.

"Now I am flying out into the wide world," said the pea. "Catch me if you can." And it was gone in a moment.

"I," said the second, "intend to fly straight to the sun. That is a pod that lets itself be seen, and it will suit me exactly." And away it went.

"We will go to sleep wherever we find ourselves," said the two next. "But we will still be rolling anyway." They did certainly fall on the floor and roll about before they got into the peashooter, but they were put in it all the same. "We shall go farther than the others," said they.

"What is to happen will happen," exclaimed the last, as it was shot out of the peashooter. As the pea spoke it flew up against an old board under an attic window and fell into a little crevice, which was almost filled up with moss and soft earth. The moss closed itself around the pea, and there it lay, a captive indeed, but not unnoticed by God.

"What is to happen will happen," said the pea to itself.

Within the little attic lived a poor woman, who went out to clean stoves, chop wood into small pieces, and perform other such hard work, for she was strong and industrious. Yet she remained always poor, and at home in the attic lay her only daughter, not quite grown up, and very delicate and weak. For a whole year she had kept to her bed, and it seemed as if she could neither live nor die.

"She is going to her little sister," said the woman. "I had but the two children, and it was not an easy thing to support both of them. But the good God helped me in my work and took one of them to Himself and provided for her. Now I would gladly keep the other that was left to me, but I suppose they are not to be separated, and my sick girl will very soon go to her sister above." But the sick girl still remained where she was. Quietly and patiently she lay all the day long, while her mother was away from home at her work.

Spring came, and one morning early the sun shone brightly through the little window and threw its rays over the floor of the room. Just as the mother was going to her work, the sick girl fixed her gaze on the lowest pane of the window. "Mother!" she exclaimed. "What can that little green thing be that peeps in at the window? It is moving in the wind."

The mother stepped to the window and half opened it. "Oh!" she said. "There is actually a little pea that has taken root and is putting out its green leaves. How could it have got into this crack? Well now, here is a little garden for you to amuse yourself with." So she moved the bed of the sick girl nearer to the window, that she might see the budding plant. Then the mother went out to her work.

"Mother, I believe I shall get well," said the sick child in the evening. "The sun has shone in here so brightly and warmly today, and the little pea is thriving so well. I shall get better, too, and go out into the warm sunshine again."

"God grant it!" said the mother, but she did not believe it would be so. Still she propped up with a little stick the green plant that had given her child such pleasant hopes of life, so that it might not be broken by the winds. She tied a piece of string to the windowsill and to the upper part of the frame, so that the pea tendrils might twine around it when they shot up. And they did shoot up—indeed you could almost see it grow from day to day.

"Now here is a blossom with a flower coming," said the old woman one morning, and now at last she began to encourage the hope that her sick daughter might really recover. She remembered that for some time the child had spoken more cheerfully, and during the last few days had raised herself in bed in the morning to look with sparkling eyes at her little garden that contained only a single pea plant. A week later, the invalid sat up for the first time a whole hour, feeling quite happy by the open window in the warm sunshine, while outside grew the little plant and on it a pink pea blossom in full bloom. The little maiden bent down and gently kissed the delicate leaves. This day was to her like a festival day.

"God himself has planted that pea and made it grow and flourish to bring joy to you and hope to me, my blessed child," said the happy mother, and she smiled at the flower, as if it had been an angel.

But what became of the other peas? The one who flew out into the wide world and said, "Catch me if you can," fell into a gutter on the roof of a house and ended its travels in the throat of a pigeon. The two lazy ones were carried equally far, for they also were eaten by pigeons, so they were at least of some use. But the fourth, who wanted to reach the sun, fell into a sink and lay there in the dirty water for days and weeks, till it had swelled to a great size.

"I am getting beautifully fat," said the pea. "I expect I shall burst at last. No pea could do more that that, I think. I am the most remarkable of all the five that were in the pod." And the sink agreed.

But the young maiden stood at the open attic window, with sparkling eyes and the rosy hue of health on her cheeks. She folded her thin hands over the pea blossom and thanked God for what had been done.

"I," said the gutter where the pea grew, "shall vote for *my* pea."

The Rose Elf

❧

In the midst of a garden grew a rose tree in full blossom, and in the prettiest of all the roses lived an elf. He was such a little wee thing that no human eye could see him. Behind each petal of the rose he had a sleeping chamber. He was as well formed and as beautiful as a little child could be, and had wings that reached from his shoulders to his feet. Oh, what sweet fragrance there was in his chambers! And how clean and beautiful were the walls, for they were the blushing petals of the rose.

During the whole day he enjoyed himself in the warm sunshine, flying from flower to flower, and dancing on the wings of the flying butterflies. Then he decided to measure how many steps he would need to go through the roads and crossroads that are on the leaf of a linden tree. What we call the veins on a leaf, he took for roads. Yes, and very long roads they were for him, for before he had half finished his task, the sun went down. He had commenced his work too late.

It became very cold, the dew fell, and the wind blew, so he thought the best thing he could do would be to return home. He hurried himself as much as he could, but he found the roses all closed up, and he could not get in—not a single rose stood open.

The poor little elf was very much frightened. He had never before been out at night, but had always slept safely behind the warm rose leaves. Oh, this would certainly be his death.

Then he remembered that at the other end of the garden, there was an arbor, overgrown with beautiful honeysuckle. The blossoms looked like large painted horns. He thought to himself that he would go and sleep in one of these till the morning. He flew there, but "hush!" two people were in the arbor, a handsome young man and a beautiful lady. They sat side by side, and wished that they might never be obliged to part. They loved each other much more than the best child can love its father and mother.

"But we must part," said the young man. "Your brother does not like our engagement, and therefore he sends me far away on business, over mountains and seas. Farewell, my sweet bride, for so you are to me."

And then they kissed each other, and the girl wept and gave him a rose. But before she did so, she pressed a kiss upon it so fervently that the flower opened. Then the little elf flew in and leaned his head on the delicate, fragrant walls. Here he could plainly hear them say, "Farewell, farewell," and he felt that the rose had been placed on the young man's chest. Oh, how his heart did beat! The little elf could not go to sleep, it thumped so loudly.

After a time, the young man took out the rose as he walked through the dark wood alone and kissed the flower so often and so violently that the little elf was almost crushed. He could feel through the leaf how hot the lips of the young man were, and the rose opened, as if from the heat of the noonday sun.

Then another man appeared, who looked gloomy and wicked. He was the wicked brother of the beautiful maiden. He drew out a sharp knife, and while the other was kissing the rose, the wicked man stabbed him to death, then he cut off his head and buried it with the body in the soft earth under the linden tree.

Now he is gone and will soon be forgotten, thought the wicked brother. *He will never come back again. He was going on a long journey over mountains and seas. It is easy for a man to lose his life in such a journey. My sister will suppose he is dead, for he cannot come back, and she will not dare to question me about him.*

Then he scattered the dry leaves over the light earth with his foot and went home through the darkness. But he went not alone, as he thought—the little elf accompanied him. He sat in a dry, rolled-up linden leaf, which had fallen from the tree onto the wicked man's head, as he was digging the grave. The hat was on the head now, which made it very dark, and the little elf shuddered with fright and indignation at the wicked deed.

It was dawn before the wicked man reached home. He took off his hat and went into his sister's room. There lay the beautiful girl, dreaming of him whom she loved so and who was now, she supposed, traveling far away over mountain and sea. Her wicked brother stooped over her and laughed hideously, as only fiends can laugh. The dry leaf fell out of his hair upon the bedspread, but he did not notice it and went to get a little sleep during the early morning hours.

The elf slipped out of the withered leaf, placed himself by the ear of the sleeping girl, and told her, as in a dream, of the horrid murder, described the place where her brother had slain her lover and buried his body, and told her of the linden tree, in full blossom, that stood close by.

"That you may not think this is only a dream that I have told you," he said, "you will find on your bed a withered leaf."

Then she awoke and found it there. Oh, what bitter tears she shed! And she could not open her heart to anyone for relief.

Her window stood open the whole day, and the little elf could easily have reached the roses or any of the flowers. But he could not find it in his heart to leave one so afflicted. In the window stood a bush bearing monthly roses. The elf seated himself in one of the flowers and gazed on the poor girl. Her brother often came into the room and acted quite cheerful, in spite of his evil conduct. His sister dared not say a word to him of her heart's grief.

As soon as night came on, she slipped out of the house and went into the wood to the spot where the linden tree stood. After removing the leaves from the earth, she turned it up, and there found him who had been murdered. Oh, how she wept and prayed that she also might die! Gladly would she have taken the body home with her, but that was impossible. So she took up the poor head with the closed eyes, kissed the cold lips, and shook the dirt out of the beautiful hair.

"I will keep this," said she. As soon as she had covered

the body again with the earth and leaves, she took the head and a little sprig of jasmine that bloomed in the wood near the spot where he was buried, and carried them home with her. As soon as she was in her room, she took the largest flowerpot she could find, and in this she placed the head of the dead man, covered it up with earth, and planted the twig of jasmine in it.

"Farewell, farewell," whispered the little elf. He could no longer endure to witness all this agony of grief. He flew back to his own rose in the garden. But the rose was faded. Only a few dry leaves still clung to the green hedge behind it.

"Alas! How soon all that is good and beautiful passes away," sighed the elf.

After a while he found another rose, which became his home, for among its delicate fragrant leaves he could dwell in safety. Every morning he flew to the window of the poor girl and always found her weeping by the flowerpot. The bitter tears fell upon the jasmine twig, and each day, as she became paler and paler, the sprig appeared to grow greener and fresher. One shoot after another sprouted forth, and little white buds blossomed, which the poor girl fondly kissed. But her wicked brother scolded her and asked her if she was going mad. He could not imagine why she was weeping over that flowerpot, and it annoyed him. He did not know whose closed eyes were there, nor what red lips were fading beneath the earth.

One day the maiden sat and leaned her head against the flowerpot, and the little elf of the rose found her asleep. Then he seated himself by her ear, and talked to her of that evening in the arbor, of the sweet perfume of the rose, and the loves of the elves. Sweetly she dreamed, and while she dreamed, her life passed away calmly and gently, and her spirit was with him whom she loved. And the jasmine opened its large white bells and spread forth its sweet fragrance. It had no other way of showing its grief for the dead.

The wicked brother considered the beautiful blooming plant as his own property, left to him by his sister, and he placed it in his sleeping room, close by his bed, for it was very lovely in appearance and the fragrance was sweet and delightful. The little elf of the rose followed it and flew from flower to flower, telling each little spirit that dwelled there the story of the murdered young man, whose head now formed part of the earth beneath them, and of the wicked brother and the poor sister.

"We know it," said each of the little spirits in the flowers. "We know it, for have we not sprung from the eyes and lips of the murdered one? We know it, we know it."

The flowers nodded with their heads in a peculiar manner. The elf of the rose could not understand how they could rest so quietly in the matter, so he flew to the bees, who were gathering honey, and told them of the wicked brother. And the bees told it to their queen, who commanded that the next morning they should go and kill the murderer.

But during the night, the first after the sister's death, while the brother was sleeping in his bed next to the fragrant jasmine, every flower opened and invisibly the little spirits stole out, armed with poisonous spears. They placed themselves by the ear of the sleeper, told him dreadful dreams, and then flew across his lips and pricked his tongue with their poisoned spears.

"Now have we revenged the dead," said they, and flew back into the white bells of the jasmine flowers.

When the morning came, and as soon as the window was opened, the rose elf, with the queen bee and the whole swarm of bees, rushed in to kill him. But he was already dead. People were standing around the bed and saying that the scent of the jasmine had killed him. Then the elf of the rose understood the revenge of the flowers and explained it to the queen bee, and she, with the whole swarm, buzzed about the flowerpot and could not be driven away.

When a man picked up the flowerpot, one of the bees stung him in the hand, so that he let the flowerpot fall, and it was broken to pieces. Then everyone saw the whitened skull, and they knew the dead man in the bed was a murderer.

The queen bee hummed in the air, sang of the revenge of the flowers and of the elf of the rose, and said that behind the smallest leaf there dwells One who can discover evil deeds and punish them also.